D0859916

JUN 2 3 2021

Strong Like the Sea

WENDY S. SWORE

SHADOW
MOUNTAIN

393 6277

Visit us at shadowmountain.com

This is a work of fiction. Characters and events in this book are products of the author's imagination or are represented fictitiously.

Library of Congress Cataloging-in-Publication Data
CIP on file
ISBN: 978-1-62972-902-2

Printed in the United States of America
Lake Book Manufacturing, Inc., Melrose Park, IL

10   9   8   7   6   5   4   3   2   1

*This book is dedicated to
kids who choose to be courageous
even when they feel afraid.*

CHAPTER ONE

꧁ ꧂ ꧁ ꧂ ꧁ ꧂ ꧁ ꧂.

Buried Treasure

Sometimes when I get home from school, I find a lucky gecko clinging to the screen door—which is pretty cool—but today I find something even better: a note from Mom.

It wasn't there when I left for school this morning, and Mom's still overseas, so someone else must've taped it to our door. Could be that Dad stuck it there before he left for work at Kahuku High and Intermediate School, or maybe Mom arranged for someone else here in Laie to leave the clue, but either way, there's no mistaking Mom's precise handwriting, each letter long and curved, stretching up and up like palm trees straining against stiff ocean winds. Bent but not broken, her words scrawl across bright white paper: *Dear Alexis, Let the game begin! Your adventure awaits.*

"Yes!" It's got to be the start of one of Mom's special challenges with treats or cool prizes at the end. That's Mom's way of staying close to me even when her work carries her far away.

I've been waiting all week for our video chat tonight, but like always, Mom's planning two steps ahead and already set her plans in motion.

I carefully peel the tape off the door and check the back of the paper for any more clues, but it's blank.

As I read her words again, my brain speeds up, questioning everything in case there might be something important I didn't see the first time—it's sort of a detective mode that clicks on inside my head.

Mom's clues might stump me at first, but I *never* give up until I figure them out and solve her challenges. I can't leave a mystery unsolved; I guess we're like mother, like daughter that way. She's super smart and basically the Queen of All Things Sneaky. That's why the navy contracted with her in the first place—her brains are her superpower.

When I solved her last challenge in less than a day, Mom promised to make my next clue-hunting mission extra tricky. And if *Mom* says it's going to be tricky, it'll take *all* my brains to figure it out. Once in a while I'll let my friends come with me on a challenge. I guess that would be . . . extra brains? Backup brains? Whatever, but usually I just tell them what I found later.

The note doesn't seem to be hiding any other clues other than to tell me the game's afoot, so I open the screen door and climb the last couple steps into the house.

My backpack thunks against the tile floor, and I tilt my trilby hat to the side like a detective on TV while I scan for anything out of the ordinary.

Overhead, the ceiling fan spins in lazy circles, mixing the scent of plumeria flowers from outside the kitchen window with the aroma of fresh-steamed rice from the rice cooker.

Nothing new on the walls that I can see. I eye the photos of my friends tucked around the frame of our favorite banyan, Castle Tree, but the newest picture is still the one of me, Malia, and Jack chowing down at a school party. Jack's frozen mid-bite, a sweet roll in his hand—no surprise there.

The living room seems the same as usual, but in the center of the kitchen table, Mom's old Triton's trumpet shell sits where the bowl of guava fruit ought to be.

Gently, I lift the eight-inch shell from the table and turn it over before cupping the shell to my ear to listen to the sea. The shell presses against the earpiece of my glasses, and a hollow *shh* whispers from the depths of the spiral, as if a tiny portal hides inside and lets only the faintest breath from the ocean seep through—a long exhale of waves rushing to shore from far, far away.

I like the sound, even if I don't like the water much anymore.

It definitely wasn't on the table this morning, so there must be a reason someone put the shell here. Maybe something's hidden inside?

I tip it back and forth, trying to see around the curve, and give it a soft shake to listen for anything rattling around, but from tip to mouth, it looks the same as always.

Cradling the heirloom shell, I pad down the hall to the glass cabinet in Mom and Dad's room to put it back on the shelf—except a compass and scroll tied with a red bow rest in the place where the trumpet shell goes.

The shell clicks softly against the glass as I swap it for the compass and scroll, close the cabinet, and rush back to the kitchen to roll out my find.

Numbers march down the side of the scroll—coordinates, I think—mixed in with Hawaiian words every local and resident knows, like *makai*, which means toward the ocean, and *mauka*, which means toward the mountain. On an island, those directions make more sense than north, east, south, and west. But Mom's directions have all that mixed up with regular compass directions and coordinates, so there's no way I can tell where it leads without following it step by step to the end.

I glance at the door, ready to go for it and find where it leads—except my map of sorts doesn't have a starting point.

The first direction says to take thirty steps mauka—toward the mountain. But thirty steps from where? From the cabinet where I found it, or from the yard?

My parents' room isn't anywhere near thirty steps wide, so that would lead right through a wall if I started in there. But where else would it be? After a few minutes with no new ideas, my stomach rumbles, and I swipe a few lumpia spring rolls from the fridge for an after-school snack.

A sticky note on the fridge reads: *Alex, Don't forget to do your chores. Love, Dad.* But I ignore it and read Mom's scroll over and over again. There's a faint watermark on the back—a palm tree over a square—but Mom wouldn't dig up a palm tree to put a square under it, so I'm not sure if that's part of the clue or if that was already printed on the paper Mom used. On the front side, the directions are clear from top to bottom and back again, but I can't find anything that says where to start.

Why make a scroll so detailed but leave off the most important part? Mom doesn't make mistakes like that, so she must've done it on purpose, believing I could figure it out.

When nothing else pops into my head, I follow Dad's

advice and change the laundry—my Friday chore. I pull the bundle of damp clothes out of the washer and let it flop into the laundry basket before shoving Dad's swim shorts and towels inside and starting the machine again.

With the basket on my hip, I slip out the screen door to our laundry lines that drape from the side of the house to a pole supporting the roof that stretches from our house out over our lanai. Dad still sometimes forgets and calls our covered cement area a porch or patio, but everybody here just says lanai. Sometimes, mainlander words sound so weird to me. Like "flip-flops," or worse, "thongs"—what kind of a name is that for a shoe? It makes way more sense to call them rubber slippers.

Setting the basket of clothes on the cement, I drape Dad's shorts over the line and pluck the clothespin basket off the step to pin them all in place.

A three-inch, dark brown oval scuttles out from under the basket, its long, whiskery antennae twitching in the bright sunlight.

A huge cockroach!

I jump back with a squeak, hands flailing, and clothespins scatter, clattering across the cement as the dropped basket bounces, then rolls to a stop. Breathing hard, I push my glasses back up onto my nose and stare at the nasty little beastie.

With his long antennae waving all over, he turns this way and that, as if looking for the fastest way out of the sun.

I shudder with heebie-jeebies, my imagination creating a hundred invisible bugs crawling all over me.

It's a big one—a B-52 bomber roach—maybe the biggest I've ever seen, and when it turns my way, I swear it's looking right at me.

I make a grab for a rubber slipper to whack it before it decides to fly at my face, but when my shadow crosses the step, the roach bursts into flight, a buzzy whir of wings and shell with sticky legs spread wide to catch hair or clothes.

Ick, ick!

I duck, pulling my hat down over my ears as the thing flies overhead into a cluster of red ti tree leaves beside the lanai and disappears.

With a shiver, I drop the rubber slipper back onto the pile with the rest of the shoes at the foot of the stairs. Good riddance.

If that bug had been any bigger, it could have carried the laundry basket off by itself.

I reach to gather the clothespins, but a big red X marks the step where the pin basket had been. A big chalk X to mark the spot where my adventure begins.

"Sneaky." I grin.

Leave it to Mom to make sure I can't start my adventure until *after* I do my chores.

I pin the clothes to the line at turbo speed, grab my compass and scroll, and stand on the X to begin the quest.

Half an hour later, I'm still following Mom's directions, walking all over Laie. At a corner, I adjust my glasses and squint at the map before checking the directions against my compass. One hundred steps mauka, then two hundred north, and—

"Hey, Alex! Wassup?" Jack glides past on his bike and circles me once as more boys from school pedal fast to catch up. "We going Sam's store. You wanna come with?"

"I can't. I'm busy." I show him the map, and he pulls up beside me for a better look.

"Eh, what is it? A new challenge?"

"Yeah, my mom left a new map. It goes all over Laie."

"A map?" He peers over my shoulder. "A map for what? Where's it goin'?"

"How would I know? I'll tell you when I finish it."

The other boys pull up and stop in a half moon around me—some barefoot like me, others not—like Kase, the newest to hang with us at Castle Tree. He moved here from the mainland a few months ago but still has a lot to learn. He waves. "Hi, Alex."

Ekolu throws me a shaka with his pinky and thumb out. "Howzit?"

"She's working on a map," Jack answers before I can. A gust of wind lifts my trilby hat, but I grab it quick and hold on.

"What kine map you get? One treasure map?" The breeze teases Ekolu's dark hair as he leans over to see my scroll.

Kase tilts his head. "What's a *kine*?"

"*Da kine* is sort of like 'the kind' or 'thing.'" I glance at Ekolu. "A whatchamacallit, yeah?"

"Sure." He nods. "Your map—does it lead to the beach?"

I scan the scroll page again. "Maybe. There's no roads or lines or anything. Just a list of numbers and directions, see? It seems like I'm getting closer to the beach, but I won't know for sure until I get there."

"I heard the last challenge led to the zip line in Kahuku. I bet that was sick." Kase eases his bike closer.

"Yeah, that was the prize—after Mom got back, we all went together."

"So lucky," Kase says. "It's like she's training you to figure out intelligence stuff like she does."

I shrug like it's no big deal that Mom could train me—or

not—no biggie. But inside, I cling to that hope tighter than barnacles on a ship. Maybe someday Mom and I could work together on tricky cases—like some special intelligence contractor team.

"What if you can't find it?" Jack asks.

"I'll find it." I've never let Mom down before, and I'm sure not gonna start now.

"This time—" Kase glances at the houses around us before leaning in to whisper, "I bet it's something even better at the end, like a ride on a catamaran or sailboat."

"On the ocean?" I wrinkle my nose. *No way.*

"Nah, brah. Not out there." Ekolu bumps Kase's shoulder. "Alex, she like something cool on island, like tickets to the RC track."

"Or a whole year's worth of chicken ramen." Jack sighs, dreamy-like. "You want us to help?"

"Only *you'd* think that was a prize." I roll my eyes and glance at my compass. "You can help if you want to, but weren't you going to Sam's store?"

Jack's stomach growls like a caged animal, and he grips the handlebars. "What say you come to Sam's store first—take five minutes—and then we help you finish?"

"Five? More like twenty-five, eh brah?" Ekolu snickers and mimics Jack's voice. "I can't decide—should I get a bag of crack seed, li hing strawberry belts, or one of every candy in the whole store?"

Sounds like Jack, all right. I wave them off. "You better go ahead. Feed Jack before he gets hangry."

"I'm not hangry—I'm starving. There's a difference." Jack takes off, Ekolu on his tail.

With a shy smile, Kase lumbers up a few steps, straddling his bike with rubber slippers almost too small for his enormous feet. "You sure?"

"Yeah. No worries. I got this." I glance up from my map and nod to my new biggest friend.

Kase is riding a tiny bike that might have fit him in second grade, making his handlebars seem no bigger than noodles inside his thick hands. Other boys grow slender and tall like banana trees that bend with the wind, but Kase seems to spread more sideways, like a banyan tree—wide and strong with solid limbs rooted to the ground.

He hesitates. "Did Malia tell you about Lowen's history project?"

"No, why?" I listen with half an ear while my brain counts the steps I've already taken and subtracts them from the total number on the scroll.

"At lunch today, he told everybody that he's been working on his history project since last summer—that it's the best thing Laie Elementary ever saw. He's got it hidden behind a tarp at his house or something."

"He's worked on it since last summer?" I tick the months off on my fingers. "July, August, September, October, November—he's been working on it for five months already? Why?"

"It sounded like he's sore you got the science fair grand prize last year and is trying to make sure you lose." Kase shrugs. "Some people get way too worked up. It's just a project, right?"

"Right." I laugh with him like it's no big deal—except it *is* a big deal to me. My mom won the history project when she was my age, and I want to show her I can do it too. How can we be a team if I can't even win the same awards she did?

"Come on, Kase!" Jack calls from far down the street.

Kase pushes off and pedals after the others. "See you later."

"See you." I sigh. If Lowen's got such a big head start, I'll have to work extra hard to even have a chance at winning. The whole thing feels a lot like cheating and stinks worse than a whole swarm of B-52 roaches, but I'll worry about it later.

Today, I'm on a mission and—bonus!—I get to see Mom over video chat tonight. No way am I letting Lowen and his stupid project ruin my day. He can go jump in the eel hole for all I care—him *and* his top-secret report.

I brush my long brown hair over my shoulder out of the way and wait for my compass to stop swaying before checking the direction against the instructions.

One hundred steps mauka.

Got it. My bare feet pace off steps as I walk up one street and down another until Mom's instructions lead me down Naniloa Loop to Kamehameha Highway, where crosswalks and 25-mph speed limit signs give safe passage for residents to get to the beaches on the other side.

A red convertible full of tourists roars by with the radio blasting—probably headed for the North Shore—and I glance both ways before running across the two narrow lanes to Hukilau Beach.

With only a couple directions left on my scroll—both of them headed toward the ocean—it's a safe bet that Mom's treasure must be hidden nearby, somewhere between me and the sea.

CHAPTER TWO

Empty Squares

Mom says girls wear a lot of hats. That's especially true for me, because almost every time she travels the world for work, Mom brings me a hat to add to my collection. I probably shoulda swapped my trilby for my detective hat on a windy day like this—but who's got brain space for practical things when there's sleuthing to do?

The breeze picks up again, and I hold tight to my hat. This one's from New York and has a stiff, sharp crown, a tiny brim turned down in front, and a short rim curled up in the back. It doesn't do much to block the sun, but it keeps pesky strands of my long brown hair out of my eyes . . . mostly.

With Kamehameha Highway behind me, I step up onto the small boulder at the corner of Hukilau Beach parking lot to check my map and direction.

I'm so close to finishing this clue my insides jitter, and I want to race the rest of the way, fast as rock crabs scurrying into the sea—except running might mess up my counting and directions. I need to follow the steps exactly so I don't make mistakes and have to start over.

Mom's map leads in a straight path toward the ocean alongside the green cement wall that borders the park.

Only eighty paces to go. *Almost there!*

I hop down from the rock, and my glasses slip right off my nose! I swoop to catch them quick before they hit the ground—or worse, the rock—and my hat flies off, but I save the glasses. Carefully, I slide them back on, backstep to grab my hat, and start counting paces.

Disaster averted—barely.

Losing glasses is the worst, 'cause the thing I'm looking for is the thing I need to *see* in the first place. I haven't lost my glasses *once* since starting sixth grade and it's already November. That's gotta be some kinda record for me.

I count off my paces past rental cars lined up along the log markers and slip deeper into the park, the sandy grass soft under my feet. The path pulls away from the wall a little and snakes through bushes before the grass gives way to pure sand. "Seventy-eight, seventy-nine, eighty."

The last step leaves me standing on the beach, dead even with the final corner of the wall. I stare down at the path, half expecting another big X or something to mark the spot, but Mom wouldn't bury anything under a main path like this. Still, it's gotta be somewhere close. My toes curl in the warm sand while I scan for anything out of place.

Down the shoreline, a couple of kids chase each other. A girl squeals with laughter as she runs away from a boy holding a slimy glob of seaweed. More keiki run after the pair, boys and girls, all of them soaking wet and laughing.

Out in the waves, a few girls bob on boards, and I squint, trying to make out if the littlest one is my bestie, Malia. I'm pretty sure she said she was going surfing with her big sisters, but with the sun shining off the water and a red-striped wind-surfer gliding between us, I can't tell if that's her paddling for a wave or not.

Malia's sisters would let me come surf with them in a heartbeat. They've invited me lots of times, but there's a whole lotta ocean between me and them, and they are welcome to it. The shore suits me just fine.

To my left, a castle of driftwood stands in the shade of a tree, the pieces tied in place with fishing line and netting that some local keiki must've found washed up from yesterday's storm.

Stretching down the beach, winding trails of color speckle the sand like sea glass above the waterline—except it's not sea glass. The storm swallowed plastic from floating rubbish patches at sea and spit them out onto the shore. Someone must've already cleaned up the bigger stuff left from high waves because only the tiny pieces remain. Another day or so and the tide and sand will hide most of that too.

I tuck the compass and scroll into the back pockets of my denim shorts and kneel to check the bushes beside the path. Brushing the sand away, my fingers slide over shallow roots and I startle a couple hermit crabs, but that's it.

Maybe something's tied inside the bush somehow? I ease the branches apart and peer through the leaves, moving from one side of the bushes to the other, but other than a paper cup, I don't see anything.

It's here, I know it. I just have to think harder, be smarter—try to think like Mom.

She wouldn't damage anything or dig a big hole if she didn't need to; Auntie taught her to respect the island better than that. So it's got to be someplace I can reach without messing stuff up.

I study the branches for anything hidden overhead and roll driftwood over, but a little worry slips in that maybe I made a mistake somewhere at the beginning of my steps today. Could I be in the wrong place completely?

I try to ignore the ocean and focus, but sunlight flashes across the waves like broken mirrors and keeps breaking my concentration. Or maybe the real distraction is knowing that somewhere out there, Mom's submarine cruises deep below the surface of that vast water. I wonder if Mom would know it if they went through a rubbish patch? Navy subs don't have portals or windows, but maybe the crew could see it on sonar or something? Could their sensors pick up plastic bags or water bottles?

Mom's probably too busy doing whatever intelligence stuff she's contracted for to notice things like that. But I do like to imagine she's thinking of me, like I think of her—especially on days like today, when we get to see each other, even if it's through a computer screen.

A tourist family with a bunch of kids all slathered in sunscreen come down the path and I step forward around the corner of the wall to let them by. With green water wings, goggles, and a snorkel stuck in his mouth, the littlest shuffles along behind the others, his feet leaving twin grooves in his wake.

"Get a wiggle on, Thomas!" the mom calls, and he waddles faster, his chubby cheeks puffing wet breaths through his snorkel. Marching straight to the ocean, he toddles onward until a wave breaks against the shore and rushes up onto the sand, sending a thin sheen of bubbles up over his toes. He squeals, patters his feet in happy little slaps against the sand, and waits for the next wave.

Silly kid. I turn for the path but spy curved lines in the stone on the seaward side of the wall. I shade my eyes and more lines appear. No—not just curved lines—they're carvings!

Whoever built the wall spaced pillars evenly all the way across, and on every pillar, shallow carvings rise from the sand and reach in gentle curves for the sky. Between the pillars, the builders left out blocks here and there, like square windows to see out from the yard. I tilt my head and study the delicate shapes worn and discolored from years of salt, sand, and surf. The grooved shapes seem random at first, but then the whole picture clicks inside my head—*palm trees!*

The curved lines form palm trees growing from a rounded beach. A different tree carved on each pillar. They're old and shallow, which is probably why I never noticed them before.

I never would have seen this from my spot on the path. It was too far back to see around the corner of the wall. I must've counted wrong or started from the wrong place or—

I groan. That's it.

When my glasses fell off, I stepped *backwards* to pick up my hat and started counting from there. I subtracted one step before I ever started counting. Of *course* I ended up short of where I needed to be.

The wind tries to snatch the scroll from my hands as I roll it out, but I hold it tight and turn it over to see the watermark on the back. A palm tree—styled in the same curving lines as the one at the corner of the wall. And beneath the tree . . . a square.

Missing bricks on the bottom mirror the pattern of square "windows" on the top, though from the pattern it seems most of them are buried—filled in by sand over the years.

I scoot some driftwood aside and kneel beside the first carving to brush sand away from the base of the wall, clearing off the part that looks like a beach line, then dig down.

The carving might be old, but it's easy to see why Mom would use it as part of her clues. It looks almost the same as our family symbol: a palm balanced on a circle. We've got an embroidered tapestry of it on the wall at home with the words "Rise Where You Stand" stitched down the side. Whatever she wanted me to find, it's got to be here.

I grab a flat piece of driftwood for a mini-shovel and scoop tiny piles of sand to the side. Another couple scoops, and sand that had been clinging to the wall collapses to reveal the hollow corner of one of those empty squares. Laying the driftwood aside, I reach in and scoop sand from the square until my fingers hit something metal.

With a fierce grin I clear the sand away and pull a tin lunch box from the hole in the wall.

"Yes!" Made of tin or made of gold, it makes no difference to me. Mom hid it, and I found it. It's perfect.

I wipe off what sand I can. No rust yet, so it hasn't been

there long. But when I turn it over to see the back, something heavy slides from one end to the other and bangs against the side.

What did Mom hide in here anyway?

I reach to open it, but a tiny lock dangles from the latch with writing scratched into the metal. Rubbing the lock clean with my thumb, I read: *Not Yet.*

Biting my lip, I hesitate. If it said anything else, I'd think it was a clue and start looking for whatever comes next, but this feels like the end. I found it. But Mom says not yet. So. . . why wait?

. . . And what's in the box?

CHAPTER THREE

The Challenge

Beep, b-beep, b-beep, b-beep!

The alarm on my watch goes off when I'm still two houses away from home. A reminder that Mom's video call will happen soon—as if I could ever forget!

Cutting across our neighbor's lawn, I slip between the plumeria tree and ti plants and hurry into the shade of our lanai. With the box, compass, and scroll, I don't have enough hands to turn off the alarm, but I hurry up the steps anyway.

B-beep, B-beep!

I pull the screen door open and set my treasure box on the mat inside the door long enough to turn off my alarm, then scoop the box back up and carry it to my room.

At my desk, I power up my computer and use a towel to wipe the last of the sand off the lunch box. The design on the side is faded, but still visible: a perfect spiral winding round and round out from the center.

I set the lunch box to the side of my desk and tug on the lock just in case it decides to magically open, but nope. It's locked.

Not yet.

If not now, then when? Maybe I'm supposed to wait for Dad to get home, or maybe wait for Mom's call? That's probably why she didn't give me the first clue until now, because waiting stinks.

The last hour before Mom calls always takes forever.

For-ev-er!

It's as if my room becomes a black hole where time slows down and the minutes turn into days. It's the longest hour of the week for sure—maybe the longest hour of the whole year.

I have a snack, sit at my desk, and fold origami. I'm not sure it actually helps the time go faster, but it definitely keeps my eyes on the paper instead of watching the second hand on the clock drag by.

I fold a frog, a bird, and a rabbit. Those are easy because Dad showed me how. But then I make up my own animal just to see what I can do. I was going for something like a dragon, but it comes out more like a mutant shark with three tails. Poor thing.

The curved bars at the top of the computer screen light up, and a window opens with an incoming call.

"Yes!" I click accept, and a video window appears with Mom's smiling face. As usual, her camera faces a wall, so I can't see much other than the oval metal door behind her, which means she's still on the submarine.

"Alexis? Honey, can you hear me?" Mom asks.

"Yes, I'm here!" I wave.

Mom gives me a shaka with both hands. "Hey, honey."

I send her a shaka sign right back. "Hey, Mom. Where are you?"

She shakes a finger at the screen. "You know I can't give our exact location, but it's safe to say that we're far to the west of you. Is Dad around?"

"His schedule says he's got another client for dive lessons, but he should be home in half an hour or so."

"I hope he makes it in time. We're moving out soon." She checks her watch. "Anything new in your world?"

"My teacher suggested we choose a role model for our history project, and I think I picked the perfect person." I spread both hands like tiny fireworks. "Nancy Drew!"

But instead of smiling, Mom tilts her head like she does when she's counting and starts typing fast on her keyboard. "Why choose her? She's not real. Why not use someone who really lived and changed history?"

My little fireworks deflate. "But she *did* change history. She's been a role model for girls for like ninety years."

"True, but imagine how amazing it would be if someone had skills like Nancy Drew, but was a real-live person who really did help save the world." She raises an eyebrow. "Wouldn't that be better?"

"I guess." This isn't going at all like I planned. She's the one who gave me Nancy Drew books in the first place. "But I can't think of anybody like that."

"And that's easily fixed. There are some amazing women from World War II that would be great for your project. I can give you a handful of names to start with. First, there's Nancy Wake—the German forces named her the White

Mouse because they knew about her, out there causing all sorts of trouble for them, but they couldn't catch her. The second woman who comes to mind has got to be Noor Inyat Khan, a Sufi princess and pacifist who wrote children's books before she became a wireless operative in the fight against Hitler."

Mom folds her arms and pauses to think, her finger tapping her arm while I grab a notepad and start scribbling down names. "Let's see, Violette Szabo stayed in occupied France and gave her life so her fellow spies could escape. Another spy was Odette Sanson, whose quick thinking saved her life—oh, and there are codebreakers too. Brilliant women like mathematicians Margaret Rock, and Joan Murray, and my personal favorite, Mavis Batey, who cracked the German Enigma code and helped win the war."

My pencil scratches against the paper.

Mavis Batey.

"Okay, I'll look those up, but no promises. I already had notecards and stuff planned out with Nancy Drew." If Lowen's already got five months of work done on his, he'll have way more than that done for sure. I'll have to bust my tail to win.

Mom checks her watch again, sweeps her long brown hair up into a bun, and ties it off with hair bands. "Fair enough, but I think you'll like what you find. So . . . did you find something interesting when you came home from school today?"

I grab the lunch box and wiggle it in front of the camera. "Ta-da! Found it."

"That's my girl." Her smile warms me right through. "Have you opened it?"

Wait, what? I cringe. "Was there a key in the square hole in the wall? I didn't see anything there, and somebody scratched 'not yet' on the lock, so I thought I was supposed to wait. Was I not?"

She holds up a hand. "*Shh.* You did perfect. I asked you to wait because I wanted to see you open it."

"See me open it?" I glance around the room. "Is the key here?"

She nods. "You already have the clue to where it's hidden. Check the scroll."

"I do?" The scroll map is so crumpled from being stuffed in my pocket, I have to smooth it flat on my desk to read it. But just like I remembered, there's nothing there other than the directional headings and steps.

"There aren't any other directions, Mom. See?" I hold the wrinkled paper up for the camera.

She taps her chin. "You know, one of Mavis Batey's supervisors had a great way of looking at things when she was stumped. He would ask, 'What way do the hands of the clock move?'"

Something moves in the corner of the room, and I watch a house gecko scurry up the wall. "How does that help? Everybody knows it's clockwise."

"Is it?" Mom's lips curl with a sly smile.

Uh-oh. That sly bit's never good; she only does it when she's stumped me. I glance at the Nancy Drew clock on the wall, but it just confirms what I said. "They move to the right. Clockwise."

"Not if you're the clock." Mom grins. "A clock would see the hands moving counterclockwise."

I imagine looking out from *inside* the clock, but shake my head. "That's cheating."

"Is it? Or is it just a matter of perspective? You've done ciphers and codes since you could read. I think you're ready for a bigger challenge."

Bigger challenge. Change my perspective. Right. I frown at the page and look it over, scrutinizing each heading for hidden clues. "I've already checked every line. There's nothing written on the page that leads to anything hidden."

"You're right." She agrees. "Outside of the original directions, nothing was written on *that* page."

"I don't—" My brain catches up with how Mom repeated what I had just said—almost word for word. If that's not a huge flashing sign to pay attention, I don't know what is. I repeat the line. "Nothing was written on that page."

I hold the paper up to the light and study the creases and folds.

Mom nods, smiling. "Now you're thinking. Just because nothing's written on that page doesn't mean the message isn't there."

Leaving the paper on the desk, I open a drawer and pull a charcoal stick from my box of art supplies.

"I use this, right?" I show Mom the charcoal.

"This is your quest," she chides. "I've already given away too much."

Okay, fine. Right or wrong, this is all I can think of. With charcoal resting gently against the paper, I sweep my hand across the page in quick, long scribbles—filling the white space with faint gray streaks of soot. Like magic, thin, white lines cut through the gloom, highlighting every random wrinkle and crease—but not all the lines are random. I color faster as cursive writing sprawls across the page. "I found it!"

"I knew you could do it." Mom's smile of approval mirrors my own as we share this moment together—a rare and precious shooting star, thousands of miles away.

Bright.

Warm.

Fleeting—and gone.

Mom checks her watch, and I feel the seconds rushing past, devouring what little time I have left with her.

She watches me like she's waiting for something—*oh, right.* I study the paper with cursive covering most of the page. It reads:

Check the compass often. Sleuthing can be tricky. Head out and search. Piece it all together.

I read it again, tapping a finger against the desk with every line. Four sentences with four words each. No way is that a coincidence. "It's a cipher."

"There you go." Mom nods. "Run with it. What—?"

"It's the first word of each sentence!" I jump up, and the rolling chair skitters across the floor. "It says: check sleuthing head piece."

Rows of hats hang over my bed—most from distant countries Mom had visited. I grab my favorite detective hat and check the seams, but there's nothing in it. I scowl at the row of hats and whisper the line again, "Check sleuthing head piece."

There! Between my bowler and newsboy hat, hangs a replica of the hat worn by Sherlock Holmes. Carefully, I lift it off the peg and peek inside.

A key slips out of the lining and falls onto the floor. I snatch it up. "Found it!"

"Excellent!" Mom claps, and I beam as ripples of pride spread through me like soundwaves.

The screen door opens, and Dad calls. "Alexis? Is your mother still on the—" He steps into my room and peers at the screen. "Elizabeth! Love, how are you?"

"Brody, you made it!" she says.

"Of course I did." He glances at me. "Didn't you check the schedule?"

"Oh, she did. She—" Mom's video connection freezes for a moment, and I hold my breath as if my hope can force the feed to work again. The screen glitches, speeding for a moment while Mom speaks. "—told me."

"How's my beautiful wife today?" Dad sinks into the swivel chair, the WE DIVE logo still shining wet from his last dive lesson, though his sun-bleached hair probably dried two minutes after getting out of the water like always.

"She's glad to see you," Mom teases.

Elbows on my desk, Dad leans closer to the screen as if that could bring him closer to Mom. His necklace pendant swings free, the carved white spiral twisting softly at the end of a leather tie.

I start to ease out of the room to give them alone time, but Mom calls, "Wait! Open it first."

The lock sticks a little when I slide the key inside and turn it, but after wiggling, it pops open with a click. Carefully, I set the lunch box on its back and open it. Inside, wax paper surrounds a carved box with a tiny glass door. And inside that, a beautiful honu hat pin rests on velvet lining—a sea turtle.

The green turtle shell shimmers as I turn it from side to side.

"I always bring you hats, but this time I thought you might like something to go *with* your hats instead. Do you like it?"

I take my trilby hat off and slide the pin into the hatband before turning it so she can see. "It's beautiful. Thanks."

Dad pats my back and leans closer to the camera. "Have you told her yet?"

"No, I was waiting for you." She taps steepled fingers against her lips and begins, "When I found out this trip was going to be so close to your birthday, I decided you were ready for something more challenging than what I've been giving you."

"More challenging?" I keep my voice steady, but I'm not sure if I would have found the key just now if it weren't for her hint.

"You knew I was working on a project before I left, I told you that." Her eyes flick to Dad and she shares another secret smile with him. "But I might have implied that the project was for work."

I blink. If it took her most of her free time to set it up, how long will it take to solve it? Will I have any time left to work on my history project and win? My stomach churns with guilt for even thinking that. Mom says she worked hard on a special challenge for me, and the first thing I do is worry about beating Lowen? I stuff my anxiety back down as best I can. "The project you spent weeks working on—it's a challenge for me?"

"Yes, and Auntie and your dad helped too."

I look to Dad. "You did?" I *want* to be excited. Really I do. And Mom's challenges are awesome, important even, but the history project is important too. I think Dad sees my panic, because he gives me a squeeze and whispers into my hair. "It'll be cool. Trust Mom."

I like being in control—or at least feeling like I'm in control. When Mom gives me a challenge, and I choose to solve it, it's fun. Mother-daughter bonding and all that. But knowing she spent so much time makes me feel caught. I don't know how to react, don't know what she expects me to do. I don't want to hurt her feelings, but that uncertainty, her expectation, feels like a riptide sweeping me out to sea.

I clear my throat, but my voice still comes out as a squeak. "Where does it start?"

"You know I love doing projects together with you, right?" Mom asks.

"Yeah." But just because she likes starting projects with me doesn't mean she has time to complete them with me. The chessboard we started to paint on my wall never got past the grid outline before Mom had to go do other things. "But will you be here to finish it with me?"

"I'll be with you every step of the way—not in person all the time, but you'll see. It's like a game we can play together even though I'm far away. Each piece I give you is part of a bigger puzzle—a bigger picture, if you will. I don't want to give too much away, but the person who has your first clue will arrive tomorrow."

"Arrive here?" This is new. "Is it the same person that left the note today? And the shell?"

"Yes." She reaches for her screen like she wants to reach right through the computer and touch me. "I know you're anxious. And this is going to challenge you, but I hope you'll see that anything worth having is worth working for. I've wanted to do this for years, and now you're finally old enough. It'll be tricky, but you can do it. Always remember, I believe in you."

"Thanks, Mom." Pretty sure that's my signal to give my parents some time together, I wave again with my pinkie finger and thumb out: a shaka to reach all the way across the ocean.

"Love you, honey." She blows me a kiss and flutters her fingers goodbye. "I'll call you next week. Same time."

"Love you, Mom." I take one last look at her smiling face and slip out into the hallway where a few family photos hang on the wall. The earliest was taken in Japan before I was ever born: Dad in dress blues, smiling with his arm around Mom, a security badge dangling from her lanyard.

The other family picture has the three of us floating on surfboards, which should be a happy scene—I seem happy in the picture—but the image feels creepy to me now with the dark ocean swelling up behind us. Dad says the dark mass inside the wave behind our smiling, faces is just a shadow—but what if he's wrong? Did he even check what was beneath us before he smiled for that picture? It could be anything.

Diplomas, awards, and certificates fill the rest of the frames in the hallway—all of them arranged in a kind of hopscotch across the wall, like the ones Mom used to play with me on sidewalks. Except this time, I *can't* play along, 'cause every square holds a certificate or award that I don't have. Every fancy frame forms another barrier between me and her.

Even when she's here, I can never really get to where she is, because she's so far above me. She thinks different, sees different—sees *more*. It's been like that my whole life. I have to watch her so close, try so hard to see and think the way she does. It's natural for her. Automatic. But I have to work extra hard to do the same things.

It's like we're different species; her all evolved, and me, still a sea slug.

The only square that gives me hope at all is the last one, a frame with two pictures inside. The photos were taken a year apart, but both show Mom as a little girl, holding first-place awards. Once for the school science fair and the other for history.

The rest might be too far for me to reach, but if I can win those two awards—science and history—I'll at least get a spot on the same wall as Mom. Maybe if I work fast, I can surprise her and get her whole big challenge thing done before she calls next week.

I walk to the kitchen with a little skip in my step. Having a plan of my own feels better. If I can solve it fast, everybody wins. Mom gets her challenge, Dad keeps his schedule, and I'll still have time to work on my history project.

As soon as I find Mom's mystery person tomorrow, I'll solve this challenge with half my brain tied behind my back.

Okay, maybe not tied behind my back, but I'll definitely figure out whatever Mom's got set up. I turn toward the murmuring voices inside my room.

"Hear that, Mom?" I whisper. "I'm ready for whatever you got. So, bring it!"

CHAPTER FOUR

Grindz

So, turns out Mom is pretty smart.

(I know, news flash, right?)

Those ladies from World War II she mentioned were amazing. How weird must it have been for them to live in a time when people thought girls should stay home and wear dresses and do girly stuff—but instead they became spies, codebreakers, and secret agents. They were super smart and could see patterns in places no one else could—and they did it in dresses and heels!

I shudder. I don't even wear my rubber slippers unless I have to. Just thinking about high heels makes my toes wiggle in protest.

I click away from one page and try another link.

If I had lived seventy-five years ago, I think I could have been good friends with Mavis Batey. She was amazing.

Her first job was looking for enemy spy messages hidden inside the personals section of the *London Times* newspaper. Sneaky spies thought they could send messages to the enemy by hiding them inside normal-looking ads and letters to the editor in the paper, but Mavis was sneakier and figured out their messages.

A car engine revs on the street, and I glance out the window in case it stops, but it just roars on by. Usually our street is pretty quiet since we're not on the main road to the university or anything, but today it seems like we've had a whole parade of cars drive by. Every time I hear a car, my chest gets all fluttery, hoping this will be the one to stop with Mom's message. But each time, the car drives on and my bubble of hope shrivels right back up. A whole day of filling up and letting down has my insides frayed.

When I get anxious, Malia's tutu always says I need to relax and think strong so I can feel more *ahonui*—that's like being really patient while still ready to persevere—but I've waited all day for Mom's mysterious messenger to bring me the next clue—how much more patience do I need?

As the car engine fades away, I turn back to my screen and click on the next page of WWII info.

Mavis Batey was so smart that when she turned nineteen, she got recruited into Bletchley Park, which was a secret superhero team of pretty much the smartest people on the planet (kinda like Mom with her clearance badge). They were the brains behind the war intel—like Jarvis, the supercomputer in Iron Man's suits, or maybe like Edna Mode's inventions inside the Incredibles' super-suits. So, Bletchley Park was basically the Avengers, but without the superhuman strength and stuff.

A quick rap on the door jolts me out of my seat faster than a flick of a crayfish's tail.

Finally! But before I can run to meet my mystery clue person, Malia's voice sounds from the lanai door.

"*Hui*, Alex? Aloha! Anyone home?" The screen door creaks open.

"I'm in here!" I grab my last page of notes and tape it up on the wall right between a poster of Nancy Drew sneaking with her magnifying glass and one of Braddah IZ holding his ukulele beneath a bright rainbow.

Malia walks in and scans the notebook pages taped to the wall.

"What is all that?" She stretches her arms up over her head and starts to yawn, but pulls back when her fingers brush some of Dad's origami creatures hanging from the ceiling. "Your family sure has a thing about paper."

I glance at my flock of origami and my notebook papers and shrug. She's not wrong.

"Why not do all your notes on the computer so you don't have to type them later?"

"I could, but I want to see it all at once. It helps me think better—like seeing my thoughts all spread out."

She jerks a thumb at the countless papers taped to my wall. "So you're saying it looks like choke papers hung all over for no reason, but it's really your brains splatted on the wall."

I smirk. "Yep. Zombies would think my wall is delicious."

"Perfect. If any show up, they can munch your wall brains while we run away. Good survival plan." She flops onto my bed and hugs a plush clown-fish pillow.

"How'd surfing go last night? I think I saw you and your sisters, but you were a ways out."

"Yeah, we paddled out right after school, but it was choppy so we bailed early."

"Did you get to use the new board, or did you take R2 out again?"

She gives a tired smile. "I used R2. But he didn't see much action. And besides, I wasn't really feeling it."

"Why? What's up?"

She shrugs. "I don't know what to do for my history project, and it's throwing me off."

"I thought you were doing a report on the leper colony on Moloka'i?"

"Naya's already doing that. Now I don't know what to do. If I do good, it'll make hers look bad, and if I don't do as good . . ." She rolls onto her side and closes her eyes. "*Ugh*, I need a new topic."

"What about something about rugby or surfing? Or that author you like so much—the one who writes about dragons?"

"Maybe." She peeks at my brains on the wall again. "What about you? That doesn't look like Nancy Drew book stuff."

"Naw, it's Mavis Batey—she's even better. In WWII, she broke spy codes that were supposed to be unbreakable." I touch an origami Pegasus so it spins slowly on its thread in the center of the room. "What topic sounds interesting to you?"

Malia pulls her feet up close and groans into the pillow. "How about the history of naps?"

I toss a plush starfish at her leg. "Is there such a thing?"

"So tired." She snags the starfish and hugs it. Her long black hair pools around her shoulders, her rugby uniform not quite hiding the swimsuit straps around her neck. "Your bed is *so* soft. You think your dad would notice if I accidentally stayed here?" She yawns again.

"Accidentally, eh? Don't you have a practice this afternoon?"

She pulls a pillow over her head. "Shh. I'm practicing my invisibility powers."

"It worked!" I hold my hands out as if searching. "Oh, no! Where'd Malia go? Her epic invisibility skills are too amazing. I can't find her anywhere." I flop across the bed over to her side. "Oh, look, I found her."

Head still covered, she lifts a finger and waves it across the plush pillows. "This is not the friend you're looking for."

"If you're so tired all the time, can't you drop one of the things you have to practice?"

She lifts the pillow to meet my gaze. "I can't. One of my sisters got a dance scholarship, but the other got one for surfing. One of those might work for me—but what if I'm better at rugby? What if I drop the thing I need most?"

"Okay, okay. I get it. It just seems like a lot." Everybody works a lot with two, sometimes three jobs, and Malia's family is no different. Scholarships are the ticket to college, so good grades, sports, skills—whatever. Malia's all in. But even a dolphin has to surface to breathe now and then.

"I can handle it. Just gimme a sec." She lets the pillow fall back over her face. "One sec."

I wait for the count of two and lean over her. "It's been a sec."

She throws a pillow, which sails past me and hits the wall right in the middle of Mom's unfinished chessboard. "Shh." She moans. "For real. Gimme a minute."

"Okay." We both know it'll be longer than a minute, but I let her sleep anyway and slip out the door to the table.

The screen door rattles, and I look up quick in case it's my mystery clue person, but it's only Auntie Tanaka. "Alex? Hello?"

"Coming!" I run to hold the door for Auntie, who kicks off her slippers at the foot of the stairs before coming inside. Balancing a paper grocery bag in one arm, she carries three more cloth bags dangling from the other.

I grab the paper bag as she bustles past. With Dad working at the school in Kahuku then teaching dive lessons till late, and Mom working overseas, Auntie took over some of the dinners. No matter what kind of grindz she makes—Spam fried rice, shoyu chicken, Kalua pork, sweet rolls, or whatever—it's all delicious.

"Ho, thanks, sweet girl. Help me put things away, 'kay?" She sets the bags on the counter and pulls out some dry noodles, cans of Spam, and vegetables. With a shrug, she slides her denim jacket off and hangs it by the door, her green and blue floral sundress flowing down to her calves. "*Ooh*, kinda chilly today."

"Small kine maybe." Anything below seventy-two is cold for our Auntie. I slide a package of dried seaweed into the cupboard. "What are you making?"

"Snozberries and rainbow drops."

"*Ugh*. Enough with the snot berries," I groan. Mom was always saying that, like it was the funniest thing ever, but it makes no sense at all. "Aw, come on. For real."

Auntie laughs at me. "Pork and noodles tonight. Tomorrow probably shoyu chicken. Matthew wants chicken katsu with curry and vegetables again, but I keep telling him there's more than one kind of food."

It'd be hard to convince him of that, 'cause Uncle Matthew Tanaka loves curry almost as much as my friend Jack loves chicken ramen—and that's saying something.

Uncle used to come over with Auntie, but now he mostly

stays home. Sometimes I think he likes his marine biology work for the university more than he likes people. It's still okay, though, because Auntie loves us well enough for both of them. When Mom was little, Auntie and Uncle sort of adopted her parents and stepped in when they had trouble. They welcomed Mom into their home until the line where our family ended and their family began blurred so much it didn't matter anymore. With Mom as their hānai child, our family is defined by love instead of blood.

Auntie's phone chimes and her ringed finger slides across the screen before putting it to her ear. "Hello?" She glances at me and then toward my room. "Is Malia here?"

"Yeah, she's in my room."

"Better get her. Her mom says she's got practice."

And that seems easy, but Malia is crashed out, her fingers loose around the pillows. Her feet dangle off the bed as I shake her awake. "Malia? Your mom called. You gotta go."

"Five more minutes?"

"Um . . . she called Auntie."

"*Ugh*. Fiiiine." She rolls out of bed and staggers toward the lanai.

"See you at school." I hold the door for her and check the street for anyone else, but nope. No mystery clue-holding people anywhere.

Sigh.

I help Auntie in the kitchen until dinner is almost ready, and Dad's car pulls into the driveway . . . alone. Still no mystery person.

He gathers dive equipment out of the trunk and locks it

in the shed before kicking off his slippers and giving me a side hug. "Mmm, smells delicious in here."

"Of course it does!" Auntie calls from the kitchen. "I cooked it, didn't I?"

"Good day?" I ask Dad, and glance at the empty street once more before letting the door close behind us.

He saunters toward the bathroom. "Yeah, but only one client ended up diving. The other got seasick before we even got to the reef. What about you? Get that report figured out?"

"I'm working on it. But I think maybe Mom was confused about someone bringing a clue, 'cause nobody's come all day. Nobody's even tried. I've watched."

"What do you mean nobody's come? I'm here, aren't I?" Auntie shakes a spoon at me.

"I know *you* are," I laugh. "But a mystery person was supposed to come bring me a clue, and they never came."

Dad chuckles while Auntie huffs, "Mystery? How am *I* a mystery? You've known me your whole life."

"Well, of course I know you—wait, do *you* have a clue for me?"

She gives me a sly smile, and I hurry across the tile floor.

"You do! Why didn't you say anything? I've been dying!"

"*Pfft.* You look plenty alive. And why would I say anything? You neva ask."

"Auntie, please." I clasp my hands together. "Can I at least have a hint?"

She raises the spoon again. "Too late to ask me now. Dinner is ready. Eat first. Talk story with your father." She winks. "Then we see."

CHAPTER FIVE

When Geckos Come for Dinner

I'm not sure what I was expecting. Another map, maybe? A code? A cipher? Coordinates? Newspapers? Any of that would make sense. But no.

After dinner, which takes forever, Auntie finally digs through her bag and fishes out a tiny bottle with a yellow string tied around the neck. "I've carried this for weeks."

I roll the tiny glass bottle in the palm of my hand. If it was made for drinks, it only holds a swallow. Only an inch and a half across on the bottom and less than three inches tall, it's shaped like the bottles people put little pirate ships in—but only if the pirate ship were small as a piece of gum.

I flip it upside down and check the bottom for markings, words, or letters, but there's nothing written anywhere. "What is it for?"

"You like me figure it out for you? Your mom said you

would know what to do." Auntie heaps noodles on a plate for Uncle Tanaka.

"Oh, I can do it. No prob. It'll be easy." My cheeks flush and I glance at Dad, but he's too busy crossing out wrong answers on the stack of math tests on the table to notice my mistake of asking for help already. Best it stay that way. "So, um, how's Uncle Tanaka?"

"He's been better." The purple and blue blossoms on Auntie's hair clip seem brighter than real flowers against her thick roll of black hair all twisted up and pinned with a hair pick. She hasn't changed much from the pictures of her and Mom when Mom was little—except for the gray wisps around her face. "Your uncle knows he should slow down, but he thinks he's the only one who can do the job. I keep telling him he doesn't have to rescue the whole ocean all by himself, eh? Other people can help too—group effort and all, but what do I know, eh?"

"Last one done!" Dad marks a score at the top of a test and circles it in red ink before checking his watch and rubbing his hands together. "That went faster than expected. So, Alex, are you ready for this challenge? You're going to love where it ends." He winks. "And no trying to needle any hints out of us. Neither of us know the whole plan, so no point in cheating."

"I wouldn't cheat." Even if I did ask, I already know the answer would be the same as always: *You're stronger than you know. Look around you, and rise where you stand.* As if that could possibly tell me anything useful. My heel bounces against the leg of the chair.

"Your mom is excited to hear all the details when you solve the challenge. But you'll need to work fast. You've got two weeks to figure out all the clues or you won't make it to the end in time."

"Two weeks to figure out what the bottle means?" That shouldn't be too hard.

He chuckles and shares a knowing look with Auntie. "The bottle is just the first step."

"Wait, this is going to take two whole weeks? What about my report?" My heel bounces faster, and my fingers tighten around the bottle, the glass smooth and cool inside my fist.

"We can carve out time for that too. We just need to schedule it in. I already made some notes for you." Dad's chair scrapes on the tile as he stands, lifts November's oversized calendar off the wall, and turns it to face me. "See? I marked out challenge time in red, and study time in blue—that could be when you work on your report."

I give him a smile because I know that's what he wants, but the calendar is bleeding red from all his marks. Was there blue on there at all? I close my eyes and take a long breath.

Dad and his schedule.

I don't remember the family "schedule" being a big deal when I was little, but recently, if something isn't on the schedule, it doesn't exist. And worse, if it *is* on the schedule, then rain, shine, or hurricane . . . we're doing it.

"Hey." Dad rubs my back and my eyes flutter open. "Where'd you go just now?"

"Nowhere. Just thinking. It's fine." The last word comes out with more bite than I meant.

"Ha!" Auntie chuckles. "That is the most *not*-fine I ever heard. You two had better talk story after I go, 'kay?"

Dad's smile falters as he looks from me to Auntie and

back again. "Ah, okay. Sure. We can talk about the schedule. Different colors maybe?"

Auntie pats Dad's side as she walks past. "Less talk, more listen, eh?"

"Right." He nods, but I know he's disappointed. All that work speckling the calendar with notes in colors and stuff— and I hate it. Worse, I stink at hiding what I feel.

"Thank you for dinner, Kamalani." Dad stacks the dinner dishes and carries them to the kitchen before rolling up his sleeves. "Next time, we could come to your place and save you the bother of cooking here."

"I know. Like old times." Auntie wraps Uncle's plate in wax paper. "But Matthew—he's . . ." She sighs. "That man. Well, anyway. Maybe later. For now, it's okay. It's not easy to help our Elizabeth—she does so much on her own. But this way, she knows you both get good food at least once a week. One less thing to worry about."

While Dad does the dishes, I put food away and try not to worry about schedules, reports, or competitions. Mostly I try not to think about anything at all—but it's hard. Just when I think I've stuffed one worry down, another pops up and takes its place like a game of whack-a-mole that never stops. Then I worry that I'm worrying too much. How weird is that? My heel bounces a little—not as much as when I'm on a chair, but enough that I catch Auntie watching me. Knowing she sees is enough to make it stop, but I itch to move my heel, or tap my thumb against each finger—or do anything other than work in the kitchen and pretend not to worry about how much I'm worrying.

"Alex?" Auntie pulls a little jar of guava jelly from the cupboard and sets it on the counter. "You like go feed the league?"

"Sure." I'm pretty sure she's just making excuses to get me out of the kitchen, but I don't care. I snatch the jelly and give Auntie a squeeze on the way out.

When I get to the dinner stump in the backyard, I pop the lid, and a dozen tiny green heads peek out from their hiding places near the stump like mini green meerkats. With bright black eyes and blue eyeshadow that matches their toes, our league of gold dust geckos scurries over warm rocks and twists down slender branches to be first at the dinner table.

Rising tall from the center of the stump, a sculpted swirl spirals around to form rings all the way across. I drop a tiny glob of jelly on every ring.

Blurring into lightning-fast streaks through grass and leaves, the geckos dart up the stump and onto the jelly-dotted swirl to eat.

With brilliant green bodies and faded red strips across their faces, our gold dust geckos lick their lips with thick pink tongues and lap the edges of the jelly. I count while they eat. Almost twenty today. Not bad.

We used to have problems with B-52 roaches and everything else, but since we started Sunday jelly dinners for the league, there are way less. Like yesterday, we still see one now and then, but it's only one. Anymore, we mostly keep an eye out for nasty centipedes under damp leaves. Dad says a big one at the farm on the mainland might be as long as my pinkie finger, but way skinnier, but here, a big one can be longer than my foot! Mean too, with a wicked bite—I've got a scar on my ankle to prove it.

"Alex?" Dad pads across the lawn while Auntie waves goodbye and carries Uncle's plate to her car.

He rubs the shell necklace he always wears and clears his throat. "Can we talk a minute?"

I shrug. "Okay."

"Are you worried you won't figure out Mom's challenge?"

"A little." Or a lot. Or maybe a really, *really*, lotta lot.

A fly lands on the jelly and three geckos strike for it at once, but only one gets to chomp the extra treat. The lucky gecko swallows and gulps, little fly legs and a wing sticking out the side of its mouth.

"So, you're worried about the challenge, and you don't like the schedule." It's not a question, more like Dad's confirming what he already knows.

My shoulders hunch. "Sorry."

Dad squeezes me in a one-armed hug and kisses the top of my head. "Hey, you got this. You'll do great. I know it."

I nod, but don't mean it.

Dad slips his hand in mine and leads me under the lanai to a plastic chair beside our old round glass table. "Hmm. Maybe we *do* need to talk story."

He sits across from me. "Help me understand why the schedule bothers you. Truthfully."

Truthfully? The word hangs between us.

With Mom gone, Dad does his best. He works two jobs—teaching at Kahuku and dive lessons after school. He never complains, even though I know he's tired. He's cheerful, he does dishes, and—if I asked—he would add me to his schedule almost anytime.

How can I complain? *Gee Dad, sorry, but I'm having an anxiety attack because I don't like the way you put colors on the calendar.* Where's the logic in that? I look away. "It's stupid."

"The calendar is stupid?" He carefully keeps his eyes on the gecko stump.

"No—" My fingers tap on my knee, and I fight to drag better words out of the muck inside my head. "Not the calendar. Me. Just me."

Dad frowns. "I'll be right back. Don't move." He jogs up the steps and into the house. A minute later, he comes back with November's schedule. "Have I ever showed you how to fold an origami gecko?"

I shake my head. What's he gonna do? Fold the schedule into one enormous gecko? It'd be as long as my arm.

He folds the schedule in half, creases it, then does it again several more times. But when he pulls the scissors out of his back pocket, I gasp!

"Wait!" I reach to stop him, but he leans away and snips along creases until several small perfect squares sit in a neat pile on the small glass table between us.

"It's just paper, Alex. And if it stresses you out, then it needs to change. So, what do you say we change some of it into geckos?" He passes me a square of what used to be his precious calendar.

Slipping another paper from the pile, Dad smooths it flat on the table and folds each corner toward the center. "When I met your mother, I thought she was the smartest person I'd ever met—that's probably still true. She's . . ."

His finger traces the lines of his paper as if the right words might be hiding in the creases.

"I'd never met anyone like her. Funny, kind, beautiful inside and out—and *brilliant*. I was so nervous at first, I got tongue-tied, while your mom spoke more languages than I could ever hope to learn. I gave her an origami butterfly on our first date, and amazingly enough, she liked it. Turns out, she loves origami like I do, with its clean, precise lines that turn a square of paper into something new."

Flipping the paper over, he reopens the first folds and makes new ones until his square looks more like a kite than a box, then waits for me to catch up.

"She already had an important job. Top-secret things she couldn't talk about, not even with me. But I fell in love, and—lucky for me—so did she."

My paper isn't as perfectly straight as his, but he nods like it's good enough.

"It wasn't so hard when we both worked overseas—me, enlisted in the navy, and your mom contracting with different forces—but then we found out about you."

I watch his clever fingers crease and fold the kite shape into something like a paper airplane.

"Make no mistake, we wanted you. Wanted you so much that we moved here to be near Auntie and Uncle. Your Mom had the better job, so I got out and became a teacher so I could stay with you when she had to go off-island for a job."

He reaches over to help straighten a flap on my paper.

"Know what's the hardest thing for me? I mean, besides being away from your mom in the first place?"

"What?" I follow along as he pinches and folds, and the new gecko begins to emerge.

"My total lack of control."

I jerk my head up. He feels that way too?

"I like order, problems that have solutions I can count on. It's beautiful to me—like this." He lifts his necklace with the bone carving of a nautilus shell. "You've seen the spirals and shells I collect. They all follow the golden ratio." He traces the curved line of the shell. "Mathematically, it follows the Fibonacci sequence as it expands using an irrational number that never repeats." He glances at me and smiles like I have a clue what he just said. "But it's more than a math problem. They call it the Divine Proportion because it occurs in nature all the time. Think of the way rose petals swirl around the center. That same spiral is in pineapples, cacti, sunflowers, the cochlea of the inner ear, the human face, ferns—even fingerprints. All of them follow the ratio. How cool is that?"

He spreads his fingers and shows me his open hands as if each finger held a jewel at the tip, and I can't help but smile at his excitement. He's like a kid with a favorite toy.

"TMI, I know. But the point is, in a chaotic world, I find peace in the small things like origami or the golden ratio. They're beautiful."

"Okay, but what does that have to do with the schedule?" I crease the spine of my gecko and watch while Dad begins a series of tight folds along the side of his creation.

"I have no control over where your mom goes—what's more—I wouldn't *want* to control her. This is her dream job. Of course I support her. But it's harder than I thought it would be to have our lives tossed about by top-secret officials in agencies that we can't talk about. So I started scheduling the things I *could* control. Replacing chaos and uncertainty with order, logic, and consistency."

Tiny, folded legs emerge on the sides of his gecko, and he holds it so I can see how it's done.

"I can control when I give dive lessons, when we have doctor or dentist visits, when I have time with you, and a million other things. The schedule is an anchor I hold to when I feel adrift."

"I know." Maybe not in so many words, but I know he stresses when we don't follow the plan.

He curls the tail in a gentle curve to the side, like a gecko at rest, and I mimic his work. "But for you, the schedule is stressful, yes?"

I breathe out a whoosh of air and nod. "It's like you said. You have control, but I don't. Not of anything—not even when to study. There's nothing left."

He dots an eye on either side of his gecko's head, sets it on the table, and hands me the pen to dot mine.

"I see. Sometimes I forget how fast you're growing up. How about we make a new schedule, and this time, we take turns?"

I set my gecko beside his. Not the same, but close enough. Family.

When Dad brings out a new oversized calendar page, he lets me make the first mark. I write "History Project" in gold— like a grand-prize trophy.

Then he draws a circle around Friday two weeks away and writes "Last Day" inside it.

We go back and forth like that until all his things and all my sleuthing days, study days, and even a play day with Malia are up where they belong. But instead of only red and blue, our new calendar is blue, and pink, and orange, and yellow, and *all* the colors. A rainbow with Mom's prize at the end.

CHAPTER SIX

Symbols & Centipedes

"So, all you have to go on is this little glass bottle?" Malia holds the bottle up for the other two girls to see as we walk home from Laie Elementary School. "What could you fit in here anyway?"

"Maybe it's for a small kine drink, like when you're only a *little* bit thirsty." Tehani reaches for the bottle, but her backpack slips off her thin shoulder, and she has to readjust the straps. Her mom wanted to get a smaller backpack, but this was the only backpack with kitty ears *and* glow-in-the-dark whiskers. Tehani would wear it even if she had to drag it behind her.

Malia passes the bottle to Tehani, who studies the bottom and turns it over. "No markings or anything? How are you supposed to know what this is?" The backpack starts to slip again, but our biggest friend, Naya, leans down and adjusts the strap for her with one hand. Naya's wide shoulders and thick frame make her strong enough to help anyone smaller than her—which is most of us.

"Thanks." Tehani lifts the bottle up high for Naya to take it, but she shakes her head.

"Naw, I'm good." Naya tosses her soccer ball high overhead and catches it again. "There's got to be more to it. Small kine like that—it's the world's most useless bottle."

"I'll figure it out." Taking the bottle back, I stare at it for the thousandth time, as if that'll do any good. During an art project in class today, I dabbed some paint on the bottom of the bottle and tried to use it for a stamp on paper, but all that did was make a mess. Jack suggested I try to make a rubbing of it like we've done with tombstone names, but the pencil marks didn't show anything different. No code to decipher, no words to figure out. If there's a code on the surface here, I don't see it.

"Eh, brah, watch out you slow pokes. Coming through!" Jack cruises past us, biking so fast he's standing on the pedals.

"For reals?" Tehani calls after him. "Where you going?"

"Sam's store!" Jack throws a shaka over his shoulder and keeps going. "Need some grindz before the rain hits."

Tehani bumps my elbow with hers. "You think he ever thinks of anything besides food?"

"Sure he does." Naya's lips curl into a sly smile. "Drinks."

I grin, and a raindrop splatters on my glasses.

"What about you?" Naya asks. "You ever *not* figured out one your Mom's clues?"

"No. I always do, but sometimes it takes me a little longer." If Mom got a clue like this bottle at her job, she'd probably be done already and on to her second clue by now. "If I could figure out how to think like her, I'd be faster."

"Maybe." Naya glances at the others, but I'm not sure if she gets it.

I try again. "Maybe it's impossible for me to think the same, sort of like a duck stretching its neck out really far and hoping to turn into goose." I flap my fingers to mimic a *nene*, the Hawaiian goose. "A duck could never be a nene—no matter how hard it tries. But that doesn't mean they can't swim together."

"Swim? Nah." Malia copies my finger flaps. "You two can fly."

Wet spots speckle the sidewalk, and I blink up at the clouds swirling overhead as they drift in from the sea. Some curl in lazy white spirals against the skirts of the mountain, while others capture treetops in misty tendrils and cling tight to the world below.

Tehani slips her arms out of her kitty backpack and stuffs it (mostly) under her shirt. "I gotta go! See you tomorrow!"

"See you!" I wave as she scurries down the street, the backpack straps dangling around her knees as she runs for cover.

As the rain picks up, drops splash off our noses, hang from our lashes, and fog my glasses. Apparently my bowler hat was not the best choice for today—tiny brim and all that. "Hang on." I pull my backpack off and hold it overhead like a second hat. "Malia, can you hold this a second?"

"Sure." She holds my backpack-umbrella while I use a dry spot on my shirt to wipe my glasses off. She and Naya don't mind the rain. They both are in and out of the ocean so much, they barely notice a little extra water.

"Thanks."

"You've got books and stuff in there. Sure you don't want

to stuff your backpack under your shirt too?" Malia watches Tehani disappear around the corner down the street. "This storm might get cranky."

"Naw, this one's waterproof. Dad got it for me for when he's diving." For when I'm sitting on the beach . . . not diving. "It's sealed pretty tight. So if the tide sneaks up, or if the whole bag falls in, it's still cool. Everything inside would stay dry if I got it out fast enough. A little rain won't hurt."

"I still don't get why you won't come out on the waves with us." Naya tucks the soccer ball under her arm and turns to watch us as she backs toward her house on Moana Street. "You can swim, and we could teach you how to surf, so what's the deal? Don't you get tired of watching the action from the beach? You'd need binoculars to see anything from there."

Malia glances at me before lifting her face to the sky, her arms spread wide as if to catch as many raindrops as possible. A distraction—her slow, silly spin gives me time to think. Of course *she* knows. But best of the best, she'd never tell.

"See?" Naya jabs a thumb at Malia and grins. "If she does this on land with just a little water, imagine what kooky stuff you're missing out there."

"Who says I'm missing out? *You* might need binoculars, but I've got my brand-new secret spyglass!" I lift the tiny glass bottle to my eye like a telescope and stick my tongue sideways. "See? Finally! I found a use for . . ."

A faint mark shimmers on the bottom of the bottle.

"No way." I flip the bottle over to check, but no, the marks aren't visible on the outside. Holding it up again, I peer through the mouth of the tiny bottle and move side to side, testing the angle. The mark only shows on the inside when the light hits the bottom of the bottle just right.

"What? What is it?" Raindrops streak down Malia's forehead, and Naya jogs up beside us.

"There's a mark inside." I set my backpack on the ground and look up through the bottle toward the lightest part of the cloud cover where the sun is trying—and failing—to shine through. The whole mark lights up, and I'm pretty sure it's a word, but not one I can read.

救援

Mom loves languages, but words come slower for me—and I can't remember if I've ever seen this character or not. "I can't read it, but I think it's a word."

I hand it to Malia and wait as she peers inside. "Whoa. Sweet."

"It'll be sweeter if I figure out what it means." Mom loaded a translation app on my phone last month, but could it scan something *inside* a bottle? Too wet for phones out here for sure.

Malia holds the bottle out to Naya, who tucks the soccer ball under her arm then tilts the bottle from side to side until it catches the light. "Nice. It's not one I know, but if you can't get it, maybe we ask my mom or grandma to help, hah?"

"Sounds good. I'll text you." I take the bottle back.

"No prob." Naya tosses the rain-slicked ball, catches it, and bounces it off her knee. "See you tomorrow."

"I better get home too. I've got hula practice, and this is gonna take more than a little brushing." Malia smooths her dripping curls off her face and shakes the extra water off her hands. Pulling hair as thick as Malia's back smooth into a bun for hula practice takes some doing. She takes a step but glances over her shoulder at me. "Want to come? You haven't practiced since school started."

"Maybe after Mom gets back. I have to solve this and work on my report." I shrug. "Dad's schedule grew colors."

"Ah, did he add pins yet? Or magnets?"

"Not yet. But he did fold the old schedule into geckos before we made this one."

"Fo' real? That's the best. Gotta go, see ya!" She waves and jogs for home as I grab my backpack.

"Yeah, see you tomorrow!" I bolt for home, but not fast enough.

A few houses away from our yard, the clouds start dumping water like someone unzipped their bellies to let it pour out all at once. As if waiting for the signal, wind sweeps through the street, each gust pressing sheets of raindrops together like schools of fish before splatting them against the ground in torrential showers.

Tiny rivulets blur my glasses, which slide down every few steps just to spite me, and when I leap over a puddle, they slip right off my nose! I catch them—*barely*—before they splash into the mud. Holding them tight to my face with one hand, I race through the rain and dash under the lanai.

I grab a towel to wipe off my lenses, but jump as thunder cracks overhead. Gray mists churn and boil beneath a low ceiling of clouds, their ghostly tendrils reaching down as if grasping for lost raindrops.

Just in case the downpour decides to flood us again, I move the slippers up a step and bring my bowler hat inside to dry. As I climb the steps, I try to ignore the high-water mark Dad painted on the stilts below our front door. My fingers tap one to the next, and I take a deep breath to still the rising tide of anxiety inside.

"It's not a flood. It's only rain, relax." I roll my neck and grasp the doorknob. What did Malia call the storm? Cranky. Just a regular storm with its cranky-pants all in a bunch. Nothing to worry about.

A flash of lightning starts me counting. On "six-one-thousand," thunder rumbles through the house, and I close the door with a satisfying click.

Water pools around my feet as I set my bowler hat on a chair to dry, drop my backpack onto one of Auntie's woven mats, and towel off. A couple minutes later and a lot drier, I flip the desk lamp on and peer through the bottle at the light.

With the bright glow right behind it, the hidden symbol shines through with fine lines. Painted, I think, not etched.

What if I hadn't looked in there? Wouldn't that have been a great conversation—*Um, no, Mom, I never did do the obvious thing and look inside, but I did paint the bottom of the bottle and squish it onto paper before rubbing pencils across it.* I groan.

Mom would never laugh at me, but then again, she wouldn't have to. I'd die of embarrassment long before she had the chance. She sees patterns everywhere, and a change in sequence hits her brain like a big red stop sign. I see the patterns too, but I don't always know what they mean. Sometimes when I see something off, it gets stuck in my head. My thoughts worm back to it again and again, the answer staying just out of reach behind swirling mists like our mountaintop; I know it's there, and I could find it if I had to, but I can't quite see it from where I am.

I open the translator app and hold the phone's camera up

to the mouth of the bottle, but it can't quite focus right no matter which angle I try. Okay, *fine*. Time for plan B.

I copy the lines into my notebook and triple check that it's right before scanning the image with my phone. Possible translations pop up:

Rescue. Relief. Aid.

"Rescue what?" I roll back from the desk and stand to scan it again from right over top, but the answer comes back the same. I slump back into the chair and stare up at my paper flock as if one of them might hold the answer, but nothing new pops in my head. My stomach growls; *break time.*

Leaving both notebook and bottle on my desk, I pad to the kitchen for a snack and flip the light switch. In the middle of the counter sits a bowl filled with the most beautiful fruit known to humankind.

Rambutan.

Okay, they're more like weird, round, red things with tiny little tentacles all over, sort of like wonky sea urchins, or maybe furry alien golf balls. But inside them is the most delicious fruit ever. They're like lychee—but way better. Kind of like a giant grape inside.

"Thank you, Auntie!" It's *possible* that Dad found time to grocery shop, but I doubt it.

I grab a knife and cut all the way around the center and pull the two red halves apart, revealing the pale, translucent center of sweetness. The second one disappears almost as fast as the first one, but I lean against the counter and take my time with the third. So, *so* good.

Across the kitchen, under the pots and pans that hang

from a metal rack, the rice cooker's little orange light glows steady on "keep warm."

Something darts past the rice cooker and slithers off the edge of the counter. A blur of orange and gray too fast to see.

Was that a centipede?

Nope, nope, nope! My toes curl and I jump to the center of the tile floor, eyes straining to check each shadow beneath the cupboards. The knife still in my hand, I squat to peer under the fridge for slithering bodies, rippling legs, or slicing pincers. Centipedes are the worst.

Fist tight around the knife, I wait for a shadow to move, but nothing does. Not under the cupboards, and not on the counters.

It's not that I want to see one, but I saw something, and the scar on my ankle prickles with remembered warnings. If it's here in the house, and I can't find it, it might find me first—and I *never* want that to happen again. I lean over the counter, set the knife down, and pull scissors out of a drawer.

Dad would do it if he were home, but if it slips past me, we could lose it for weeks. I can't risk it.

Fingers tight around the scissors, I take another step toward the wall. The blur headed that way, didn't it?

My gaze slides up the wall toward the picture frames—and it moves.

I suck a breath as a tiny head shifts, bright eyes staring back at me.

A lucky house gecko.

Gray-blue with orange spots, he clings to a picture frame of Grandma and Grandpa Force and lifts his chin as if to scold me for interrupting his bug hunt.

The little guy is on a mission, and I'm blowing his cover.

With legs wobblier than seaweed, I lean against the counter and drop the scissors as the gecko strolls across the picture of Dad's old farmhouse.

Inside the frame, Grandma and Grandpa Force stand frozen with pale arms raised mid-wave on the steps of a white wraparound porch—they would never call it a lanai like we do. For them, it's all porches, beef, and potatoes. Probably never had a bite of poi in their lives. They're the reason I get cards from the mainland every Christmas and birthday like clockwork, and I send thank-you notes back. They ask about school, talk about the weather, and dream about getting together one of these days . . . which is a lot like someday . . . which is a lot like never.

The gecko races across the next picture, where Mom and Dad smooch in front of Rainbow Falls on the Big Island. It's way newlywed and sappy, with all the hand-holding and mushy stuff.

Obviously grossed out by all the kissing, our gecko leaps off the picture frame and lands on a photo of Auntie and Uncle grinning from the bow of Uncle's boat, *Sarge's Barge*. Auntie wears a swimsuit with a lavalava tied around her waist, her warm brown shoulders encircled by Uncle's strong arms.

The gecko hops onto the wall, his magic sticky-toes splayed wide as he skitters across the smooth wall and hangs there, over Auntie and Uncle's picture.

I've seen that picture a million times—can close my eyes and *still* see every detail: flowers in Auntie's hair, Uncle's Spartan race bandana, and their new puppy, Sarge, a brown and white fluffball barely big enough to peek over the gunwale of *Sarge's Barge.*

Except this time, a scrap of paper sits tucked into the corner of the frame—and it's stamped with the same mark as the one inside the bottle.

⊙ ⧬ ⬒ ⬡ ◗◯⟆⟆ ⬡◯⟆⬡⬡ ⟆◗⟆

CHAPTER SEVEN

Deep Water

The gecko licks his eyeball with a pink tongue that slimes up over his brow and darts back into his mouth. He studies me with wide eyes split down the center by black irises drawn tight into a vertical line. Whatever bug he was chasing must've got away, 'cause he settles onto the picture and turns his whole head to watch as I ease close enough to pluck the paper out of the frame.

I check the back side for more clues and hold it to the light, but there's nothing there, so I flip it back and stare at the symbol again. My app says it means "rescue," but it might as well read "Mom was here," because it means the same thing to me.

救援

The gecko curves its whole body and stretches one arm out, the fat, lined pads of its front toes grasping at the air like it wants to read too, but its tail flops over the frame and it clings tight to the wood again.

With the gecko's tail dangling over their heads, Auntie and Uncle smile out at me from the photo like they're waiting for me to figure out the rest of the clue.

"I know, I know. There's something more," I agree, but nothing on the picture seems out of place. The beach behind Auntie's house, the boat, the dog, some coconut trees and bushes to the side—nothing weird to see. At least, nothing on the *front* of the picture.

"Time to move, buddy." I lift the picture off the wall and lower it to the floor until Mr. Gecko jumps off and scurries behind a bookshelf in search of more bugs.

Something knocks against the back of the picture and bumps my hand as I stand up. When I turn the frame over, a tiny glass stopper swings back and forth, dangling from a yellow string attached to the top. Mom's swirling handwriting scrawls across the backing, spelling out a single word:

RISE

"Ha! Found it!" I glance at the space where the gecko had disappeared and raise the picture so he can see it if he's still back there in the shadows. "See? Mom *was* here."

Cradling the picture with one arm, I trace the loops of her writing with a finger. "Okay, so, 'Rise.' You mean, like . . . get up and go now?" I glance at the rain splattering against the window. "Or like find another clue on the family crest?"

Just in case, I check the back of the tapestry, but there's nothing there.

I roll the glass stopper back and forth. Maybe it means go at moonrise? Or sunrise?

Would Auntie already be headed to work at sunrise? She goes in pretty early, along with loads of other residents and students who work at the Polynesian Cultural Center—PCC for short—to teach tourists about Polynesian cultures.

Or maybe "Rise" could be the name of a new program there? I know there's a luau and special shows besides all the little villages of different nations like Fiji, Samoa, and Hawaii. But maybe there's a new presentation I haven't heard of yet?

I don't know, but whatever it means, Auntie's definitely in the middle of it. *She* gave me the bottle, and the new paper clue was tucked in the corner of a picture of her and Uncle. I grab the phone and text her.

Found the picture clue. Can I come over?

Rain patters against my window in waves. First a light smattering, then a downpour, and then light again. I scowl at the storm. Is the worst of it over or not? I wish it would make up its mind.

Either way, it's gonna be real wet. Better walk, not ride my bike. Probably it'd take less than ten minutes to get there if I hurried, and Dad's umbrella would keep the rain off as long as the wind doesn't blow too hard. I'd stay dry—mostly.

My phone chimes.

Wait till rain stops. Check weather in 30 min.

Not the answer I want, but I guess that gives me time to study. I scan the history notes on the wall. "Okay, Mavis, looks like you're up. Let's do this."

My computer screen flickers as I click past news reports

of typhoons forming in the Pacific and pull up references on Mavis Batey.

Notes fill my pages. Red and blue are Dad's favorite colors to use, but I mark Mavis's key biographical dates in yellow, her accomplishments in green, her family things in purple, and on and on. With colors clinging to my notes like bits of sea glass, the pages whisper their secrets at a glance.

When the patter of rain on the roof finally stops, I grab my oilskin hat and head for Auntie's house.

There are nine hundred and eighteen steps between our house and Auntie's. I know because Mom counts them under her breath every time we walk. Once, I counted how many mailboxes, cars, and driveways there are between our house and the roundabout near Hukilau Beach and wrote it all down so she would know the counts already. I thought maybe one less thing for her to worry about might make more space for me.

Mom thanked me but didn't stop counting things on her own. I guess her numbers sound better than mine.

Snuggled between Kamehameha Highway and the beach, Auntie and Uncle Tanaka's house sits behind a stone wall with gnarled Hau trees twisting up around the gate. Dad says the solid metal gate was Uncle's idea, and the person-sized door to the side was Auntie's.

Weathered hinges creak as I swing the heavy wood door open, slip inside, and close out all the traffic behind me. Lush trees, flowers, and bushes line the edges of the walls from decades of Uncle's and Auntie's gentle gardening. Colored stones border the flower beds in patterns from when Mom used to spend her afternoons here, before she had to work all the time.

The first message I ever figured out says "I love you" in Morse code, with sky blue for dashes, yellow for dots, and green for spaces.

Out of habit, I steer clear of the stinky fruit under the noni tree and hop over another of Mom's patterns laid into the bricks of the pathway; a pigpen cipher that spells "Ohana"— *family*.

Cracks between the bricks glisten where rain had kissed each nook and cranny during the storm. It won't stay wet long, though. Already, patches of blue sky push the clouds aside, and sunshine warms my skin as it peeks through the holes to chase the last of the mist away.

I ignore the front door and head for the lanai on the side where three Hala trees stand guard over the pathway. With their shaggy heads and towering roots rising out of the ground like legs, they seem to perch on the tips of their toes, waiting for the right moment to run across the yard and find a new spot—but of course they never do.

Tucked under the lanai, a half-full basket of long, slender lauhala leaves waits to be woven into mats, baskets, hats, or maybe something else for PCC. Part of their mission is to pre-serve Polynesian traditions like Auntie's weaving, so she teaches Polynesian university students how to do that or make purple poi paste from taro roots if they don't know how already.

Auntie's tried to teach me, but I'm not great at weaving,

and patience isn't my strongest thing. But I do love to hear her play the ipu gourd while others dance the hula. She's amazing.

"Aloha, Auntie!" I call through the screen door, and wait for permission to enter.

"Over here!" Auntie calls from the backyard.

I jog around the side of the house to the open grass that slopes down to the sea. About halfway between, Auntie sits on a log in the shade of coconut trees while Uncle works on his boat in his red Kahuku T-shirt, cutoff jeans, and slippers. He's shorter than Dad, and maybe a little more wiry, but he's just as strong from a lifetime of hiking shorelines and riding waves. He used to run, too.

"So, what's this you found?" Auntie pats the towel draped over the log beside her.

Treading across the lawn, I pull the glass bottle with the stopper from my shorts pocket. "I found a glass stopper behind the picture of you and Uncle in the boat, and it fits in the bottle. Did you know it was there? I thought maybe—"

A deep bark rumbles over the sound of the waves as a furry mountain rises up from the firepit behind Auntie and glares at me.

I slow, but Auntie turns and nudges the enormous dog aside with one hand. "Hey, you behave. Get. Alex is ohana, and don't you forget it."

"Hi, Sarge." I flutter a few fingers at the mammoth Newfoundland, but he ignores me like always and lumbers over between us and Uncle before flopping down on the grass. Sand clings to the tips of his long white and brown hair where it dried into crusty icicles. Strings of drool swing from his jowls and splatter slobber-drops across the grass as he huffs once in my direction and lays his head on his paws.

Auntie clucks her tongue. "What? You think she'll take Uncle's time from you? He has plenty time to share."

"I do not. Haven't got one thing done all day." With his back to us, the sun shines bright on every white strand that speckles his long black hair.

"You've worked plenty. And when's the last time you visited with our Alex, eh?"

Wiping his hands on a rag, Uncle glances my way and gives me the tiniest of smiles—so quick it barely moves his wispy beard and mustache before it's gone again. "Good to see you, Alex."

"She's got something from Elizabeth," Auntie says. "One of those hidden messages. Come look."

"You go ahead. I hear fine from over here."

"Shame; is that the best welcome you can do? Why not just show her the door?" Auntie shakes a finger. "You keep pushing everyone away and someday you'll find no one there when you need it most."

"I don't push them away; they go on their own." Uncle pushes his copper glasses up with the back of his wrist and turns back to his work.

"*Pfft.* And the wind doesn't blow. Fo' reals!"

"They do what they want! The day I invite people in for more trouble is the day pigs fly."

If I didn't already know better, he might've hurt my feelings, but that's just how Uncle is, so I try to keep out of his way as much as I can. His *"Go away"* is loud and clear without him ever saying another word. It's Auntie I came to see anyway.

A tourist family walks by on the beach, their children splashing in the surf. Over and over, the kids dart out and back, their laughter rising over the *shhhh—shhh* of waves crashing softly as they roll in from the deep and wash over the sandy shore.

I hand Auntie the little bottle and sit beside her on the log. "See how the stopper fits? The yellow string is a match too. And I found this." I take my oilskin hat off, fish the square paper out from between the liner and the sweatband, and show Auntie the matching marks from the bottle and paper.

She's still holding up the bottle to peek inside when Uncle sets his tools aside and walks over. "Have you been into my samples? Those aren't toys. You didn't dump out the vial, did you?"

"Hush, she didn't dump out anything. Our Elizabeth made a challenge for Alex, and it seems you're a part of it." She passes him the square. "Read this."

Uncle tilts his head back to read through the bottom part of his glasses as Sarge shoulders his way between us, his long tail knocking against my knees as he gazes up at his favorite human.

"Sarge, ow!" I lean away, but his tail beats a steady rhythm. *Whap, whap, whap!* He wags fast and hard like maybe he's hoping his tail might sweep me right off the log and out of the yard.

"It's marked inside the bottle too." Auntie passes him the vial, and Uncle scowls at it as he squints inside.

"My phone says it means 'rescue,' but I'm not sure if it's right . . ." I scramble off the log and stand out of Sarge's reach behind Auntie.

His hand shaking, Uncle checks the bottom of the vial and growls, "That's what it means, but what good is a marked-up vial? I can't take samples with this. It's ruined."

"I thought maybe there might be something here to match it." My voice feels very small even to my own ears, but under Uncle's prickly gaze it's a miracle I can talk at all.

"Fo' real, Matthew?" Auntie chides and Uncle snaps back, but I stop listening when I see the new stones curving around the base of Auntie's banana tree. The 'rescue' character is painted in blue on a yellow stone, and a string of colored rocks follows after. Yellow, yellow, blue, green, blue, yellow . . . The colors fade as my brain focuses on the pattern. Morse code again. I pull my notebook from my bag and check my notes. Dot dot dash—a U in Morse code. And more: dash dot, dash dot dash dot, dot dash dot dot, dot.

UNCLE

Morse code. Together, Mom's clues in the rocks say, "Rescue Uncle."

I watch him as he grumps back and forth with Auntie. ". . . but why not use a marker or paper? Why ruin the bottle?"

"You'd give that girl the moon if she asked. What's one little bottle to you?" Auntie laughs.

How could I possibly rescue Uncle? He's a marine biologist—and super smart. He's been working for the university since before I was born; getting samples; teaching students; doing all the things that keep him so busy and gone on the water and on the reefs. Mom and Dad both talk like he's so much fun, and I think he used to be—I might even remember it a little—but he's been grumpy for so long, I can't remember what his laugh sounds like. It's like all of his happy sailed away one day, and grumpy was all that came back.

I scan the yard and spy more color-coded rocks by the breadfruit, banana, and papaya trees.

WORK, TOGETHER, HELP, OHANA

Help Uncle rescue things for work? I turn the words over, rearranging them in my head. Together, help Uncle rescue work family? What would be his work family that needs rescuing?

"Do you rescue things in the ocean?" I blurt, and Uncle blinks at me while a sly smile slides over Auntie's face.

"I collect samples to test water quality and—"

"Turtles, dolphins, sea lions—my Matthew would rescue the entire ocean if he could." Auntie beams at him.

"Well someone needs to do the work," says Uncle. "And there's only so much a man can do by himself."

By himself. An idea wiggles into my head and I bite my tongue to keep it from popping out of my mouth. Is this really what Mom meant? The waves rumble onto the sand, and beyond them, deep blue stretches to the horizon with vast sky above and impossible depths below.

Deep water strong enough to snatch people from the shore.

Deep water with hidden creatures.

I shake my head and step back, but no one here is asking me to do anything. It's only Mom and me, arguing inside my head.

I don't have to do it.

Auntie and Uncle can't make me.

Dad won't make me.

Mom won't make me. But if I don't, I'll never find Mom's next clue—won't finish the challenge. It'll be over, and I'll have to tell Mom I couldn't do it—that I couldn't keep up, that I wasn't smart enough—that I quit because I'm scared of things I can't even see.

Dad's voice echoes in my head. *"You've got two weeks."*

Two weeks to figure it all out. Or two weeks to fail.

I've never failed a challenge yet. And I'm not going to start now. I squeeze Auntie's shoulder. "I think I know what Mom's clues mean."

They watch me, Uncle grudgingly, Auntie expectantly.

I lift my chin and take a breath. "I need to help Uncle with his work."

CHAPTER EIGHT

Brain Freeze

"Wait, you're going with Uncle Tanaka to collect samples?" Malia sets her rainbow shave ice on the only spot on the cement table *not* covered by my notes—if I can even call them that. Maybe a better name would be scratch paper of failed attempts. For all the good they've done, Malia could call them scribbles and still be right.

"Yeah, I'm pretty sure I'm supposed to help him 'cause Auntie only gave me this index card with all these jumbled up words *after* I asked Uncle if I could help. But why? I mean, if I'm supposed to figure out this new clue, why make me offer to help first and *then* give it to me?"

A Japanese white-eye swoops in and flutters under the table between us and Malia's older sisters. With green-yellow feathers and a gray belly, the white-eye hops across the patio pecking at this or that. But after a few seconds, he flies off toward L&L Hawaiian BBQ. Seems chickens already cleaned this area out.

Malia turns my new clue card over. "What does it mean?"

"I'm not sure yet. I had to use a Caesar cipher to change the letters on the card before I could read it at all. Now the letters are good, but they don't all make words yet. It's a tricky one."

She passes the card back to me. "No, I mean, is this card going to help you when you're working with Uncle Tanaka?"

"That's the problem; I don't know." The door to Angel's Ice Cream, Smoothies, and Shave Ice swings open, and one of Malia's sisters walks by. I lower my voice. "Does it mean I'm supposed to work with Uncle every day? Or only on special days? No idea."

I sip my pineapple float and scowl at the mess of papers surrounding the oversized index card with Mom's coded messages. I've had it for two days, but I'm still not sure what Mom means by it.

Sometimes it's easy to think like she does or at least see what she'd notice—like how many tables there are on the patio outside Angel's. She'd know how tall the umbrellas are that rise out of the center of every table: three red, three orange, and three yellow. Nine of them. Mom would know that. She'd probably know how many windows and doors lined the parking lot too, but I don't think that would help with this clue.

"Was Uncle Tanaka excited you wanted to help?"

I wrinkle my nose. "Well, after I asked to help, Uncle sort of sputtered and choked till his face turned all purple before Auntie made him go inside . . . so maybe *that* counts as excited?"

"Sure. Let's pretend he's so excited he can't hardly stand it." Malia smirks and stabs a spoon into her shave ice a couple times to mix in the evaporated milk topping. "You think you'll get to put stuff in those little bottles?"

A rooster with long black tail feathers crows and flaps his wings. Perched on top of a car with surfboards on the roof, he crows again and puffs his feathers. *The show-off.*

"I don't know if we'll use bottles. Maybe? I'll find out this weekend when I go with him."

"But I thought he works—" She glances at Jack and the guys walking out of Angel's with their heaping shave ice cups and whispers. "You know, out on the ocean."

"*Shh.* Don't jinx it. He works by the shore too—with tide pools and stuff. Maybe we'll do that? No one said we had to go way far out or anything." I swirl the cardboard straw in my half-melted pineapple float and take a sip as the boys settle at the next table over.

". . . and then Tehani's mom says I'm gonna be the tree. A tree!" Kase holds his arms out like a palm tree with a spoon in one hand and a towering bowl of rainbow-colored shave ice in the other. "You think it's 'cause I'm tall?"

"Hey! Watch it." A man behind Kase stops so fast his safari hat slides off, and he teeters on his tippy-toes—his face close enough to Kase's shave ice that his nose almost touches it. Right behind him, a lady in a sparkly sun hat and matching miniskirt holds their Pizza Hut box high overhead to keep from smashing it into her date.

"Sorry." Kase pulls his shave ice back and steps aside.

"Unbelievable. No regard at all." The tourists grumble and stride past to a sit at a table near the end of the patio.

"So does that make me a good tree or a bad one?" Kase sits next to Ekolu at the table beside us.

"Brah, at least you didn't end up a reindeer." Ekolu points to his face. "She says I gotta wear a red nose. On this! You can't mess with perfection. No way."

"Naw. You want perfection? This is perfection." Kase stabs a spoon into his rainbow ice tower. "You're a close second—maybe."

"Second!" Ekolu sits up straight, his spoon hovering over the shave ice. "Second to none, brah. Prove me wrong. I'll take you on right now."

"Ooooh." Kase grins. "You're going down. First one to finish wins."

"Don't do it." Malia picks up another paper to study. "You should quit now before it's too late."

"Oh, it's happening." Kase sits across from Ekolu, his spoon at the ready. "On three."

"You'll hurt your brains." Jack takes another tiny bite of ice.

"One." Ekolu leans over his bowl.

"Lolo boys." Malia slides a paper aside and reads the next.

"Two." Kase raises an eyebrow.

"Remember last time?" Jack nibbles his ice. "It did not go well."

"I've been practicing!" Ekolu grins. "Don't distract me."

"Don't encourage them." Malia passes Jack a page. "Have you seen Alex's notes?"

"Three!" Kase and Ekolu shovel scoop after scoop into their mouths, plastic spoons flying so fast they almost blur.

Jack stands behind Malia and scans the table full of papers. "Whoa, you think you have enough notes? What's it for—history?"

"Nope, it's part of Mom's challenge."

Slurping and smacking, Kase and Ekolu wolf down the tops of their shave ice and dig into the bottom half.

"You got it figured out?" Jack savors another spoonful, his dark brown eyes scanning the table.

"No," I grumble.

"She had to decode the *code* first to try and figure out the real code." Malia glances at me. "Right?"

"Yeah, I couldn't read any of the words at all until I figured out that Mom used a Caesar cipher—you know, with all the letters moved over like this." I point to an ABC list on the table with a second set of ABCs beside it, except shifted over so all the letters are one letter off.

$$A = B$$
$$B = C$$
$$C = D$$

"I had to work out how to shift the alphabet. Left, right, how many spaces—like that—before I found real words."

"You got it?" Jack slides into the seat beside Malia and picks up a page.

"I think so. Shift all letters one space to the left, and that TUBOET word turns into STANDS."

Ekolu—or maybe Kase—slurps loud as they wolf it down.

"Can you guys even taste your shave ice?" Malia asks, but the boys barely give her a glance, their eyes locked on each other as they shovel spoonful after frozen spoonful into their mouths.

I pass my new, corrected card to Jack. "But some words still don't make sense; like, who is Janob? And why spell

KOOL with a K instead of a C? Plus there's the AND with the initials S and T over that."

```
J AN OB    STANDS 3.14159        S
              HE      READS: T
                        PERSEVERANCE
      BEST < 1.61803398875       E
             ALL                 N
                                 G
          K       (SHELF)        T
    S     O       SHELF          H
    T     O
    A N D L       SHELF
```

I shrug. "There's got to be a second code or cipher or something, but—"

Shrill squawking erupts, and Ekolu and Kase jerk their feet out from under the table like the floor turned to lava.

In a blur of feathers, a speckled hen flaps her wings and clucks like crazy-pants as she rushes past us with ten fluffball chicks scurrying along behind.

"What the—" Kase stands and watches the feathered train dodge from table to table to the feet of the tourists with the pizza. The hen's squawks change to contented clucks as she gathers her brood around a pizza crust.

Leave it to tourists to feed chickens in the middle of a restaurant patio. More chickens here just means more poo. The safari hat man rips off more crust and drops it on purpose.

Malia and I share a look with Kase, and he raises a brow. "Tourists. No regard at all, eh?"

I open my mouth to tease him back, but a weird, slurpy-sucking sound rises behind us.

"Hey!" Kase yelps and grabs for his shave ice as Ekolu raises his bowl to his lips and slurps the last of it down. "No fair!"

"Boom!" Ekolu throws a double shaka. "Totally fair. No one said stop. Who's the best? *Me.* That's right. I'm awesome." But like a glitch on a screen, Ekolu's smile cracks and he gasps, drops the spoon, and grabs the sides of his head. "*Gah!* Ow—brain freeze! *Aagh!*" He pants with his mouth wide.

Jack snickers but barely looks up from my clue card. "Told you to slow down, brah. You need every brain cell you got."

"Hold your tongue against the roof of your mouth. It warms up faster." Malia half turns in her seat.

Eyes shut tight, Ekolu snaps his mouth shut and grits his teeth.

"I'll get you some water." Kase jumps up, dodges a couple more tourists, and ducks into Angel's again.

I can't help but feel bad for Ekolu, his face brighter than ginger flowers. "You okay over there, Ekolu?"

Teeth gritted, he shakes his head and whimpers. "Ugghhh!"

Kase bursts out of the shop and hands Ekolu a cup of water. "Here. This'll help."

Ekolu grabs the glass and gulps it down, the red in his face draining almost as fast as the water. With a cough, he gives a weak shaka. "Mahalo, brah. That was bad."

"Yeah, that's what you get for cheating." Kase swirls the last of his shave ice around his bowl. "And you suffer for nothing, because that win doesn't count."

"Does too count. I won," Ekolu pouts.

"Did not."

"Did too. Keep talking and we'll have to duel it out at Castle Tree."

"As Loremaster of Castle Tree, I declare your challenge invalid." Kase licks his spoon.

"That was just a title we made up for you because you're new here. It doesn't mean you get to 'declare' things forever," Ekolu grumbles.

"Sure it does." Kase grins. "No one else wrote anything down. I'm grandfathered in as Loremaster."

"What? 'Cause you brought a notebook to a tree fort? Who does that?" asks Ekolu.

Who knew that by letting him write down our made-up lore about the coolest banyan tree in town, the rest of the Castle Crew and I were forever handing all the power to Kase—all because he was the first kid who thought to bring a notebook and pencil.

Jack turns the corrected clue card to face me. "Were you being serious about not knowing what any of these mean?"

"Yeah, I don't know, but I can figure it out." I always do. At least, I hope I can. "I'm missing another layer, another code . . . or something. It's complicated."

"Maybe you just *think* it's complicated; simple answers can be right too."

"Mom doesn't do simple. I mean, she works in counter-intelligence. She breaks codes in her sleep faster than I can read them out loud. I just have to try harder."

Jack sets the card on the table between Malia and me. "Well, then I think you should stand in the corner until you figure it out. Get it? Stand in the corner?" He snickers, but then quits when I don't join in.

"Rude. Thanks, but no thanks." Can't he be serious even once?

Jack taps the corner of the card. "No. Fo' real. *Stand* is in the corner. See?"

"What?" Malia and I lean over the cement table—and he's right. The letters all together spell STAND—bent in half and tucked in the corner. Like shave ice sliding down my neck, shivers prickle my skin. "The words aren't in a second code—they're word puzzles!"

I hug Jack around the shoulders, and he grins even wider. Leave it to Jack to remember the fun stuff. Silly fun and games, that's Jack—so different from my mom.

But it was Mom who made the clue. "Wait, *my* mom sent me word puzzles?"

"Sure. Why not?" Jack shrugs. "You gotta have fun too, right? Change it up."

Would Mom be disappointed if I got help to figure it out? I chew my lip and push my glasses up again. I see patterns and numbers and things just like she taught me, but this—who would think to break a word in half? Not me. But Jack gets it. And besides, Mom's gonna call in two days. Imagine how cool if I got the whole thing done! Maybe Jack's right; it's time to change it up and let friends help.

"Hey, guys, come look at this. Jack solved 'Stand in the corner.' Do you see any other ones?"

Ekolu and Kase crowd around the table with Malia, Jack, and me.

"So if we figure this out, does that mean we're super

spies?" asks Jack. "I solved the first one, so I get choke kine spy points."

"Spy points. Yeah, brah. We should have code names." Ekolu raises his hand. "I call Aquaman."

"That's not a code name." Malia tilts her head—looking at the card from different angles.

"I'm gonna be Agent Double-O Ramen." Jack smirks. "But that's top secret, so don't tell anyone."

"What's with the weird spacing?" Kase taps the card. "Janob is all spread out."

"Oh!" Malia beams. "That's because it has the word *an* inside the word *job*. It's *an inside job!*"

"That's got to be it." I scribble notes on a page. "That sounds right. So far we have 'stand in the corner' and 'an inside job.' What else?"

"Maybe KOOL means 'look' but upside down?" Ekolu says. "Oh! You gotta do a handstand!"

"I can't do a handstand. First, my glasses would fall off, second—doesn't matter. It's not happening."

Ekolu holds his thumb and finger a half-inch apart and squints at me through the gap. "Maybe small kine handstand?"

"No—" Kase points at the sky. "It means *up*. Like LOOK UP!"

"Look up, yep. Sounds good. Next?" I underline the words.

"Check those two groups with the numbers—both have one word underneath the rest." Malia twists the end of her thick braid around her finger. "That's got to mean over or under or maybe on top?"

"The first one is under," Jack says. "It's like the

stand-in-the-corner one—except with the HE *under* the STANDS 3.14 . . ."

"That's pi!" Kase smacks his fist against his palm. "Three-point-one-four-one-five—HE understands pi!"

"But who is HE? And what's with the choke numbers after that?" Ekolu grumps.

"Let's see, SHELF three times, with a circle around the top one," Malia says at the same time as Jack blurts, "Top shelf!"

I check my notes: *Inside job, Stand in the corner, Look up, Top shelf, He understands pi*. "It's directions on how to find something, I think. But what's the starting point?"

Kase pulls his phone out, and his thumbs patter against the screen. "This says that 1.618 number is something called the golden ratio."

There's only one person I know who loves that ratio, and with that, the rest becomes easy. "It's my dad! He says the golden ratio is the BEST over ALL! And the last one is from the statue of Ahonui at Kahuku High and Intermediate School. The bronze plaque talks about Strength through Perseverance. I've seen it."

I grin at my brilliant friends. "The next clue is inside, in a corner, high on a top shelf, at my dad's work. We can take the bus there Friday right after school."

"Agent Ramen and Agent Aquaman rule!" Ekolu fist bumps Jack and they pull away with squid-like fingers. "We definitely count as spies."

Malia snorts, and Jack glances at the rest of us. "What? You guys didn't even pick a code name."

I pull my sun hat down tight and gather papers into my

backpack. "I don't need to. My mom's already smarter than any spy. She's cool, like Mavis Batey."

"Bet a real spy could find the clue in like ten minutes flat," Jack teases.

I narrow my eyes. "If a normal old spy could find it in ten minutes, I'll do it in nine."

"You're on." Jack rubs his hands, a wicked sparkle in his eye. "And winner picks the spy code name for the loser."

CHAPTER NINE

Saisei

Enigma: An inexplicable person or thing that is baffling, mysterious, and perplexing.

I underline the definition—twice.

Basically, *Enigma* is the perfect name for a German code machine that was supposed to be unbreakable. But maybe they should have called it the *almost*-unbreakable-machine, or the really-tricky-to-read machine.

Was it hard? You bet.

Unbreakable? No.

I study the pictures that Mrs. Keala, the librarian at Laie Elementary, let me print out for my poster board. One shows the Enigma machine from the outside, and another has it sliced in half to show all the parts inside.

Shaped sort of like a weird old typewriter, the Enigma machine had all these gears, wires, and rotors that randomized messages so no one could read them. Without the secret daily settings for the machine on the other end, no one could break the code—or at least that's how it was supposed to work. But a bunch of smart people like Mavis Batey found human errors from enemy soldiers who sent the messages—patterns and mistakes that helped them out-think the machine. Sometimes they'd use their girlfriend's name or a swear word for the key, and the codebreakers could use that to figure out the rest of the message.

One time, Mavis figured out the Italian Enigma machine's code and saved loads of lives by warning of an attack before it happened. She was a civilian like Mom—and smart. *Brilliant*, even. And yet, she was sworn to secrecy just like all the other people who worked at Bletchley Park. They couldn't talk about it—not even with their kids.

Wouldn't that make parents—even the moms—enigmas to their own children?

For thirty years after the war, Mavis Batey couldn't talk about her war work—at all. Way too classified. Her kids didn't know anything about her codebreaker stuff. For all they knew, Mavis was just super good at Scrabble—she'd *always* win.

I lean back and run my fingers along the brim of my third-favorite hat, the newsboy. It's poofy enough to stuff all my long brown hair up inside it if I want, and the front brim is wide enough to shade my eyes but not get in the way. Seems like a good reporter-kinda hat for doin' history project stuff.

The interview with Mavis Batey goes on about the things she did—things she figured out. But all of it was top secret. The list of things she knew (that she could *never* share) must've been enormous.

So many secrets.

So many questions unanswered—and not just about Mavis.

Mom too.

How many classified things has Mom promised not to tell us? We know she does intelligence and counterintelligence stuff, but she never tells who, what, where, how—or anything specific. Is there a limit to how many secrets one person can hold inside her brain? Even computers run out of memory space sometimes. Does she think about classified things at home when she's walking, or counting, or spending time with me?

When she's gone working, am I in her thoughts at all?

Thirty years is a long time to wait to find out.

I check my watch. Twenty more minutes before Auntie comes to pick me up. Plenty of time to get more work done on my report—especially since Dad says I can't go to Kahuku High till tomorrow because it wasn't on the schedule for today.

He loves his red and blue marks on the schedule so much, it makes me want to make lots more of them—real thick. In fact, we could paint over the *whole* schedule in blue and red, make it a big flat blue and red flower. That way, if Dad says something isn't written down, I can point to the schedule and say, "Sure it is. It's right under that big red blob."

Perfect!

"Alex, I found these World War II books back in the office. You want them?" Mrs. Keala sets a stack of books beside me and leans over to see my screen. Her heirloom bracelets clink together, each carved with delicate gold flowers surrounding a Hawaiian word or name.

"Yes, please. Thank you." I slide the biggest book onto my

lap and flip through pages of tanks, airplanes, and soldiers. "Mrs. Keala, is it okay if I leave my stuff here and read these on the couches?"

"Sure, and if you want to check them out, just let me know. Leave whatever you don't want on the table." She pats my shoulder and turns to help a couple keiki with their arms full of picture books.

I tuck my backpack under the table and slide the chair in before carrying the new books to the wide green couches in the reading corner of the library. The zigzag carpet is soft enough to make a good reading spot, and the green couches around it are nice, but the best place in the whole library to read is on the giant inchworm. It's enormous, but I take a spot on a couch because only tiny kids are allowed to sit on the worm. When I was little I used to sit on a low spot between its humps and imagine it could move if it *really* wanted to—a sea dragon to take us on a ride around the school and maybe even across the ocean.

But that was a long time ago—before Mom taught me how to find a different kind of magic inside numbers, words, and patterns.

Page after page, I search for anything about Bletchley Park or codebreaker girls, but mostly it talks about war machines and battles and things—not secret stuff or spies.

The library door swings open and a boy yells directions, "Don't drop it! I spent months on that thing."

I hop up to peer around the stacks.

A group of boys carry something tall and wide and all covered in black rubbish sacks and taped closed so no one can see what's inside. Lowen leads the group, sweat sticking his straight black hair to his forehead as he strains to hold up whatever it is. He glances behind him. "Mrs. Keala? Where can I put my report?"

"Already? I thought you were bringing it next week?" She clears a few books off the top of some shelves to make space. "You must've been working really hard to get it all done already. Very dedicated."

"Yeah, my dad works afternoons all next week. So we brought it early. Make sure no one sees it. Okay?" Lowen and his friends grunt and strain as they lift the thing onto the shelf.

What does he have in there anyway? Sandstone instead of poster board?

"If you really want to keep it covered, we can." Mrs. Keala centers his project on the shelves a little more. "But you should be proud to show it."

"I am! It's the best ever. But I don't want anyone to steal—" He spies me standing beside the stack. "Hey! No peeking. You hear? It's off limits to you."

"I wasn't gonna peek." What's he even talking about? "What do I care what your stupid project is?"

"Hey." Mrs. Keala stands between us. "That's not any way to talk to each other. Be nice."

"She'll steal my idea." Lowen folds his arms and scowls at me. "For science project last year, I did a report on ocean currents, and next thing I know, her project has ocean currents and tides and everything. And then she won! I'm not taking any chances."

"That's not fair. I didn't copy off yours." I glare at him. I picked the ocean because it's Dad's favorite place in the world—I mean, I might not go diving with him anymore, but at least with a report, we can talk about the ocean and it makes him happy. "Besides, you don't own the tides. I never copied you."

"Says you. You're a no-good, rotten cheat!"

"Okay, okay, enough." Mrs. Keala guides Lowen and the other boys toward the door. "Time to go home."

I try to stuff his words down where they don't sting, but like steam venting from a volcano, it leaks through till my face is as hot as the lava in my guts. He called me a cheater.

A cheater!

I don't even care that he wants to keep it a secret. I'm used to secrets. It's the idea that he thinks I'd cheat off of *him* that boils me.

I grab my stuff, slide my slippers on, and open the door.

"See you bumbai." Mrs. Keala waves.

"Yep, see you later!" I step out under the covered path.

Keiki run around the grass by the little statues outside the library.

"Tag! You're it!" A boy with curly black hair down past his shoulders pokes a freckled blond kid and off they go. Barefoot, they dodge and squeal and rush past me to the outdoor stage for school assemblies before running across the sidewalk to the fire-truck playground on the other side.

As I turn to walk along B building, a brown mynah bird walks out of a first-grade classroom onto a hopscotch in the middle of the sidewalk, but then scurries back inside the classroom when I get too close. Finches, doves, mynahs, you never know who's coming to class when the door's wide open. Sometimes I share my rice with them at lunch.

Inside the front office building, I slow by the giant gecko

statue garden—my favorite spot in the whole school. With of-
fices and covered sidewalks on all sides, the gecko garden sits
under a tiny patch of sky as if someone cut a room-sized rec-
tangle in the roof. As big as a reef shark—except with black
and orange skin and legs—our mascot gecko statue hovers like
a guardian spirit over the flower garden, his three smaller gecko
brothers of black, blue, and green stuck to the wall behind
him. I know they can't move, but after a lifetime of geckos
running around at home and all over, I watch them out of
the corner of my eye, half-expecting them to change positions
now and then just for fun. Part of me thinks that would be the
coolest ever, but the rest of me thinks the big one might try to
eat us . . . so maybe not.

At the entrance to the school, I lean against the half-circle
sculpted on one of the gates and wait for Auntie, my newsboy
hat cushioning my head against the metal.

When the Tanakas' white car pulls up to the school, I hop
down the cement steps and open the side door. Auntie scoots
her ipu gourd and basket-weaving things from work over to
make room for me. A few minutes later, we're pulling into her
driveway.

"Glad you can help today. If we wait any longer to mow,
we'll need machetes to cut a path to the mower." Auntie carries
her double ipu gourd to the house to keep it safe till she goes
back to PCC again. "Mow the backyard first, then the front.
Okay, sis?"

"Kay." I take off my backpack and set it on the floor of the
car for safekeeping while I work, but when I turn back around,
a huge wet nose sniffs my glasses and leaves a trail of slime
across the lens. "*Aaah!*"

Almost nose-to-nose with me, Sarge licks his lips and sniffs me again. A slobber-string of drool hangs from his sand-dusted jowls, and foamy wet drops splatter my shirt.

"*Oof!* Ew, Sarge. Back up." I lean away from the sea-flavored dog breath, but he leans in closer, sniffs, sniffs again *real* deep . . . and sneezes all over me.

I wipe my cheek. "*Ugh.* Auntie? Where's Uncle?"

Her back to me, she props the house door open and slides her ipu inside. "He's had a couple of bad days—you know, not feeling well—but don't tell him I told you that, eh?" She glances at us. "Hey! You big whale. Leave our Alex alone."

Sarge obediently faces Auntie but sits on my foot, his shaggy rear end leaning hard against me all the way up to my knee.

I never thought of dog butts being super heavy, but Sarge weighs more than me, and I'm pretty sure his butt is full of bricks.

"I'm warning you." Auntie shakes a finger at the massive dog. "No treats for a month if you keep this up."

Sarge groans and lies down, and I heave my foot out from under him. He's pretty much blocking every path out from the car, but I don't dare step over him 'cause if he stands up under me, he could gallop off with me like a runaway shaggy pony.

Sidestepping, I finally clear Sarge, pull the mower out from the covered patio, and push it onto the lawn.

Sarge trots past me, so close his tail thumps against my hip on the way by. And when I get near Uncle's boat, Sarge huffs and paces me, always standing between me and the boat.

"You don't have to protect his boat from me," I grumble. "You can keep it."

I reach for the pull string to start the mower, but something moves nearby in the water . . . something that is *not* waves.

I squint for a closer look, but whatever it is dives under and hides, a distorted, dark shape lurking under the surface.

Is someone snorkeling—spying on us? Could a spy from Mom's work find his way to our island? I stand on my toes, partly to see better, and partly to make it easier to run away if a creepy bad guy pops up out of the ocean.

But no, I hadn't seen a face mask. It can't be a person. Maybe a seal?

Sarge splashes into the shallow waves by the dark thing in the water and waits with ears perked and tail wagging.

Uncle walks up beside me, his hands around a teacup of something foul-smelling.

I lift my chin toward the black thing. "Something's in the water by Sarge."

Uncle takes a sip. "Mm-hmm."

"Should we call Sarge away? It might be dangerous."

"Maybe we go have a look then, eh?" Uncle drains the last of his cup and sets it on his boat. But when he walks to the shore, the thing in the water moves straight *toward* him!

Sarge backs out of the way, his tail wagging.

A wave rolls over the shape and it rides the motion onto the shore—not a seal but a turtle. Its brown, scaly head lifts toward Uncle as it pushes itself farther up onto the sand, but it's not shaped like any turtle I've ever seen. Instead of the round disc shape, its body waddles back and forth, the shell more like a saddle, or maybe a deformed hourglass.

Uncle squats out of reach of the waves, where the ocean

stretches up onto the sand as far as it can reach, spreading thin and clear like melted butter. With quiet patience, he waits as the turtle approaches.

I've never seen a turtle like it. Not green sea turtle, not loggerhead. Nothing I can think of has a shape like that. "What is it?"

At the sound of my voice, the turtle whips around and beats a fast retreat into the sea.

I cover my mouth. "Sorry. I didn't mean to scare it."

"Saisei is shy, but determined." Uncle stands up and watches her go. "I keep telling her she should go be with her family over on Turtle Beach, but no. She always comes back. Laid a clutch of eggs here last year and everything. Go to your family, I say. Be with other turtles, I say. But she comes back every time like she thinks *I'm* her family." Uncle shakes his head wistfully. "Do I look like a turtle to you?"

He's so straight-faced, I can't tell if he's teasing or not. "Um, no?"

"Bah." He walks slowly back to the house, Sarge at his heels.

What was that all about?

After a minute, I pull the mower string and the engine roars to life. But as I push the mower back and forth, I keep watch on the place where Saisei disappeared. Now and then, for just an instant, a dark head breaks the surface, and I wonder if she's watching me back.

CHAPTER TEN

Invisible

"Ten seconds and counting," Jack croons from below as I balance on a chair and reach for an envelope taped to the top shelf.

"Shut it," I hiss, my fingers barely grazing the corner of the envelope but not enough to grab it. "Almost got it."

"Nine. Eight. Seven. Six . . ."

"Need help?" Dad calls from his wide metal desk at the back of the room.

"I can do it." I grit my teeth. "One more second."

"Three. Two." Jack bounces by my chair.

"Got it!" I snag the envelope as Jack yells, "One! Time's up, I win."

I hop down off the chair. "Not! It was a tie."

"No, I win." Jack prances backwards, waving his phone with the screen flashing zero.

"Not!"

"I win a hundred percent."

"Not—times a million."

"Uncle Brody, you saw, right? She lost."

"No way. Tied all the way." Slippers slapping softly against the tile floor, I weave through empty chairs to Dad and bounce the envelope in my hand. It weighs more than it should for such a small package.

"I'm staying out of it." The keys on Dad's computer click a steady rhythm, the desk lamp accenting the shadows of each finger like ghost crabs hiding beneath his hands. "That's between the two of you."

Bright posters of natural spirals line the ceiling of Dad's upstairs classroom: a snail shell, a rose, a hurricane, pineapples, pine cones, the side of a human skull, cacti, a human ear, sunflowers, galaxies—all of them with the spiral graph drawn over top to show the golden ratio math equation.

"Ready for your code name?" Jack matches my steps.

"Only if you are. 'Cause we tied." Carefully, I rip the envelope open and peek inside, where white paper wraps around something flat and heavy.

"Ekolu and me looked up stuff with 'hat' in the words— you know, research—and we found a sick name for you." He bumps my elbow. "Ready for it?"

"If I say no, will it go away?"

"Definitely not." He spreads his fingers like starfish. "Code name: Shatter."

Full stop. Shatter? Like glass? "Why would you name me that?"

"You don't like it?" His grin fades.

"You think I'm broken?"

"No—not like that. You shatter codes and da kine, same as the lady in your report. We thought about Hatrack or Crosshatch, but none mo bettah than Agent Shatter. Give it a day. You'll see."

I roll my eyes—hard. Once Jack's brain catches hold of something shiny, it wraps around tight as an octopus on a face mask and won't let go.

The thick white paper crinkles as I unwrap the package and gaze at the copper swirl inside. Polished to a burnished gold, a nautilus shell shimmers in my hands. Deep in the creases of its perfect spiral, dark green tarnish winds round each curve, slicing through the shine like lines of fine seaweed curled on sand.

"Whoa." Jack traces the spiral and glances at Dad. "Is this the prize? Did she win?"

A shivery rush rolls through me as if someone dumped a sack of leaves over my head, the edges prickly and fragile against my skin. Could it be the end? Does this mean I can show Mom on her call tonight that I solved her riddle? She'd smile, of course. Proud that I figured it out—maybe even call me her mini-me like when I first figured out her patterns at Auntie's house years ago.

But Dad doesn't cheer. He watches me with the same focus he uses when plotting out graphs and charts—like my reaction is one more variable to plug into his equations. His chair squeaks as he leans back and folds his arms. "What do you think, Alex? Is this the end?"

"Would you tell me if it was?"

"Would you want me to?"

I sigh. Would it kill my parents to give a straight answer? Having my question thrown back as another question turns every conversation with them into a test. Sometimes I don't want to worry about which answer is right. And how many wrong answers do I get before I fail the test? If I'm wrong one too many times, will they give up on me?

I turn the shell over, tracing the spiral—identical on both sides. A perfect example of Dad's golden ratio—except for the cork sticking out of the mouth of the shell.

Leaving the white wrapping on the desk, I hold the shell with the cork upright and wiggle it out. It pops free and a few liquid drops slosh onto my hand. The scent of lemons fills my nose.

"It's full of lemon juice." I pass the cork to Jack.

He sniffs it, frowns, and hands it back. "But why?"

"Because it's not the end. There's more; another clue to find something else." I wedge the cork into place again. I don't know what lemon juice has to do with the golden ratio or nautilus shells or anything, but if Mom left it for me, then *she* thinks I should know—but I don't.

I sigh. "How many more are there?"

Dad sits up. "Your Mom took weeks to set this up. Would you really want it over already?"

I shrug. Dad's been better since we did the schedule on the calendar together, but the pressure is still there to finish on time—or else. Something important will get messed up if I don't finish on time. And every day I don't finish is one day closer to disappointing everyone. Maybe I don't want a challenge. Maybe I want to ride my bike to Sam's store to get Spam musubi and crack seed and li hing strawberry belts like Jack does.

Dad waits for a proper answer, but I groan, pulling my

sun hat down over my face, the brim pressing the bridge of my glasses hard against my nose. Did people working at Bletchley Park ever get tired of figuring things out?

"Alexis. Look at me." Dad uses his teacher voice, but I can't see him past the yellow fabric of my sun hat, and since I can't see him, I can almost pretend I can't hear him either.

The chair creaks and his fingers lift the brim of my hat. "What's wrong?"

Jack shifts restlessly beside me, and I almost groan again. I wanted this clue to be the end, but it's not. *Again.* I know I'm supposed to have patience and persevere—and I will. But, it's hard without Mom, and the clues aren't done, and I think about her all the time . . .

I take a breath. I'm supposed to shatter codes—not myself. Mom would be stronger than this. "Sorry. I'm just tired. We ran around the field a bunch for PE and Lowen almost tripped me—he says it was an accident, but I don't know—and then we took the bus here right after school." I sigh.

"Maybe you better turn in early tonight so tomorrow goes better." Dad turns his computer off and stands, but when Jack and I get up and head for the door, Dad calls after me. "Don't forget your paper."

My paper? The only paper I had was blank. I pluck the crumpled sheet off the desk and turn it over to check again, but both sides are empty of words. A clean page.

I stare at the paper. Why would Dad want me to take a blank paper with me? Blank paper wrapped around a fancy vial of lemon juice? *Unless* . . . I suck a breath and spread the paper out on the desk as flat as I can.

"I can only think of one reason Mom would give me

lemon juice *and* a blank paper." I smooth the sheet, paying close attention to texture, but other than creases, it seems normal—so far. Flipping it over, I smooth the other side. "Only one way to find out."

"Wait, find out what?" Jack reaches for the paper, but I pull it back and eye Dad's desk lamp—a real old one with a base shaped like a scuba diver frozen mid-swim over a reef. I bet the light bulb is almost as old as the lamp, which is perfect.

"Hold on, Jack. Can you take the lampshade off?"

"No prob." He unscrews the top, lifts it off, and sets it aside. "You supposed to do something with the lemon stuff?"

Silent in his chair, Dad waits, the slight bounce of his chair the only crack in his careful mask.

"No. I think it's already been done." Paper in hand, I glance at Dad and Jack. It would be so much better to try this alone. I know what I'm supposed to do, I think. But I can't be sure. And in about five seconds, either we'll see something really cool . . . or we won't, and I'll look really, *really* dumb.

I lift my chin. "Here we go." Carefully, I hold Mom's white paper an inch away from the light bulb and wait, letting the light warm the paper.

Like a marshmallow being roasted over a campfire, brown lines appear and spread in toasted swirls as I move the paper across the bulb. The darker the lines, the brighter the paper seems as words appear one by one across the page. Written in lemon juice, the invisible message transforms into charred curves penned in Mom's perfect, elegant scrawl.

When the last curl ends, I lay the paper on the desk and read.

In the place where we met, a sea turtle holds the key.

"So, not the end," Jack says.

"Nope." I turn the words over in my head. *In the place where we met.* It could mean what it says, or not. "Now I gotta figure it out."

Dad doesn't have a scuba lesson today, so he gives us a ride home—and that more than anything tells me that I found all there was to find at his school. Otherwise he'd have said something like he did with the paper.

As we pass Mālaekahana campground, my mind drifts, my thumb tracing the swirl of the nautilus shell. The radio murmurs local news stories: how the storm caused erosion and collapsed a section of highway by the North Shore that's closed for repair; authorities were called in to protect a monk seal basking on a popular beach when tourists swarmed in for photo ops; meteorologists warn of a super typhoon forming off the sea of Japan, but Hawaii is not forecasted to be in the direct path of any major storm. They report other stuff too, but my thoughts are filled with the riddle. *In the place where we met, a sea turtle holds the key.*

By now, I've repeated the words of the clue inside my head so many times, they're seared into my brain as much as they're burned on the paper.

By the time Dad drops Jack off at his house by Wahinepe'e Street, I'm already making a list of things I need to tell Mom on our call tonight. I can't tell her I finished the challenge, but at least I can show her the bottle, the Morse code from Uncle Tanaka's house, the rebus picture puzzles, and the lemon writing.

In my room, I arrange the copper shell on my desk so she

can see it first thing when she joins our video chat. Will she be surprised I got this far? Or disappointed I wasn't further?

The clock in the corner of my screen reads 5:57 p.m.

I move the shell from one side of the desk to the other so it catches the light. Can she see the shine all the way on the other side of the world? Maybe.

5:58 p.m.

I tap the sides of my papers, the stack straight, lemon message on top, picture words under that, and my latest notes on Mavis Batey under that. Should I arrange my pencils straight like Mom likes? Probably she can't see them from the camera angle anyway.

5:59 p.m.

I smile at the screen, my own faint reflection grinning back at me.

My nose itches but I don't move to scratch it because I want my smile to be the first thing she sees.

Wiggling my eyebrows helps keep my mind off the itch.

6:00 p.m.

In a constant loop, I check the time, the little bars that say the internet is working, the screen where Mom's face should be, the clock, and round again. I know the second I look away, she'll be on, because Mom is always on time. She's never missed. Ever.

6:01 p.m.

Cheeks burning, I hold the smile even with eyes watering from trying not to itch my nose.

6:03 p.m.

I rub my nose with my arm, refresh the page, and line a pencil straight with the edge of the desk.

6:10 p.m.

Dad peeks in. "Did Mom call?"

"Not yet."

He checks the screen and then his phone before pursing his lips. "Okay. I'll be in the kitchen. Call when she comes on."

"Okay."

Dad walks into the kitchen and turns on the news. The local weather jingle plays before Dad turns the volume down.

Heel bouncing against the wheel leg of my chair, I set a pencil in line with the rest of the row and refresh the page again.

And again.

6:30 p.m.

Dad brings in a steaming bowl of udon noodles, sets it down, and glances at the line of pencils marching across my desk, each sorted by size, length, and color. He pats my shoulder and murmurs, "These things happen sometimes. Don't let it worry you." Except the extra lines between his eyes tell the truth of his worry even if his lips can't.

With extra tabs open for email and maps, I click through news articles as Dad murmurs to Auntie on the phone in the kitchen, his voice too low to hear the words. I walk to the door to see Dad better, but he sees me coming, holds up a finger to stop me, and pulls the phone to the side to whisper to me. "I'm sorry, I need to make a few calls, but I don't want you to worry, okay? I'm sure everything is fine, and we'll hear from your mom soon. Understand?"

I nod because he wants me to, but I'm not sure he believes the words coming out of his mouth.

"Maybe work on your report, okay? I'll check on you later." He flashes a quick smile—where his mouth forms the shape but none of it reaches his eyes—steps into his room, and shuts the door between us.

"Well, okay then. That was weird," I whisper, retreating to my desk. There really wasn't a reason to shut me out. I wasn't going to listen in—well, maybe I was. But only because Dad's voice sounds sorta off, like he's real mad at someone. Mad, or maybe worried.

I listen for his door to open again, but he doesn't come out. I guess I can knock or yell for him when Mom calls. Because she will call. Of course she will. Dad *says* she will.

7:10 p.m.

For real. The most punctual person on the planet is an hour late. What's going on? Where is she? I try to remember everything Mom mentioned about where she was, but there's not much. She's west of here, so maybe off-shore near Japan somewhere? I mean, she can't tell me exact locations in case spies hear, but it's a start at least.

Seems like the Sea of Japan's been on the news lately, but there's no way to know if Mom's there, right? She could be anywhere. Subs like hers can circle the whole earth, but she can't tell us where she's been—not even after she gets home. She has rules for all the secrets she carries. I learn more about where she's been from the hats she brings home than from anything she says. I'm used to not knowing where she is. Everything's fine—normal even.

My fingers tap from one to the next and back again.

7:40 p.m.

Dad's words are clipped as he argues with someone on the phone with his bedroom door shut tight. "What do you mean you don't know? Then get me to someone who does."

My breaths come shallow as I sit quiet as stone and wait. A cold hollowness bores through me, swapping my insides for caverns of ice. I can't think—don't *want* to think what it all might mean.

Dad's a farm kid, a veteran, a diver, a teacher, a collector of perfect spirals, and a math guru. He's laid back but in control. Always.

I don't recognize the voice spiked with worry and frustration that spills through the keyhole and pools in the space between us. Dad never loses his cool—not like this.

". . . yes, Elizabeth Force. No, she's not an officer. She's civilian. What? That's right, civilian . . ."

The murmuring from inside Dad's room comes and goes, but the door doesn't open.

8:00 p.m.

Cold, the bowl of udon perches on the corner of my desk. Untouched.

Reports of a super typhoon in the Pacific pour from stone-faced reporters across the web, their alarms and images flickering across my glasses.

8:30 p.m.

Meteorologists warn . . .

Could grow to rival the strongest super typhoon ever recorded, Typhoon Tip of 1979 . . .

Catastrophic for anyone caught in its wake—on land or at sea . . .

Every click, every new screen pierces and cankers inside my head like venomous urchin spines. Barbed words and reports hook in tender skin and won't let go.

Super storm.

Waves pound my heart against the rocks.

Destructive wind speeds.

I try to surface, to connect. I hit refresh. Refresh. Refresh.

Category four, category five.

Maybe she's not there. Maybe I understood wrong. Maybe Dad was upset about something else.

New tabs with windows pop up across the top of the screen.

9:00 p.m.

I try to lie to myself, pretend everything's fine and this is all a mistake . . . but I know who Dad was arguing about. I know he's worried.

I know, and I can't hide. Not from him. Not from the reports. And there are so, so many reports. With the sound on the computer turned way down, I turn off the light like I've gone to bed. Dad would want me to go to bed, I think. But the reports surge across the screen and I can't look away.

Huge waves wash over sea walls and flood streets. Reporters in raincoats hang on to their plastic rain hats and clutch microphones tight as they talk through rain and wind.

I grip my desk as the storm reaches through the computer and captures me. I hear the rain, imagine the wet, and watch the destruction with wide eyes as news reports drag me under.

Super typhoon.

Sea-level pressure dropping dramatically.

Casualty reports.

Missing people.

Search for higher ground.

Someone clings to a tree surrounded by churning water as rescuers push to reach them. More people stand ready with ropes to pull lost souls to safety should they fall to the torrent.

What country? I can't tell. There's so much, it feels like the storm has swallowed the whole world. Worry steals my breath and fills my lungs until I choke.

I'm drowning.

I click on tab

And I

. . . after tab

can't

. . . after tab.

breathe.

CHAPTER ELEVEN

Castle Tree

I dream of ciphers, of spirals, of shipwrecks and shells.

There's laughter too. But it's cruel.

Hidden beneath the surface beyond the shore, eely-black ripples weave back and forth, watching, waiting for me to step back into the ocean so it can finish what it started all those years ago—except I won't go in.

I know better.

But I'm not the only one close to the ocean; Mom's there too.

And the ocean, tired of lying in wait for me, looks to Typhoon and lends strength to the winds. And the laughter builds and roars as Typhoon grows and pushes Mom's submarine down

and down

and down,

deep into the black.

It rolls and spins, and seaweed tangles fast round my legs as I scream, *take me instead!*

I'll go in.

I'll jump, I'll swim, anything—just leave her alone. But laughter rumbles on and on, and I wake with the taste of salt on my lips.

With a breath so deep it chokes me, I kick the blanket wrapped around my legs off my bed. It slides to the floor, and I run to the desk.

Maybe it all was a nightmare; maybe none of it was real.

But there are the blinking dots above the line that used to say, "Waiting for host to join video chat." Now it reads, "Meeting time expired. Failure Code: 103. No host detected."

She never logged on.

Not once.

I waited for hours and hours, and I should still be in the chair now—except Dad must've carried me to bed in the middle of the night and covered me.

I spin in the chair and try not to think.

Sunrise slices through my window blinds to pry shadows from their hiding places and paint the bellies of my origami creatures pink. Each folded creation speaks to time with Dad or Mom.

The dragon Mom gave me when I won the science fair, the fox Dad folded when I solved Mom's last challenge. A lot of kids take time with parents for granted, but my time with both of them together is numbered by folded papers like imitation stars.

I turn away, but gold rays slide down the wall till my notes begin to glow fiery orange, and I can't help but look at the screen again.

Meeting time expired.

I should turn the computer off. Except, I *can't* turn it off.

What if she calls?

I shake my head at the false logic of that idea. She's not calling. Think about it. She can't, or she would've done it already. Something big wouldn't let her call home. The meeting is expired and the link won't work anymore. But turning it off? I won't do it.

I can't.

It'd be like shutting Dad's oxygen tank off while he's still on a dive.

I leave the screen on, a life preserver floating out to sea.

Sleep is impossible, but so is sitting still—and if I look at the screen even one more time, I'll go mad.

I tiptoe down the hall, over woven grass mats and across cool tile where Dad snores softly on the couch, the muted TV flickering with weather channel images of a giant white swirl rotating far to the west over the Pacific.

Seems Dad can't turn the screen off either.

I step out onto the lanai and keep going. Faster and faster. With legs pumping, feet churning over concrete and gravel, I cling to a life-vest of speed.

As long as I'm moving, I don't have to think of storms, or submarines, or empty screens. So I run uphill because my heart isn't strong enough to endure the gloating sea—not when its cruel laughter still lingers from my dream.

When I run out of road, I cut sideways across perfect gardens, past fountains, palm trees, and white stone walls set on the hill, then back onto roads again until cement gives way to soft grass.

Sharp as a centipede sting, my side aches so hard I gasp. One hand on my ribs, I limp past Tree Field and finally bend over to catch my breath in the shade of the great banyan tree. Head down and hands on my knees, sweat drips off the tip of my nose and falls to the grass as my hair hangs damp and snarled. When I can breathe again, I smooth my hair away from my face best I can, but I have no hat, hair tie, or pick to keep it out of the way.

A breeze rustles leaves high in the canopy of the banyan tree and twines through hanging roots to cool my face and tease my ratted hair.

It's the Castle's way of welcoming me home.

Perched on top of the university hill, Castle Tree lords over its domain with hundreds of roots trailing from its branches like jellyfish tentacles. The young ones sway in the wind, some of them thin as vines not yet touching the ground, but others pierce the earth and stand thick as trees.

I climb over and through, reaching higher until I reach the heart of the Castle, a natural room with a slanted dirt floor and walls made of roots.

Here with my Castle Crew friends, we've fought a thousand battles defending our secret kingdom from unseen foes. With sticks and imagination, we slash and parry, poke and block. We scurry up and down, ducking under and through the web of roots, chasing our invisible enemies away across Tree Field, until Castle Tree is safe again.

I thought my friends and I were the first to ever imagine Castle Tree to be a real castle in a magical kingdom, but turns out, Mom already knew how many vines made up the walls inside the heart. She played here too, even kept the perfect stick "sword" leaning against the same nook in the roots as I do. More sticks sit in a hollow on the other side of the room, ready for our Castle guards. Seems it's always been the perfect place to shield or conquer a hidden realm, depending on what game we play.

Today, my game is called "Pretend last night didn't happen."

Hidden inside the protection of my castle walls, I sweep chunks of sandstone and limestone aside and sink down onto a bare patch of volcanic red soil. Tiny green shoots push up through fallen leaves that crowd the roots and edges of my secret room. Breathing deep, I rake the damp soil with my fingers, crumbling handfuls inside each fist as I sort the chaos inside my head.

Maybe everything's fine. Maybe Mom's okay. Maybe.

Maybe not.

Nestled in the heart of Castle Tree, I hug my knees, rest my forehead on my arms, and rock back and forth. *One, two, three*—this place is a kingdom of pretend. *Four, five, six*—and while I'm here, I'm Queen. *Seven, eight, nine, ten . . .*

Queen of pretending.

I can pretend that Mom will be fine. And if I pretend hard enough, it's sort of the same as believing. Maybe if I try hard enough, I can believe that she's safe.

Safe, steady, and strong.

I imagine that belief cutting through the tangle of nets twisted inside my chest, freeing my heart, and letting me breathe again.

Ninety-eight, ninety-nine . . .

I rock and tap every number with my toes.

. . . Seven hundred thirty-six, seven hundred thirty-seven . . .

I keep counting, keep pretending, until my little room in the heart of the tree is all there is left of the world.

The canopy whispers peace to my soul and I forget to count, or think, or worry. Just me, and the banyan tree. Hidden by secret passages through roots and shadows, I could live here forever, a clown fish safe in her anemone.

Castle, my friend, playmate, and protector.

A root cradles my head as I lean against the tree, my insides still shaky but empty of the panic that used to be there.

A gecko scurries across the red dirt floor and disappears into a pile of leaves on the far side. Birds flutter through the branches, and flying things buzz from one sunbeam to the next.

"Alexis, you up there?" Malia's voice from below shatters the spell.

I rub my eyes with the back of my wrist and blink up at sunbeams winking through the leaves from high over the canopy. How long have I been here?

I should answer, but . . . I don't.

"Alexis . . ." The crunch of Malia's feet on fallen leaves circles the tree, but part of me still wants to pretend, and I listen in silence.

"So . . . I heard about the missed call."

I rest my head against the Castle's living walls and close my eyes.

"And the typhoon."

I groan. More of a soft exhale, but it's enough.

"Ha! Heard you. I knew you were up there."

"No," I mumble. "Nobody's here."

"Okay, darn. I'll keep looking. Thanks."

That almost makes me smile—not quite—but almost.

She slips through the roots into the heart of the tree, slides down beside me, and drapes an arm across my shoulders. "I'm sorry you're upset."

"Last night was awful."

"I know." She squeezes me tight against her side, and the cold inside me loses the worst of its bite. "But it's still just a storm. And your dad says submarines are strong. There are no reports of a sub being damaged or lost or anything. He says he was going to talk to you this morning and tell you not to worry, but you snuck out early and ran off without your phone."

Not to worry? Why not? *He* was worried. I'm sure of it—or at least, I think he was. Was it really a misunderstanding?

She pulls my phone from her pocket, clears her throat, and speaks with a fancy made-up accent. "Eh-hem. I beg your pardon, miss, but I've been sent to deliver this speaking device to the beloved Queen Alex of Castle Tree. Is she here?"

"Nope."

She gasps and stands, then dashes to the side of the inner room, her hand against her chest all dramatic. "No? Queen Alex has fled the castle? I must find her. I've sworn an oath. I must search the kingdom until I find her and report to Lord Brody Force—" She cups her hand to her mouth for a loud fake whisper. "That's the queen's father, you see. He wishes to hear from her forcewith." She tilts her head and raises a questioning eyebrow at me. "Foresooth? Forth with?"

A soft smile steals across my lips, and I shrug. "I don't know how to say it either."

"Whatever. ASAP then." Malia flicks her thick, black hair over her shoulder and drops back into the fake accent. "Might you know where Queen Alex hath gone? You could join me in my quest—be my squire and stuff."

Play? Part of me wobbles at the thought, as if *I'd* been the one tossed around in the storm last night and not those reporters on the computer screen. I glance around the natural room. What was my plan anyway? To hide here all day? My stomach growls. I didn't eat the udon noodle dinner Dad made last night, and I was sleuthing after school before that, so the last time I ate was . . . lunch yesterday?

I take a breath and stand, brushing leaves and red dirt from the seat of my shorts.

"Well?" Malia rolls a finger forward, waiting. "Have you seen her?"

"Sorry. Nope. She ran off to live with a dragon—or maybe a dragon ate her. I can't remember." I'd been pretending to be invisible all morning, pretended so hard I almost disappeared. But Malia found me, and broke that spell, because that's what BFFs do. So I let her pull us into a new game of pretend where typhoons aren't a thing, and moms aren't missing.

"A dragon, I hear you say? No! Not my lady! I must avenge her. Where is this foul dragon?"

I slide my stick-sword from between the roots in the wall. "I refuse to tell."

"You fiend! Queen Alex charged me to protect the kingdom—and if you're not her, you're a trespasser!" Malia stuffs the phone in her pocket and pulls a stick from our stash on the other side. "I shall smite you with my smite-y stick."

She jabs her stick at the air, and I swat it aside. "Your smite-y stick is nothing against me. I will prevail . . ." I glance at my chosen weapon. ". . . with my stabby-staff."

Malia flashes a wicked smile and swings low and slow. "We'll see."

I twist away and dodge her sword by sliding between roots. Our swords clack together.

Crack, crack!

With a lunge, she slips through my guard, the tip of her stick barely grazing my foot. "Ha! Tagged you!"

"I still have one foot!" As per our battle rules, I hop one-footed onto the Castle balcony—a wide but short cliff of limestone surrounded by banyan roots. As I clear the tight vines, I spin and tap Malia on the shoulder. "Got your sword arm!"

"No big. I have an extra one. You're going down!" She lets the arm hang limp and swaps the stick to the other hand. "Oh yeah, going down like seaweed."

"What?" I wrinkle my nose. "What does seaweed have to do with any—"

Tap, tap, tap! Malia tags my other leg and both arms. "Haha! Now whatcha gon' do?"

"Cheaterpants." I let my sword fall to the ground.

"You were distracted fair and square. I win!"

"Win? No way, man, I could still—"

"Still what? Breathe on me?" Malia laughs and throws an arm around me. "Come on. You lost fair and square. Admit defeat."

"Never."

She picks up both sticks and tucks them away. "I came, I saw, I smited."

I sit and dangle my feet over the edge. "So, O great one, how'd you even know I was here?"

"Coconut wireless." She sits beside me and bumps my shoulder with hers. "You know how it goes, eh? One of the aunties saw you running flat out without your hat, and told someone who told someone who told my mom, who asked your dad."

"So everyone knows?" I groan.

"What did you think would happen? We figured you'd come here, but I'm supposed to text him when I find you."

"Traitorous spy."

Across the grass, a car putters by on its way around campus, and I wish I could take back my panicked run this morning. If the coconut wireless saw me running, then the whole town knows. Under the watchful eyes of hundreds of aunties, word travels faster than a crow could fly. Neighborhood Watch got nothing on the coconut wireless. Half the time, our parents know more about what we did each day than *we* do by the time we get home.

So everyone knows now. That's great. Just great.

"Ready?"

When I don't answer, Malia leans closer. "Do you think your mom would want you to sit here all day? Is that what *she* would do?"

"How would I know what she would do? I can't ask her because she didn't *call!*" I chuck a limestone rock off the cliff and grab another, not really mad anymore, just giving voice to all the things stuck inside my head since last night. "Did the coconut wireless know about the storm too? One of the biggest storms they've ever seen. And Mom's at sea, probably right in the middle of it. Why else would she miss a call?"

"You should call your dad. He says the people he called would know if the sub had sunk. It hasn't. So whatever's going on, your mom is okay. And besides, she set quest stuff up for you. I think you'd hurt her feelings if you didn't try your hardest to finish the game she started for you."

"I don't know." Don't know what to say, or do, or how to feel. "I'm not feeling it."

"Come *on*. Your mom already left you directions on what to do next, and even if the worst happens—which it won't— would you really want to live the rest of your life knowing that you decided *not* to finish the last challenge she set up for you? You want to throw away her last gift?"

I open my mouth but she cuts me off. "Do you know how many times I've wished that my mom would do something like that for me? Make a special quest or treat or scavenger hunt—anything just for me? With us it's always 'get to practice,' or 'what are your grades,' or 'are you reaching your goals,' or whatever. I know you think your dad's schedule is harsh, but I have to do stuff all the time. *All* the time. Your schedule would cry if it met mine."

She tosses a rock off the cliff onto the grass below and stares after it as she twines her fingers through one of her dark curls.

"Isn't that what you want? That's the goal, right?"

"Yeah, but, it's *everything* I do. I run as hard as I can—but it's a race that never ends. Every day, always the same thing. And then there's *your* mom, who spends weeks just to set up something special . . . something out of the ordinary that's only for *you*. You really gonna throw that away?"

"I'd finish a hundred challenges if it would get her home safe," I mumble.

She stands and holds out her hand. "I know, but you don't have to solve a hundred challenges. Just this one."

"Fine." I take her hand, and we wind through Castle Tree and down to the lawn.

"Hurry up." Malia tugs my hand. "You're gonna be late for your appointment with Tanakas and I'm gonna be late for hula practice."

I gasp. "Oh my gosh! I totally forgot about Uncle."

"Yeah, I don't think Uncle will wait for you if you're late. So you better run. I'm running too—except the other way."

"Okay." I turn to go, but stop to give her a hug. "Thanks for finding me."

She bear hugs me back and lifts me off my feet. "Always. Now go! Uncle might leave early just to get rid of you."

"See you!" With my hair flying free as I sprint across Laie, I make sure to wave at the aunties on the way past so they know all is well. I still worry, and I'm definitely not perfect, but at least I know I'm not alone.

CHAPTER TWELVE

Tests of Tides

Malia wasn't kidding when she said that Uncle waits for no one. By the time I fly through the Tanakas' gate and into the backyard, Uncle is already pulling a double-seater kayak out of the yard and down to the beach, the keel leaving a deep groove in the sand.

Auntie stands with a canvas bag over her shoulder as she watches Uncle from the edge of the lawn, her hands on her hips. Her yellow skirt ripples in the wind, though her hair is twisted up tight with a carved white bone pick.

Hip-deep in the surf, Sarge wags his tail, his whole attention focused on something dark brown bobbing up and down with the waves. With the next roll, its head clears the water and disappears with a splash, shooting away into the deep. Apparently, Uncle's turtle, Saisei, isn't thrilled to see me.

"Wait! I'm coming!" I leap over the sitting log by Uncle's bigger boat, a fresh coat of paint on the "Sarge's Barge" letters.

We're taking a kayak? Seriously? Why not just wrap us in seaweed and ring a dinner bell?

"See now, Matthew!" Auntie chides. "I told you Alex would come. But do you listen?"

"*Huff, huff!*" Sarge heads right for me, his enormous paws splashing water everywhere as he bounds out of the surf with long slobbers whipping back and forth like shoestrings dangling from his drooping jowls.

I run faster, trying to avoid the drool monster, but he swerves and skids to a stop sideways in front of me before shaking his whole body like a washer on spin cycle.

"Hey!" I curl away from the wet whirlwind as water, sand, and things I'd rather not think of splatter me. Wiping my glasses on my shirt, I try to slip by behind him, but he backs up, tail wagging as he blocks my way.

More woolly mammoth than Newfoundland dog, his bright, intelligent eyes follow my every move. He pants with a big doggy grin, his tongue lolling to the side.

At the shoreline ahead, Uncle reaches the water and pushes the kayak in.

Waves lift the small craft up and drop it against the sand again, the boat teetering side to side as Uncle soldiers on, pushing the kayak into the ocean's embrace.

On the beach between us, waves break and stretch into thin sheets of water that fill the hollows of Uncle's footprints.

He's not waiting for me.

"Wait! Uncle, I'm here. I'm coming!"

Another minute and I'll miss my chance to go with him. I take a fake step to the right then dodge left to get around

Sarge, but he dashes in front of me before I can reach Auntie. "Aw, come *on*, Sarge!"

Auntie tsks at the canine troublemaker. "What? You think she gon' steal your braddah? Let her go."

Sarge licks his lips and whines, his paws shifting nervously.

"Don't you give me that look. No arguing. Sit."

Whump! A hundred and fifty pounds of gigantor dog sits right on my foot, pinning it to the ground. He leans against me, soaking whatever dry spots I had left. Solid as a black and white furry mountain dropped on my toes, he cements me to the grass with his butt.

"Oof!" My arms flail as I try not to fall over.

"Move, you big lump." Auntie wags a finger at Sarge. "So jealous of a tiny girl? Shame. Shame on you!"

With a heave, I yank my leg out from under Sarge, who falls over onto the grass with a dramatic grumbly-groan.

Under Auntie's stern gaze, the grumpy horse-sized puppy lies still while I tiptoe around and look up to meet the gaze of an even grumpier Uncle Tanaka standing almost waist-deep in the waves.

"Um, sorry I'm late."

"Bah." Uncle holds the kayak steady with the bowline, his glower dark as thunderclouds.

"Your father left a bag for you." Auntie slips the canvas bag off her shoulder and passes it to me. Inside are all the things I should have thought to bring: towel, canteen, granola bars, lip balm, sunscreen, a waterproof case for my phone—and my fishing hat.

Auntie leans in close. "If you're going to make a habit out of running wild across town with no slippahs, hat, or phone . . . you should keep an emergency bag here so your dad doesn't have to run things over in a hurry, yeah?"

"Dad's here?" I scan the shadows under the palm trees of the yard. But he's nowhere that I can tell.

"No. He's at work, but he said to tell you to be helpful, have fun, call when you're done, and come home safe. He came by as soon as Malia texted that you were on your way. He had to go teach a class for some mainlanders. It was on the schedule."

"I'm sure it was." The corner of my mouth quirks up as I pull the floppy hat on and slide the chinstrap bead up tight. So Dad brought it all over, and he didn't even stay to scold me. True, he had clients to get to, but still. A gentle warmth seeps inside like stones basking in the sun. "Tell Dad thanks for me."

"Tell him yourself. You've got a phone." Auntie tsks, but her smile shines through in her rich brown eyes.

Mom might love me with riddles and codes, but Dad loves me with golden spirals and supply bags. I'll have to do something extra nice for him to say thank you. Maybe pick up some li hing strawberry belts or crack seed from Sam's store on the way home.

Uncle clears his throat so I know he's done waiting, and I trek down the sand.

Water grasps at my toes and shivers race up my legs as if I'm stepping onto shards of glass instead of crossing the water's edge. Everything in me says, *Danger! Run! Don't go in there!* But Uncle's watching, and I know he'd never let me help again if I back out now. No help means no clues, and no way can I let a little paralyzing fear get in the way of solving Mom's challenge. Like Malia says, the challenge was for fun before, but now it matters more. One step after another, I force my way in, cool waves slapping against my bare legs as I wade up to my knees.

I clench my fists and eye the waves. If the water comes up to Uncle's waist, it'll hit my armpits before I reach the kayak. Forcing each step, I make it till the waves strike my waist and splash up my chest, until I can't see the ground, and my feet refuse to go any farther. There might be *things* in the water. My breath speeds up and I try my hardest not to think of anything, but shadows of long, powerful bodies and snapping teeth seep past my shields.

All I have to do is take a few more steps . . . or fly. They feel equally impossible at the moment.

"Uh, can you please bring the kayak closer? Please?" I hate to ask, but it's better than giving up.

Uncle scowls but lets the kayak drift closer on the next wave, the bowline still secure in his hand.

"Right." I grab the sides of the kayak with both hands, but every time I try to get in, it tips, nearly dumping his stuff in the water.

Grumbling something I try hard not to hear, Uncle steps close enough to hold the kayak steady for me while I climb into the front seat. He jerks his chin. "Life vest's behind the seat."

"Oh, right." The blue vest slips over my arms easy, and I click the straps into place like Dad taught me. Even after I wouldn't go out on the water anymore, Dad still drilled me about water safety when I waited on the shore. I think it's a leftover Marine thing—or maybe just a parent thing.

The kayak rocks with a series of larger waves, and I throw a leg over each side for balance.

With me settled, Uncle hangs on to the bowline but turns away as he adjusts his vest.

Something splashes behind me, but I don't dare turn to see. A couple seconds later, Sarge bounds through the waves and lifts a sodden, webbed paw onto the side.

I squeak as his weight half tips me to the side, but Uncle barks an order. "No room for you today. She's in your spot."

Sarge groans again and sits in the water, still head and shoulders above the waterline even in water that was over waist-deep on me. His double coat of fur floats around him like seaweed, lifting and falling with each wave. After a long, wistful gaze at his master, Sarge sighs and sniffs my leg. Quick at first, he sniffs my knee and thigh, then breathes in deep and licks his nose with a long pink tongue. Our eyes meet and he stares back steady and strong as if to say, "If *I* can't go, he's *your* responsibility. Keep him safe."

Gingerly, I reach out to scratch Sarge behind his ear, and he leans into my touch and closes his eyes.

"Blasted thing. Whoever made this should be fired. Can't believe . . ." Uncle takes a few steps toward shore but keeps his back to me and grumbles under his breath. I can't see what he's doing, but he keeps fidgeting with his vest. Veins pulse on the side of his face, which is getting redder by the second.

"Let me, let me." Auntie hikes her skirt and ties it up in a quick knot by her thigh before wading in. She brushes his hands aside, clips the vest for him, and gives him a kiss. "You two have fun. Be good, eh?"

"I almost had it," he grumps.

"I know you did." She pats his shoulder and winks at me.

Uncle pushes the kayak out farther and climbs in behind

me, my stomach lurching as the craft tips one way and then the other while he sits down to paddle us out from shore.

Gritting my teeth, I pull my feet in and hold on.

A wave hits the bow and splashes my face. For every stroke forward Uncle makes with the paddle, another wave pushes us back. We bob up and down, and part of me wishes the waves would win this crazy tug-o'-war between the sand and the sea and shove us back on the beach where it's safe.

As is, Mom's instructions to help Uncle are the only thing in this world that could have gotten me this far.

"Paddle's behind you," Uncle says over the sound of the waves, and I give a jerky nod. I want to help—that's why I'm here—but my traitorous fingers stay clamped to the sides of the boat like a starfish stuck to a rock at low tide.

Free of the waves breaking near shore, we slice through the swells. Dark patches of coral sweep beneath us and I hold on even tighter. Anything could be hiding in those shadows. Eyes open or closed, my nightmares won't let me forget it.

The farther we go, the tighter my grip on the sides of the kayak. Every dip and rise leaves my stomach somewhere behind in the troughs of the waves. Seems like they always come rolling in three sizes. Regular, large, and supersized. Malia likes riding the supersized ones on her surfboard, always coasting along the front of a wave as it crests and rolls into a barrel behind her. Total confidence. Total control.

But me, in a kayak like this? A leaf on the wind has more control than I do.

A series of waves hits us from the other direction. The biggest splashes my face, and my glasses slip right off my nose. I tear my hand from the boat and snatch the lenses right before they drop into the sea. How could I forget my swim goggles? Nothing about my morning was planned, but still. I grit my teeth. I'd rather kiss a squid than have to tell my parents I lost my glasses again.

The waves calm down by Temple Beach and a smaller swell pushes us onto the sand about a hundred feet from the base of Laie Point. Uncle jumps out and pulls the kayak higher onto the beach with me still in it, useless as a sea slug. It takes me three tries to get my glasses back on with all the jitters bouncing around inside my head like someone's sending Morse code over my nervous system.

I'm shaking—but not from cold. I haven't let myself be that far out in the water since the day the sea tried to take me.

"Grab a vial from that box. I need a sample from the wash here." Uncle pats a tackle box of sorts tied down to the floor behind my chair.

Graceful as a seal on land, I half flop, half roll out of the kayak to my knees in the sand and open the box. Inside, rows of little glass vials wait empty, and I hold one up for Uncle, but instead of taking it, he nods his head toward the point.

"If you're not going to paddle you could at least learn how to do samples."

"Coming. Sorry." I hurry around a boulder and wait while Uncle studies the wash that leads back to the Foodland bridge.

"This part of the shoreline changes with the tide and storms," Uncle says. "I've seen rough seas push sand up into the Foodland parking lot past the bridge down there, with saltwater all the way to the bridge. Sometimes it's like now, where the sea leads a little way in, but leaves a sandbar before the bridge, and another pool of water after that. And sometimes the whole wash is dry." He nods. "Pass me the vial, and follow me."

I wade into the wash beside Uncle. His glasses must fit way better than mine, 'cause they don't slip at all when he leans over and dips the glass bottle down into the water until his whole arm is under the surface.

"See here?" He pulls the stopper from the vial so air bubbles escape from inside, rising up quick to pop at the surface under his chin. "For this study, I don't want samples from the surface. It needs to be more than a foot down."

He slides his gloved thumb over the mouth of the bottle and stands up. "Then you cap it off . . ." With the bottle in one hand and the stopper in the other, he slowly moves them together. But the closer his hands get, the harder they tremble until water sloshes out of the shaking vial like a little sprinkler.

Uncle glares at the bottle, his mustache twitching, and he turns away from me before trying again. After a minute, he flourishes in triumph. "Got it."

Less than half full, the little vial holds more air than water as he holds it aloft.

His elation fades as he follows my gaze and examines the bottle. He sighs. "It might be enough. Maybe."

As he looks down, low waves roll through the wash, their reflected sunlight painting his face in flickering light. For one brief moment, his grumpy mask falters and I glimpse frustration and pain behind the disguise.

He wades out of the wash, leans against the truck-sized boulder of lava rock, and pulls a little notebook from his pocket. "It's, uh . . . better to have more. But this'll probably work. We have to record the date, time, depth, and location where we gathered the sample."

As I watch him struggle to open his notebook, I can't help but compare this man to the Uncle in Mom's stories. The Uncle Tanaka *she* knew was full of laughter and loved adventure. I remember all her stories, everything she ever told me on our walks, and none of them—not one—mention his hands shaking.

Something changed with him, and when it did, it took his laughter with him.

Could this be why Mom wanted me to help him?

Uncle's wavy black ponytail rests over one shoulder, and he scratches his short beard with the back of his hand before writing in his notebook with a quavering hand. "Wash at base of Laie Point . . ."

I look down at my hands—small, and a little pruny from all the water, but steady. Well, if his hands don't work right, maybe he could use mine. "Could I try to take the sample?"

His eyebrow lifts as he studies me. "I already got it. Weren't you paying attention?"

"I know, but I thought I could do it again—kinda like practice so I can make sure to do it right."

He purses his lips and then hands the half-empty vial to me. "Well, I suppose that'd be alright. But don't open it until you've already got it under the water. No contaminating the sample."

"Okay." Tiny silver fish dart away as I wade to the center of the wash and thrust the bottle as deep as I can before pulling the stopper. Air bubbles tickle my chin, and a wave drenches the side of my face, but I press the stopper in to close it tight.

The vial is clear and full when I wade out and pass it back to Uncle.

He grunts in approval. "Good."

We go from place to place across the bay, sometimes by the shore, sometimes out on the water. Each time we stop for a sample, I try to ignore the dark reef and deep water below and focus on the task. Dunk, fill, stopper the vial, and hand it to Uncle. Move to a new spot and do it again. We get the job done, but it's mostly in silence.

In Mom's stories, she and Uncle talked about loads of stuff like the scientific method, facts, and ocean creatures all the time. But this Uncle seems determined to say as few words as humanly possible. Maybe he just likes the sound of the waves . . . or maybe he just really doesn't like me. Probably he wishes Mom was here instead of me.

I understand, because I wish that too.

After an hour, the wind and waves calm to almost nothing, and I ask a question just to break the silence. "So, how many more samples do we need?"

"Almost done. One more from the eel hole should do it."

My hands freeze halfway to the water. Did he say eel?

Now it's *my* hands that shake.

I *know* he means the wide circle of clear sand surrounded by reef. That "eel hole" doesn't actually have eels in it—at least no more than the normal ocean. My brain clicks through the logic. But I still imagine a Godzilla-sized eel snaking up from a hidden tunnel wide enough to swallow a house. There's no eel that big. Even the viper moray eel that haunts my dreams could never be *that* big. The hole is just a natural formation around a bunch of sand. Sand in the middle of reef. Nothing scary. It's illogical to be afraid, and I know it.

But there's nothing logical about my fear.

When my grip on the sides of the kayak doesn't stop the tremors, I tuck my hands under my armpits, tight against my sides.

We slice through the water, more glass than waves, a hidden world slipping by below us. Shadows of fish streak across the browns of the reef as we fly over the submerged landscape. Dips and hollows, coral and seaweed. And all at once, the reef disappears.

"Reach as far down as you can for this one, hah?" Uncle turns us to face the ocean and we stop in the center, surrounded by a ring of coral.

Without moving my head, I peer down into the clear water. Be logical. It's sand. Just sand. Eel hole is a local name for the place, nothing more.

Except, why would there be coral everywhere but here? What kind of eel or creature could keep this open? How huge would it have to be to carve it all out?

"Alex?" The kayak shifts as Uncle Tanaka leans close and taps my shoulder. "Hey, if you're tired, we can head in right after this. One more, okay?"

One more, and I can go back to land. I close my eyes and take a big breath. "Okay. One more." I pull one of the last vials out of the case and lean to the side, but I can't make my hands go that last inch into the water. We float on gentle waves over the maw of the eel hole with me hovering at the water's edge. That last inch, as impossible to cross as a force field.

Come on. Just do it. *Do it!*

The trembling moves up my arms and races down my body until my knees bounce and my teeth chatter. If I give up, I'll never find the answers to Mom's clues. I have to do this. I *will* do this. Just put the bottle in the water and close it up.

One, two, *three!*

"Alex, what's wrong?" Is that irritation in Uncle's voice, or worry?

"I got this!" Teeth gritted, I lunge for the side, pushing the bottle down into the depths. It's the bravest thing I've ever done—or maybe the stupidest.

The kayak tilts with me. *Too far.* And my hands are way too far down to grab hold of anything.

My scream is cut short as water fills my mouth, and I'm swallowed into the depths of the eel hole.

CHAPTER THIRTEEN

Friends and Fears

Sounds stop.

Light shifts.

Bubbles slip from my lips as I tumble upside down, hair tangling my fingers and face like fishing lines.

Somewhere above, a muffled voice calls my name. "Alexis! Swim!"

A current rushes across my skin, pulling me away from shore. Saltwater blurs and stings, and the shadow of the reef looms close as something dark moves in the water. Something *alive.*

"*Alex!*"

A creature of the deep, coming for me.

Not again!

I spin away from the creature and kick for land. With powerful strokes, I scoop water behind faster and faster. My head breaks the surface and I gasp, the shadows behind growing ever bigger inside my head. Throat burning, I push hard for shore.

"*Alex, wait!*"

Memories of another time, another place, fill my head with dread. Alone and swept out to sea, crying for help that could not come. I'm helpless. Lost, a plaything to a monster.

No! Not again—*never* again. I can't stop, can't let it take me.

I keep swimming, leaving the eel hole and its phantom monsters behind. The deep sand gives way to shallow reef and I swim even faster.

Don't touch it. Don't look!

A pale strip of beach teases ahead, the mountain's green expanse towering in the distance. Nothing else matters. Only land.

A wave catches me, pushing toward shore, then pulling away. But I break free, my toes digging into the sea floor as I claw through the last of the water.

Safe at last, I stand shivering on the sand. My throat burns as I double over, my stomach cramping with swallowed seawater.

"Hey! You okay?" A tourist lady in a bikini emerges from under a wide umbrella and runs to me, her face and shoulders glazed red from sun.

I cough, gag, and gasp again with legs weak as lauhala leaves. Crumpling to hands and knees, I wheeze in jagged breaths, my hair plastered to my cheek and tangled round my arm. Chicken skin erupts across my body and I moan through chattering teeth. "It tried to get me again. *Again!*"

"What did? Should I call someone?" The lady's long-nailed

hand pats my shoulder with nervous flutters like a finch flitting to and fro.

"Alex! Alex!" Uncle's stern voice pulls me from the fog inside my head, and I remember the kayak, Uncle, and the vials for the first time since plunging into the sea.

I roll to my back and blink at the fuzzy image of Uncle Tanaka racing up from the shore toward me. He skids to a knee beside me.

"Did you hit your head? Are you hurt?"

"She said something tried to get her," the lady says.

"No." I didn't hit my head, did I? I cough again, a retching, violent hack that wracks my body, and I curl forward until Uncle's strong hand cradles my forehead.

"Look at me," he orders when my coughing subsides, and I blink up at him. "Follow my finger. Up, right, left . . ."

As my eyes trace the lines he makes, his other hand cups my cheek with a gentle, trembling warmth.

"Is she dead?" A little girl in water wings peers over Uncle's shoulder with wide blue eyes.

"She'll be fine." Uncle pats my back.

Uncle, the girl, the lady, tourists—everyone looking at me. The crowd swells—a blur of bright colors. Did that lady have a cell phone pointed at us? Not cool. I roll away from the gawkers and push up onto my feet. "Sorry. Oh, man. I'm fine. Really, I'm okay. Sorry."

"Sorry?" Uncle follows with arms half-raised, ready to catch me if I fall. "You have nothing to be sorry for."

My first few steps are jelly, but after a few more my body feels like my own again as strength trickles back into my limbs.

"We're okay. Thank you." Uncle waves at someone behind us but stays by my side.

At the waterline, some keiki tug Uncle's kayak up onto the shore.

"Mahalo." Uncle inclines his head to them and they fade away, probably running off to tell the adventure of the mad girl who freaked out and swam up on shore as if the jaws of death were after her.

I'm still not sure that they weren't.

"I should have been faster," Uncle says. "But when you went over, you knocked the paddles out with you. I reached for you, but you took off like a marlin and left me in your wake." With an arm around me, Uncle's voice grounds me as much as the sand beneath my feet, and my shivering subsides. "I thought you'd reach for the kayak—I was right there with you—but the way you swam . . . Fast as anyone I've ever seen."

He waits for me to talk or something, but I don't know what to say. With the adrenaline and shakiness draining away, all I feel now is stupid.

I gave in to my fear, which caused my fall and swim through blind panic, when a perfectly good kayak waited right there. Shame settles across my shoulders.

"What say we talk story for what scared you so bad." Uncle sits beside me on the sand, his arms resting palm up on his knees.

When I don't slide down beside him, he starts talking anyway as if we're two old friends visiting on the beach with no worries at all. This whole year, he's barely said more than two words to me at a time. So why now?

I want my dad—worse, I want my *mom*. A lump twists

in my throat and I look away down the beach and take a step toward home, blinking hard. If I left now, I could be home in ten minutes or less. Dad would still be gone, but I could wait there, and he'd come home after work and fold origami with me, and I could pretend today never happened.

Palm trees sway in a gust of wind, but their fronds mush all together in a blurry green blob at the top of each fuzzy brown line. I frown and rub my eyes. Maybe the saltwater did something to—*my glasses!*

Both hands fly to pat my hair, shirt, and shorts. Nothing. I scan the ground, squinting best I can, but my glasses are nowhere.

Can today get any worse?

Slowly, I smooth my hair from my forehead to the top of my head where my hat is supposed to be, but isn't.

Yep. It's worse.

I lost my best fishing hat. My bag might still be in the kayak with the phone and stuff, but I can't tell from here because it's all just one big yellow blur.

"You know why I work with the ocean?" Uncle scoops a handful of sand and lets it sift through his fingers.

"Mom says you like sea creatures," I mumble. Can I still figure out Mom's clues if I never go out on the water again? As in never ever, as long as I live?

"I do like the creatures, but the real reason is that the sea keeps *my* fears away." He waits like I'm supposed to say something, but I don't know what to say. How could the ocean keep anyone from being afraid? It's strong, unpredictable, always changing . . . and sneaky. Thieving, too. It steals hats, glasses, *and* moms.

Sitting crisscross beside me, Uncle's voice is calm and quiet. "There's no shame in being afraid. Only a fool fears nothing."

If not being afraid makes someone a fool, does being terrified make someone smart? "I didn't mean to panic. I forgot the kayak was there."

"No, it's okay. Sometimes people worry about regular things, like crowds, or the dark, or spiders." The sand runs out onto the pile below Uncle's hand and he scoops it up again. "It's normal. But sometimes something unexpected overwhelms us and creates a new fear inside us, something fierce and wild that springs out at us when we least expect it, again and again. That kine harder to kill—more like cockroaches scurrying inside cracks and behind walls."

Great. So now I have the ocean *and* cockroaches to worry about. I slump onto the sand beside him. Sometimes I forget that I haven't always been afraid, that this isn't normal. Without turning my head, I watch Uncle from the side of my eye. Here, sitting at the edge of the sea, he is more at peace than I've ever seen him. Steady and secure. Even his hands seem to drink in the stillness; only the faintest of tremors remain. Slowly, I draw my feet up like his. "So, why would the ocean make you feel safe?" The sea is a lot of things, but safe isn't one of them.

Smile lines crinkle at the corners of his eyes. "Seems strange to you, I know. But there was a time in a war when I thought I'd never see another drop of water. Sand everywhere. Dry and blistering hot. Every breath pulled moisture from our lips and left our tongues as dust. I'd never breathed anything like it. With sandstorms and sweat, sand coated the inside of our ears, stuck between our teeth, and crusted the inside of our noses. Salt and sand burrowed into the pores of our skin."

"Crusty sand up your nose? Sounds scratchy." How many tissues would it take to get all that out?

"Rough as sandpaper, yeah. It rashed our skin like sunburns. We carried over a hundred pounds with body armor, helmet, and equipment. Our sweat washed sand into our eyes as temperatures soared over a hundred degrees. Every. Single. Day."

"If you didn't have water, how did you get the sand out of your eyes?" I swivel toward this gentle new Uncle.

"We blinked. A lot." He blinks at me really big and silly a few times. "Took a while to get it out sometimes. At the end of the day, we shook sand out of our clothes, our boots, our socks—but we could never get rid of it."

The kayak tilts against the sand, and Uncle tosses a shell into the sea. "I used to dream of water."

Did Mom know this about Uncle? If she did, she never told me.

"After some bad things happened, I got sort of mixed up inside my head until I started to believe that I would only be safe if I could be near water."

"Like home base?" In my fast escape, the shore felt like that to me.

"Exactly like that. As long as I'm near the ocean, I'm not afraid." He gazes out at the brilliant blue sea and breathes deep. "Loud noises still bother me sometimes, and when they do, I go out to my ocean and let the waves carry my fears away."

I dig my heels into the damp sand. What would it be like to have endless beach with no water? I've never been more than a day's walk from the ocean in my entire life. It's always there, always waiting. Lurking in the background. But I think I used to like seeing it there, peeking through the trees like an old friend. I'd forgotten that. "So when you're out on the water, it's like your happy place." Like my Castle Tree. Or like Dad's golden ratios.

"Exactly." Uncle nods. "Now you know how I chose my profession. So, what about you?"

"Me?" That's a weird thing to ask. "I'm twelve. I don't know what I want to be yet."

"No. I mean, you swim like you were born to water. But something happened, I think. And now you're afraid. Will you tell me why?"

It's strange that I never noticed the laugh lines at the corners of Uncle's dark brown eyes before. Were they always there, hiding under all the frowns? Are they different lines, or do they take turns going up or down?

"Alex?"

"What?" I hug my knees and count the snail shells between Uncle and me. Twelve. There's twelve shells between us. How many shells are between Mom and me? A million? A billion? More? Shells march from my feet to the water, not straight like a line, but here and there, a zigzag of snails and sand.

"If you tell me your story, I promise to help you find whatever clues your mom left for you. I'm good at solving codes and riddles—who do you think taught her?"

I look up, the shells forgotten, and he nods. "It occurs to me that the reason she wants you to help me is so that I can help you." He cups the side of his mouth and whispers. "She's sneaky like that."

So . . . Mom wants me to help Uncle so Uncle can help me? Mom's sneaky, all right.

"See? You know what I mean. You can lend me your hands, and I'll lend you my ears. It's a fair trade, but only if you talk to me."

Talking about the bad thing is almost as scary as going into the ocean. That's why I *don't* talk about it. Never ever . . . except something about Uncle makes me think that maybe just this once, I can.

I twist my hands in my lap. "I don't like to remember it."

"You're stronger than you think. Take your time." Uncle watches the horizon instead of me, and somehow that makes it easier.

"So, Dad had a scuba class on a shore dive a few years ago." My voice cracks, and I clear my throat. "Beginners need help with everything. Fins, tanks, all of it. It has to be done right so they can waddle out to sea . . . but it took forever." I gaze out over the glassy water of the bay, clear and perfect—same as it was *that* day, when I was tired of waiting while they flailed and tripped over their own flippers. Pink, featherless penguins all tangled up in diving gear.

"I saw something out over the reef. A turtle maybe. It disappeared before I could really tell. I thought I could see it if I got out there fast enough. I was *dying* for a peek." I take a shaky breath. "I almost did."

"Turtles are docile."

"The turtle didn't scare me. The ocean did." How can someone who loves the sea and everything in it possibly understand?

"What happened?"

"Dad told me to wait—said we'd go out together so I could snorkel above the class during the lesson, but I went out without him." My swim goggles were pink. I wrinkle my nose. What a weird thing to remember. "I was sure I only needed a few minutes cause snorkeling's easy, and I was *fast*. But I was stuck with all these tourists making noise and splashing. I thought they'd scare the fish away for sure, so I went first, ahead of all those people. Ahead of Dad."

"Did your dad know you left without him?"

"Not at first. Dad was focused on his clients, and I didn't say anything. I just swam out. The water was clear as glass." I wave at the endless ocean. "Visibility forever. Seemed like I could see the whole reef at once—a whole rainbow of coral."

I see it still. Anemones with crazy tentacles drifting back and forth, spiky sea urchins waving purple spines in the world's slowest sword fight. "A jack fish bigger than me cruised along twenty feet below. I almost followed him until I saw the cleaning station full of bright yellow tangs. At least fifty were swarming over a green sea turtle, picking at its shell and cleaning its skin.

"I floated there and watched for a while." I lick my lips. This was the part where I usually try to wake up, and I glance at Uncle, hoping he'd ask for something else—anything else, but he only stares out to sea and waits for me to finish the story.

My fingers knot in my shirt. "So the turtle leaves the cleaning station and swims toward me with a few fish still picking his shell clean. Out of nowhere, these big waves roll over us and a strange ripple goes through the water. The turtle starts swimming weird— like flapping its fins to go fast, but he wasn't moving hardly at all. He beat his flippers hard, but still stayed like twenty feet away—at least I didn't *think* he was moving. He was, though. We *both* were moving. The turtle was swimming, and I was caught in a rip tide."

"Rogue waves can do that," Uncle says. "Dangerous situation."

"I tried to swim sideways to get out of it like you're supposed to, but the current kept getting wider like it was following me. The turtle left or got swept away or something. I don't know. But there was this one last rock jutting straight up out of the water, coming up fast, but I grabbed on."

"You caught onto a rock?"

"Yeah, my fingers caught on lava or coral, I don't know. I grabbed on as hard as I could and screamed for Dad, hoping he'd come if I held on long enough. I thought I heard him calling for me, too. But something powerful churned in the water beside me . . . this huge, dark thing with gleaming white teeth rising up from somewhere inside the rock—a viper moray eel." I close my eyes, but the memories don't stop. "It came straight at my face with its mouth open. I jerked back so fast I almost did a backflip. I kicked and splashed away as fast as I could."

Uncle nods like he can see the whole thing.

"I had to let go—but then it was just me alone, with our island getting farther and farther away. The ocean had me and it wouldn't let me go."

"I see." Uncle stands up and holds a hand out for me. "Kamalani told me you were rescued once, plucked half-drowned from the waves far out from shore, but I didn't know the details. Who got you out?"

"Some guy in an outrigger canoe saw me and brought me

back." I let Uncle pull me up and then I brush the sand from my shorts. "It probably sounds dumb."

"No. A ten-year-old keiki swept out like that? I can imagine how it would feel like the ocean conspired to take you away."

Conspired. That's it exactly. It baited me with something I wanted to see, tricked me and pulled me away, and when I grabbed onto something, it sent a viper moray to shake me loose.

I shiver.

Uncle bows his head. "Thank you for telling me. I already promised to help you with your challenges, but I think I can help you with this too. Do you trust me?"

Trust him? Grumpy old Uncle Tanaka? I bite my lip. The man I know never smiles, but this new Uncle makes me wonder if he was all bark but no bite. Maybe this really is the man Mom remembers. And if he's good enough for Mom, he's good enough for me. "I trust you."

CHAPTER FOURTEEN

Water under the Foodland Bridge

Okay, so maybe I *want* to trust him, but when Uncle asks if I want to ride back in the kayak I almost throw up.

Yeah, get back in the water today?

No.

Just no.

No power on earth could get me back in the ocean today.

At first, I worry Uncle will be disappointed or grumpy when I say I'll walk back along the shore, but instead of arguing, he pushes the kayak into the water and keeps pace with me in the shallows. Far enough to be able to paddle and keep the waves from forcing him onto the shore, but near enough to stay even with me.

Me walking, Uncle paddling, we make our way to Tanakas' beach. Well, at least I *think* of it as Tanakas' beach since it's in their backyard, but really, all the beaches on the island are public access. People could walk around the whole thing if they wanted to—except for raw, jagged places where waves smash against the rocks over and over. Reckless and relentless. Some water just seems a little angrier than others. Laie Point is like that, with spray rocketing into the air like a volcano erupting water. Anyone trying to climb around the base would get pounded against the rocks before they made it halfway out.

It doesn't take long to walk back to Uncle's house, but when we're still a couple hundred feet away, Sarge stands in the surf facing away from us with his tail wagging.

Uncle waves for me to stop, comes into shore, and walks up beside me, the bowline to the kayak trailing behind him. He points his chin toward Sarge. "Looks like we have a visitor."

I squint, but with my glasses lost somewhere between the eel hole and shore, I wouldn't even know the black and white blurry blob ahead was Sarge if it weren't for his size. I mean, how many buffalo-sized black and white furballs can there be around here? "I can tell Sarge is over there, but he's blurry. I lost my glasses."

Uncle studies my face. "Ah, I thought there was something different about you," He murmurs. "On the far side of Sarge, there are two dark bumps sticking out of the water. Can you see the dark shape? Right in front of Sarge's nose."

I put a finger on the outsides of my eyes to squinch my eyelids, but I still can't make anything clear. "Um, kind of. I think I can see a shadow there. Or maybe I just want to. I'm not sure."

"It's Saisei. You remember her from the other day?"

"The turtle? Yeah, but she disappeared so fast, I didn't really get a good look at her."

"She's shy. But she's been following us most of the day. I

expect she gave up and went home when we didn't go back out in the kayak." He taps his finger against his salt-and-pepper beard. "Her being shy has never been a problem before, but now . . . how do we get her used to you?"

Why would I want her "used to" me? I'd rather stick to land creatures: cats, dogs, birds—even geckos! Air-breathers. That's what I want. Okay, so technically she *is* an air-breather, but I like the kind with no flippers. "Wait, did you say she was following us?"

"Sure. She was swimming below us for most of the voyage. I'm surprised you didn't see her when you fell in."

Maybe I did, but without swim goggles, I wouldn't know what she was—but there was that shadow in the eel hole swimming right at me . . .

"I know how you could see her—if you got in the kayak and hunkered down, she probably wouldn't know you were there, and I could pull you right up beside her."

I narrow my eyes at him. "Are you trying to get me back in the water?"

A grin creeps across his lips. "It doesn't really count as *in* the water. It's only a few feet."

"So it's only a *little* bit in the water? Next you'll say water's only a *little* bit wet. Nice try. But no, thanks." Now grumpy Uncle's *teasing* me?

"Small kine water." He holds his pointer finger and thumb a centimeter apart and peers through the trembling gap.

I snort, "How about, *no* kine water." I start off again and Uncle chuckles and hurries to keep pace while towing the kayak behind him.

When we're halfway there, Sarge whips his head around,

barks twice with a deep *huff huff,* then bounds toward us with big happy leaps. Behind him, the shadow vanishes into the surf.

I brace myself for a hundred-pound butt to smush my foot or for a wagging tail of terror to knock me over, but Sarge only circles me once with a wide doggy grin and then trots to Uncle's side. I cringe as a long string of drool slimes Uncle's hand, but he doesn't seem to mind and gives Sarge a good scratch behind the ears.

Auntie steps out from under the trees and waves. "Hey! Howzit? Why you pulling the boat? Did you have trouble?"

My cheeks heat as I open my mouth to apologize for all the trouble . . . again . . . but Uncle beats me to it.

"Always with the worrying. Everything's fine. I wanted to stretch my legs, you know? Exercise, like you always tell me. Maybe I'll join the Iron Man competition next, eh?"

First he jokes with me, now he's covering for me? This is definitely not the same Uncle I saw this morning. So why the change after my freak-out? Maybe he feels sorry for me?

"Why stop at Iron Man? There's the Triathlon and Spartan races too. Those runners better watch out now that you're joining the competition." Auntie gives Uncle a kiss on the cheek. "Though, you might need one or two more walks before the race."

"I just walked all the way from way over there." Uncle jabs a thumb behind us. "The crown is as good as won already."

Auntie's laugh fades as she looks me up and down. "Decide to take up swimming again?"

"No. I mean, not on purpose."

"Ah." She slides a quick glance at Uncle. "What did you do? I told you to be nice, you big grump. You okay, Alex?"

"I—" Uncle raises his hands, but I answer for him.

"He was nice. Promise. Hardly grumpy at all."

"Hardly grumpy, eh?" Auntie crosses her arms, eying us both.

"I swear! It was . . ." I glance at Uncle. No way can I say *fun*, but I learned a lot, and he's different than I thought he'd be. I discard a few more answers and settle on, ". . . good?"

"Good, huh? Maybe so." She wraps her warm arms around me, gives me a squeeze, and turns to Uncle. "I have to finish one project for work, but we need some things. You like go store?"

Uncle slides his fingers through hers. "For you? Anything." He curls their clasped hands up and kisses the back of her hand.

She lets me go and playfully taps his chest. "What, you think sweet talk gon' get you out of trouble? Don't forget, I know you too well."

"I'm counting on it." He touches her cheek and bows his head to rest his forehead against hers.

I drop my gaze to Sarge and give him a good scratch. It's not like Auntie and Uncle were smooching or anything, but the way they radiate love—tender but solid—feels way too private for me to be standing there gawking at them like a crane.

Uncle clears his throat. "I can run to the store, but let me put samples away first."

Together we pull the kayak far onto the shore, and I help lift and carry it to the yard.

We set it down by the shed, and Auntie brushes sand from her hands. "Alex, can you get the car keys while I help Matthew gather the samples?"

"Sure." I skip past the sitting logs and Uncle's boat to the screen door under the blossoming plumeria tree and slip inside. The scent of flowers follows me inside, but as I venture deeper into the house across the linoleum floor, the aroma of steamed rice mingles with a savory BBQ dish that makes me drool almost as much as Sarge.

In the living room, an aquarium with coral anemones and bright colored fish stands along the wall behind the couch with a whole school of colors. You'd think he'd get enough fish-time with an entire ocean in his backyard without bringing some ocean inside too, but I guess not.

Beside the lanai side door, Auntie's key rack perches like a cuckoo clock on the wall with a triple stacked roof on top. On the front, a carved map of Japan decorates the Barbie-sized double doors that hide the rows of key hooks inside.

Key fobs make it easy to tell which keys are for cars, but other keys hang beside them. Little silver keys for filing cabinets, a short key for a mower, house or office keys, and a brass key attached to a ring with a turtle. I pluck the car key fob off the hook and close the door.

On the way past the fish tank, I kneel on the couch to watch an orange-striped clown fish and electric blue damselfish dart around the anemones and coral in a game of tag. Above them, a blue-striped emperor angelfish swims regal laps around the tank. I'm pretty sure it's a baby 'cause the white spaces between the blue lines turn yellow when they grow up.

A statue of a Japanese building with a tiered roof like Auntie's fancy key holder rests in the center of the tank with little silver fish darting in and out of the doors.

Once upon a time, when Dad was still in the military and

Mom was working one of her first overseas jobs in Japan, my parents first met by a Japanese temple that looked a lot like that. There's a picture of it in their bedroom. A pagoda, I think that's what it's called.

I push off the couch to head outside, but freeze when my brain replays the words from the lemon juice clue in Dad's classroom: *In the place where we met, a turtle holds the key.*

Glancing over my shoulder at the temple-shaped key holder, I shake my head. "No way." But when I open the door and slip the turtle keychain from the hook, it's perfect. It fits the clue right down to the turtle keychain holding the key. And Mom made sure I'd help Uncle, didn't she? She *knew* I'd be here. It's got to be right.

With car keys in one hand and the turtle key in the other, I run out to Uncle and pass him the car fob before spinning to Auntie. "Look what I found! Do you know what it goes to?"

She turns the turtle keychain over while Sarge sniffs the back of her hand as if to see what the fuss is about. "Isn't this yours, Matthew? I noticed it a while ago but forgot to ask about it."

"Not mine." Uncle shakes his head. Beside him, Sarge sneezes, flinging slobber drops all over our legs.

"I think it's Mom's next clue." Too excited to care about the drool, I hold up the key to read the numbers stamped into the face. "It says, three one four. *Oh!* It's pi again. The first numbers of pi are 3.1415. But what's it go to?"

"Looks like it's small enough to be a key to a post office box," Uncle says.

"See?" Auntie shoos us to the car like this was the plan all along. "It's on the way. First post office, then Foodland. Same parking lot. No problem."

"Yeah, yeah, we go," Uncle grumbles. "Is five minutes rest too much to ask?"

"Today, yes. Post office, then groceries. Rest after."

We pile into the car and stop by my house to get a spare pair of glasses, which means I get to choose between black, bejeweled cat-eye glasses and blue swim goggles with yellow-tinted lenses. Dad found the sparkly cat-eye pair on sale once and thought I'd like them—he was wrong. Come to think of it, he's the one that bought the new swim goggles too, thinking I'd use them next time I swam with him, but a layer of dust covers their original packaging on my shelf.

It stinks that I have to wear glasses when most of my friends don't need them at all. How's that fair? Reluctantly, I put the cat-eye pair on and look in the mirror. If I had been born a long time ago, I'd probably think they were cool, but with all those fake diamonds plastered around the frame, it looks like they got in a glitter fight and lost. "Why would anyone wear this on purpose?" It makes me want to grumble like Uncle.

Standing beneath the flock of origami creatures in my room, the room feels empty without the computer screen on. My own personal ghost town. Dad must've turned everything off this morning after my lolo run to Castle Tree. My notes on Mavis Batey still cover the wall around my desk, but a whole lifetime has passed for me since Mom missed her call. It's been ages since last night—years even. Time does funny things when worry and love jumble together. I glance at the clock. Another hour and a half and Dad will be home. With luck, maybe he'll have news about Mom.

On the way out of my room, I grab the last banana lumpia from the fridge for a snack and snag my sun hat with a floppy brim. If I have to wear these sparkly things on my face, at least I can keep the sun from shining off them and bouncing sparkle rays into space.

Uncle doesn't seem to notice the glasses when I get back in the car, and we drive the rest of the way to the post office in comfortable silence.

The Foodland Plaza is home to all sorts of great places like Foodland Grocery, Chinese food, Angel's Shave Ice, and . . . Laie's post office. We glide past all the other stuff and pull right up to the post office's hallway entrance. The office has super short hours, but the hallway is always open for the PO boxes that line the wall. I jump out to search for the number. "Three one three, three one four! It's here!" I might have squealed a little.

The key slides in the hole and turns with a click. I bite my lip as the tiny metal door swings open, and I peer inside the gloomy void. A long, narrow box tied with ribbons rests on the metal.

"What is it?" Uncle stoops to watch as I reach in and pull the box out.

"I don't know, but I think I like it." The red silk ribbons untie with one tug, and I shimmy the top of the container off and pass it to Uncle. Inside, a canvas scroll with dark wood knobs at each end rests in the silk-lined box. This scroll is way fancier than the first one that led me to Hukilau Beach and the lunch box.

Uncle peers over my shoulder as I set the box aside and unscroll Mom's message.

A painted, odd-shaped oval lies on its side with wavy lines and speckles around it. Inside the oval, a whole bunch of perfect circles slice right through the canvas with a letter of the alphabet above each one.

I search for a pattern, but the letters seem totally random. No order. No cipher. No nothing. It's just a jumbled-up alphabet over a bunch of holes inside an oval. Could the spacing of the holes mean something like with Morse code somehow? If Mavis Batey were here, she'd probably have it figured out in no time, but I don't see it. "This one's tricky," I mumble. "I can't see a pattern. I need to look it up on the computer and see if anyone else has seen pictures with holes like this."

Uncle raises a bushy eyebrow. "You could do that, or you could go under the bridge and see where it leads."

"Bridge?" I turn the scroll on its side. "There's not a bridge here. What do you mean?"

He holds up the top half of the box. In the center, someone sketched a picture of the Foodland bridge from the side and added a faint dotted line disappearing underneath it. "What say we go walk under the bridge a skosh?"

"Heck, yeah!" This is gonna be the easiest challenge yet! Not only did we find Mom's clue, but we got a picture map of where to go to figure it out. I stuff the ribbons in my pocket and tuck the empty box under my arm before grabbing Uncle's hand and tugging him down the sidewalk. "Let's go! It's gotta be the Foodland bridge over here." Mom probably tucked something up in a corner under the support beams of the bridge. "Come on!"

Uncle matches my pace as we stride along the covered sidewalk and pass storefront after storefront. "Always in such a hurry. Between you and Kama, I'll be an Iron Man–Spartan racer in no time. You're probably plotting it together. Can't hide your evil plan from me."

"No, you just *think* you figured our plans out. My mom's a sneaky genius and she's teaching me everything she knows! *Muahaha!*" My laughter fades from evil mastermind to nervous giggle. *Uh*, did I really just tease Uncle like that? I'm not thinking straight. With the next clue so close, my stomach jitters like it's gonna run across the parking lot all by itself!

A few minutes later, we reach the far end of the parking lot where the grass dips into a wash that melts into sand under the Foodland bridge. As part of the Kamehameha Highway, the bridge is never silent for long, especially since these two little lanes connect everything on this half of the island.

I've been here a bunch of times before with Mom on our walks, but this time, instead of a shallow sheen of water over sand, there's a good foot of water at the edge of the grass. The closer it gets to the bridge, the deeper the water. And beyond the bridge, it goes deeper still. There's not one drop of sand or rock to stand on that isn't already under water. What is it with me and water today? "No way."

In the pool at our feet, a school of silver fish flow from one side of the wash to the other in perfect unison like metallic ribbons flashing beneath the surface. Mom can't mean for me to go in there, can she? She *knows* I don't go in water anymore. There must be another clue, some other way she meant for me to go . . . But even as I think it, I know that's not true.

This is why Mom made the picture on the box so clear and easy to understand. She knew I'd never believe it otherwise. "Aw, Mom. So not cool."

Uncle peers down the wash. "Remember what I said about this wash channel changing with storms? Sometimes waves carry sand all the way to the parking lot here and bury this pool, but this time it left the pool deeper here, and—" He squats to look under the bridge. "Shallow farther in with a sandbar. You saw that from the other side."

I duck to follow his view and sigh at the island of dry sand rising up from the water on the other side. At least it's not full all the way to the ocean. Okay. Only a little water. I can do this . . . maybe. "How deep do you think it is under the bridge?"

"Foot and a half, maybe. Less than two."

I can feel him studying me, like I'm some marine animal about to do something really interesting—but I already decided I won't go back in the water.

I stand frozen, caught between two powerful currents: curiosity and fear. The only way I can solve Mom's clue is to step into the water, but didn't I promise myself no force on earth could get me back in the water? I glance at Uncle, half expecting him to admit he set it up—a huge conspiracy between him and the ocean—but even he's not *that* grumpy.

Why would Mom do this to me? Clearly I can't go forward, but . . . I can't leave without Mom's clue. My hands break out in sweat as my anxiety spikes up. "Come on, I can do this." I shake the stress from my arms and take a steadying breath, but when my feet refuse to move for the third time, my voice comes out in a whine. "Why did Mom have to put it down *there*?"

"Don't worry." Uncle grins. "It's only small kine water."

CHAPTER FIFTEEN

Small Kine

Small kine water? I give him the stink-eye, but Uncle just grins wider.

"Bah!" I grumble. He may be the kahuna on all marine biology things, but who really knows what's down there? There could be all sorts of things hiding under the sand or in the shadows. Cars driving over top wouldn't have a clue of what lurked below.

Why make a bridge here at all? It's obviously a man-made riverbed. It's got cement walls down both sides and everything. "Why'd they build a waterway that starts right here by a parking lot and ends at the ocean? It's only, what—a few hundred feet long?"

"See behind you? The long dip in the grass? It's a natural depression. Laie is a flood zone. You know heavy rains sometimes bring water down from the mountains and fill the streets, yeah? It's why so many here build their house on stilts—they prepare for the floods they know will come sooner or later. If there was no water channel, no way through to the ocean from here, the next heavy rainstorm could flood everything on this side of the highway.

Okay, fine. So maybe they have a good reason for the water here, but it's still mean that Mom added this path to my challenge. I stare down at the water below. On this side of the bridge, saltwater mixes with fresh runoff to make a brackish soup, so probably there's nothing big hiding up here, but that's how hiding works: you don't see hidden creatures until they jump out and try to get you.

"So, we go look, or just watch those little fish all day?"

I jump at Uncle's voice. How long was I staring at the water anyway? I swallow. "I think . . . uh, I think that one of us has to go in there and look under the bridge."

I glance at Uncle hopefully, but he doesn't volunteer. Instead, he extends a hand toward the water. "Ladies first."

Why does it matter to him if I go in the water or not? Okay, fine. I'll just step in and . . . My leg muscles flex, but my foot is stuck fast to the grass. Not just stuck, but rooted, like my heel transformed into a banyan tree vine, burrowing deep down through the ground all the way to lava rock.

The other foot doesn't do any better. I can step back, but not forward. A short circuit in my brain with malfunctioning feet sensors. I blow out a breath in frustration. "Stupid. *So* stupid."

"Can't step in, can you?" Uncle sidesteps so I can look at him better.

I shrug. If I could, I would've done it already.

"Remember what I said before about how these kinds of

fears are bigger? It's not your fault that you feel afraid, and you're certainly *not* stupid. It's your mind and body's way of protecting you." Uncle leans against a tree and steps out of his rubber slippers.

Still rooted to the side of the shallow pool, I watch him from the corner of my eye.

"You like codes, right?" He steps to the edge, letting his toes curl over the little drop-off.

"Yeah, but Mom knows way more than me."

"She's lived more than twice your lifetime. Of course she knows more. That's not the point. You read Morse code, right?"

"Yeah."

"And ciphers?"

"Sometimes." What does it matter? How can that help me move when my feet won't listen?

"I bet that means more times than not. What about maps?"

"Sure. Everyone knows how to read maps."

"Only if they have the right key or legend to understand them. Kamalani mentioned you're doing a report on a code-breaker? Someone from Bletchley Park, yeah?" Uncle asks.

Whoa, why would Auntie tell him about my report? "Yeah—what does Mavis Batey have to do with the ocean?"

"This Mavis was a real smart lady, correct?"

"She was brilliant."

He taps his beard and nods. "Brilliant enough to see patterns and clues from enemies in messages, letters, and numbers. Same as your mom can do with language, colors, and shapes. Same as *you* can do."

"So, what? Everyone can."

"Not everyone." He raises a finger. "Most people would

never look at a line of colored rocks bordering a flower bed and understand it was a code. To the rest of the world, it's just pretty rocks. But to you, it's a message. You understand there's more to this world than what's on the surface."

"So, Mom showed me how to look for things. Malia's family taught her to surf, Jack's dad showed him how to lay bricks. It's nothing special. We just learned different stuff." Maybe I was a little better at figuring things out than others, but that's no biggie.

"Exactly. You learned to see hidden messages in a land above water, but I've spent my life studying things most can't see *below* the water." Uncle steps down into the pool and faces me. "What if I told you the ocean speaks in code?"

"The ocean can't read." I know I'm a kid, but come on.

"I never said it could read. I said it speaks to us in code." He folds his arms, and I fold mine. I can play the waiting game too. If he wants to say something that makes sense, I'm listening.

"I can prove it to you." He points at the schools of silver fish swirling between him and the bridge. "Those fish move in perfect unison. How do they know to turn at the same time?"

"Maybe they see the one next to them turn and then they copy each other?"

"It's more precise than that. Each fish can feel the vibrations of the fish around it. They can tell from the vibrations what they need to do even before they can see it. They school together, creating a bubble of safety that confuses predators and increases their chances for survival—all because they communicate in ways no one can see."

I frown at the school of fish. "Okay. But that's not really a code."

"Not to you, maybe," Uncle agrees. "But it sends a message to the fish throughout the school. The purpose of a message is to communicate. And they do.

"So, you know there's vibrations, but marine life can use colors too. Octupi and squid use bright or even flashing colors to warn predators off or attract mates. But unless you know the code for which colors mean what, you won't understand. Let's say you saw a cuttlefish with zebra stripes; what is it trying to say?"

"You're teasing. How can a cuttlefish know what a zebra looks like?"

"It doesn't know, but a cuttlefish *does* change his colors to black and white stripes that look a lot like zebra stripes when he wants rivals to know how tough he is. Vibrations, colors, sounds, shapes, even chemicals." He tilts his head to the far side of the pool. "In fact, there's a hermit crab right over there using chemicals now."

"A hermit crab?" How would it know what to do with chemicals?

"Better hold that scroll higher."

I jerk it up by my chest to check for any damage, but it seems okay. "Why?"

"I'll show you." Uncle reaches for my hand and I grasp it without thinking. Next thing I know, he's tugged me splashing across the pool to a shallow patch of sand where a hermit crab creeps between rocks below the surface.

Note to self: never take Uncle's hand near water. Too sneaky. The way he ignores my jerky shudder when water sloshes up to my knees, I almost believe he did it on accident . . . almost.

"See how the antennae and mouth parts move?" He grabs a reed from the bank and dips it near the crab. The tiny antennae move faster and the crab inches away from Uncle's stick. "They're constantly tasting for chemical signals to tell them if there are predators or food sources nearby. It communicates a message, same as your codes do."

He tugs me toward the bridge. "What say we look for the code your mom left for us? You think it's under here?" Ducking under the edge of the bridge, he pulls me behind him into the gloom.

My gaze darts from one side of the bridge to the other, ready for shadowy eels to rush at us any second, but nothing does.

"Check the corners on that side. Do you see anything?" Uncle lets go of my hand, and I think about bolting out of there, but I'm already in the water and he seems so relaxed . . .

I dip under each support beam and peer into dark corners, paying special attention to the graffiti in case Mom left a clue there. Other than some swears and things scrawled across the cement, there are no real messages that I can see. I guess I should have known that she would never vandalize anything—not even the underside of a bridge.

"Step into the light. Let's have another look." Uncle holds a hand out for my scroll box and shows me the bridge drawing. "The dotted line goes under the bridge and on through to the other side. Whatever we're looking for must be farther on."

With tall cement walls on either side of the wash, there's only one way we can go: makai, toward the ocean. Round rubber-and-glass floats hang from trees in someone's yard, where they've arranged them over a stinky noni bush with its white fruit scattered on the ground and reeking worse than rotten cheese. Shaped like lumpy, rotten potatoes, the smell makes my stomach churn. "Oh, gosh. That's awful."

"This?" Uncle wafts the smell toward his face. "You get used to it. It's good for tea." He taps a disgusting fruit. "They say this is good for many things in the body—and it keeps fleas away."

"So you drink stinky noni tea on purpose so you don't get fleas?" I don't have fleas either. But I sure don't drink that.

He gives me a flat look. "The flea deterrent is for Sarge. Lower blood pressure for me."

"You give this stuff to Sarge? Poor dog."

Uncle leads me along the watery path, always choosing the shallowest part.

When we finally reach the sandbar, I look over my shoulder at the little cars passing over the bridge on the highway. We've gone farther than I thought. But how far are we supposed to go? There's no way to scale the cement walls lining both sides of the wash without climbing through someone's yard. It's all private property.

"Come." Uncle tugs my hand and we walk off the sandbar and back into the water on the other side. Here, the channel curves slightly, and the cement walls down both sides grow taller, the tops of the walls far higher than I could reach. Around our knees, waves roll in from the ocean ahead where Laie Point and Temple Beach join.

"Uh . . ." Suddenly the little path doesn't seem separate from the ocean at all. The waves cruise right on in here, so what's to stop dangerous creatures from swimming right in? I slow, but before I can stop alltogether, Uncle tugs my hand, pulling me out of the mouth of our narrow, walled world.

"I know they make you nervous, but waves are an important part of the ecosystem." Uncle glances at me over his shoulder. "Every wave at high tide brings fresh nutrients and microorganisms to feed the reefs and tide pools. Waves replenish the food supply of plankton and other tiny creatures that feed bigger ones on up the food chain. It's all connected."

"Okay." Chicken skin races up my arms as the sandy bottom drops deeper and water splashes up over my hips. I shiver, my fingers clutching Uncle's hand like crab pincers. Waves slosh against my sides, but Uncle leads me up and out onto the sandy shore beside the entrance.

The enormous boulder we saw when I took the first sample for Uncle sits beside the mouth of this man-made wash. Hours later, I've come full circle and am back where we began.

We could have gotten here by walking down the shore on dry land and not through all that water. *So why make me walk through it?* I want to yell at Mom, or at least demand answers. But with my feet on the sand, my mind clears and I know the answer before I ask the question. We might have been here before, but Mom couldn't have known Uncle would take me here. And besides, we never had Mom's scroll before. This time, I can find her next clue.

To our right, the cliffs of Laie Point jut out to sea. To our left, Temple Beach stretches far down the shore, and right in front is that same big boulder—an oval lying on its side. I open the scroll and compare the rock to the painted, odd-shaped oval with wavy lines and speckles around it.

"The scroll has a picture of the boulder." I tilt the drawing so Uncle can see. "The wavy lines must represent the ocean, and the speckles are sand, and inside . . ."

I hesitate, studying the small circular holes cut right through the paper inside the drawing of the oval. Each hole with its corresponding alphabet letter written above. "I should have recognized it before—the boulder, I mean. It has the same shape and everything . . . except it has too many holes in the picture. The rock doesn't have near that many."

"No way for you to know," Uncle says. "Could've been a drawing of anything. Maybe a rock, maybe a sponge? Only way to find out is to be brave enough to take the next step. And Alex, the girl who just walked with me into the waves despite her fear, is a very brave girl indeed."

"Whatever." I roll my eyes, but he leans close.

"Do I look like I'm lying to you?"

His dark eyes bore right through me and I slowly shake my head. "No."

"Good. I may not always say what you would like to hear, but I promise you, I'll always tell you the truth. And the truth is, you *are* brave."

Heat flushes up my cheeks and I don't know what to say, so I focus on the scroll instead. I count the holes on the rock against the holes in the picture in case the ratio matters some-how, but that doesn't help. Maybe the lines behind it mean something when they line up with the real-life rock? But the squiggly lines only represent waves, and they're never still enough to count for anything.

I bite my lip, hold the scroll in front of me, and step back along the sand until the real rock is far enough away to appear the same size as the oval in the scroll. I circle the rock until two short lines I had dismissed as more waves on the scroll line up with the cement walls at the mouth of the wash we just came through.

The moment those walls lines up, several dark spots on the rock show through the holes on my scroll. I gasp and wave for Uncle to come quick. "I got it! It's not a code, it's a puzzle piece. When I hold the scroll in the right spot, the rest of the picture shows through. I need a pen!"

"How about a pencil?" Uncle helps me circle the holes on the scroll that line up with the holes on the rock until each matching one is marked.

I read the marked letters written over each hole, but they spell a nonsense word: SHELILESDBACCVACOS

Three of the holes on the scroll have no letters marked next to them at all. I frown at the letters and blank spaces. They make exactly zero sense to me, but at least it's a message. I can figure the rest out later.

"Looks like you got the message. What say we go get those groceries, eh?" Uncle takes a step toward the wash.

"Sure." I roll the scroll up and take a few steps to follow him back to the Foodland bridge, but the deeper water pulls my gaze. Did I see a shadow in the water? Or was that a reflection from the dark rocks on the cliff?

Then Uncle is there again, holding my hand and leading me onward. "Did you know turtles make noises to communicate with each other?"

"I've never heard a turtle noise."

"Their sounds are mostly out of human hearing range. Sounds so deep, they travel long distances under water. But we can hear some. Hissing, a kind of cluck noise, or even a high-pitched whine sometimes."

Before I know it, the smell of the noni fruit fills my head and I wrinkle my nose as we pass. Did we really travel so far already?

Uncle keeps spouting turtle facts. "And then there's the baby turtles, which squeak at each other while still inside their eggs. We think it might help them coordinate their hatching so they all hatch at the same time. That's their best defense against predators—to rush to the ocean all at once."

We duck under the bridge, slosh through the last pond area, and step onto the grass. Soaked from the ribs down, but otherwise okay.

Uncle steps into his slippers and waits for me.

"You know," I say as I take the box from him and put the scroll back inside, "you think you've got everyone fooled, but I've cracked your code too."

"What do you mean my code? I have no codes." Uncle trudges up to the parking lot, but I'm not letting him off the hook that easy.

"You pretend to be grumpy, so that's the message you're communicating to the world, but the truth is . . ."

Uncle slows and half turns his head. "What?"

I take a breath. "It's fake—the way you act all mean, sharp, and bristly. 'Cause really, you're just pretending. You swell up like a spiky puffer fish to scare people off, but on the inside, you're a marshmallow."

CHAPTER SIXTEEN

Hidden Magic

After Uncle buys some pork manapua buns for dinner and drops me off at home, I lay out the canvas on the table and snap a picture so I can text the mystery message to my friends.

SHELILESDBACCVACOS – Any ideas?

I know I can figure it out on my own eventually, but Jack really helped crack the last one fast, so why not give the rest of Castle Crew another try? Besides, with their brains working on that, I can make fried rice as a bonus sorry-I-freaked-out-and-ran-away-this-morning thing.

Spam chops up easy, and I dump it into the frying pan to sizzle while the first few text guesses pop up on my phone. Naya thinks the three empty spaces on the scroll means three words, like a spacebar—which makes sense.

Jack texts: *If it's an anagram, it spells saliva belches!*

I text back: *Not long enough. Still missing dccos. Try 3 words.*

Malia tries: *Loss beach advice—missing cls*

Naya: *Cave belch socials = uses all letters*

Jack: *haha—burping in caves with friends?*

I add carrots, peas, and cabbage to the pan with an egg and let it crackle with rice and Spam until the whole house smells like fried rice.

Ekolu sends a smiley and shell emoji with: *basic cave shells—doc*

Something about "beach" and "cave" sticks in my head. Didn't Mom show me a cave by Clissolds Beach once? I'm sure she did, high in the rock at the base of Laie Point there. I check the letters against the name.

That's it! My thumbs fly over the screen: *Got it—Clissolds Beach cave! TY! Go with me later?*

Malia and Jack both text that they can, but I have to wait for Dad before I can go. We still need to talk.

By the time Dad drives up, hangs his scuba gear under the lanai, and drapes his towel over the line, I've got the rice and manapua on the table with napkins folded into frogs on each of our plates. I wish we had rambutan to make it real fancy, but I ate the last of the red fruit already.

He opens the screen door and sniffs. "Fried rice? Is Auntie here?"

"Just me." I pull the chair out for him. "Sorry I ran off this morning."

He sits down, but holds an arm out for me and pulls me in close to kiss the top of my head. "I'm glad you're okay. I'd have come for you myself, but Malia said the aunties already told her where you were. I was scheduled back to back, but still. Do you want to talk about it?"

Talk about Mom being gone? "Do you know anything new?"

"Not yet. But these gaps in communication happen sometimes with military submarines. She's all the way across the ocean and—"

I wave a hand to cut him off. "Not right now. Please." Unless there's something new—some fresh hope that everything will be fine, or reason for why she missed the call, then talking won't help anything. My chair scrapes against the tile floor as I settle across from him. "Just tell me one thing—do you believe Mom is okay?"

He looks me straight in the eye so there's no mistake. "I do."

I take his belief and stuff it inside to strengthen my own. Mom *will* come home. And we *will* be together again. "Okay."

He pauses with the manapua roll halfway to his mouth. "Hey, you're wearing the glasses I bought you. Feeling confident today?"

"Uh, sure." I try to smile, but it feels more like a grimace as he bites into the soft roll and closes his eyes, savoring the flavor. I know I should tell him about my glasses being gone, but a small part of me is still hoping I might be able to find my glasses again so I can pretend the whole disaster never happened. Besides, I need to focus on the *new* clue, not a soggy sad thing. "Can I run to the beach later?"

"Not by yourself. Buddy system, Alex. No more running off alone. Besides, you should be focusing on Mom's challenge, not playing around on the beach. You don't have much time left." He jabs the roll toward the schedule with all its colors.

"I know, that's why I need to go. I think Mom might have

put something in the cave by the point. *And* I won't be alone."
I show him the phone screen. "Malia and Jack will go with
me."

"To Clissolds Beach already?" Dad takes a bite and studies the calendar. "Better than I thought. How'd you get so far
today?"

I grin. "Easy, I got Uncle on my team."

The next morning, Malia and I ride our bikes to the PCC
side of Laie Point as planned, but Jack sends a text that he has
to go do yard work for somebody and can't come.

"Wait, Jack is doing yard work? On purpose?" Sure, he's
always first in line for adventure, but yard work?

"Maybe they're paying him with Spam musubi?" Malia
guesses. She sends him a teasing text, *Any food there?* But he
sends back, *Sorry busy.*

So weird.

Pine needles crunch under our feet as we slip through
shadows of beach almond and ironwood trees. I step carefully
so I don't get pricked by quarter-sized pinecones and long seedpods, but Malia wears slippers, so she doesn't have to watch as
close.

As the prickly needles and giant seedpods give way first
to grass and then sand, we wind through piles of driftwood
along the waterline and watch for tiny sand-colored hermit
crabs. Any other day, we'd build racetracks of sand to see whose
hermit crab creeps over the finish line first, same as Mom did
when she was a kid. Way better than sandcastles any day.

As we near the rocks of the Point, a'ama crabs skitter
sideways, streaking away from us into grooves and cracks. It

amazes me that something stuck sideways can move so fast, but they do. Fast as minnows darting from light to shadow, they're here and gone in a blink. Behind them, black snails creep along above and below the waterline on rocks jutting up from tide pools. Sometimes we let them cling to our fingers, their little eyeball tentacles testing the air. Ekolu sucked one out of its shell once and ate it. He said they're way salty and dared me to do it too, but I like my food to *not* be alive when I eat it. I mean, *eww*. Food that's already dead should be a rule.

Malia and I climb past the first few tide pools, high above the waves where green naupaka leaves with their tiny white half-flowers blanket most of the rocks. With one last glance behind us, we slip into a wide crack.

"See anything?" Malia wedges her slippers against the sides real careful so they don't fall down into the crevice.

"Not yet." I climb farther in and the space narrows, the sides forming a natural cave. We search for a marking of some kind, but there's only rock with naupaka branches and leaves curled into the space between.

I hunt for patterns, messages, anything, but it all seems pretty normal—until I spy a flat rock darker than the rest wedged way back in the crack. Reaching as far in as I can, I grab the stone, and my fingers touch something metal and not-stone behind it. I pull the stone out of the way and pluck a breath mint tin out of the crack. "Got it!"

It's jammed shut, so I try wiggling the lid. No luck.

"Love you," Malia says.

"Uh, thanks?" I mean, we're best friends and all, so I guess I love her too, but . . . I slide my fingernails under the edge.

"No," she laughs. "Look!"

169

Cradled in her hand, a naupaka leaf clearly reads "Love you" in brown scratches across it. And once I see that message, a dozen more wink at us from the branches inside the crack. I read one after the other:

Strong,

Brave,

Smart,

Kind,

Beautiful,

U got this,

Brilliant

Each leaf could describe my mom perfectly, and I wonder if maybe it is all about her, until I read the last three leaves.

My girl,

I ♥ U,

Alexis.

I tuck the tin into my shorts pocket, reach out, and cradle the last leaf. "Did Mom write all this?"

Malia turns them over one by one. "Had to. She probably stood right where you are with a needle or thorn and scratched the words on these leaves while they were still growing. With letters this brown, they've been here a while."

I imagine Mom, climbing up inside here to hide the tin, but staying longer to write words of love for me to find. I climb up and peek over the edge, half expecting to see her on the beach below, but it's only Malia and me alone with driftwood, sand, and waves as far as I can see. Even still, I hear Mom's voice whispering to me with every word, "Alexis, my girl, I love you."

We've seen words written on leaves a hundred times, even

picked swears off a few bushes now and then, but this time feels different. Expectant. As if she waits on the other side for me to speak back.

"Do you have something I can write with?" I pat my pockets and scan the rocks.

Malia snaps a narrow, dried twig off the naupaka branch. "Try this."

I search for the youngest leaf I can find and hold it from behind while I scratch an answer onto the new leaf: Love U 2.

We search the rest of the leaves one by one and check the cracks for any that might have fallen. And even then we linger, because something in me wants to hold this message, this moment with me for as long as I can. We almost take the leaves with us when we climb out, but they seem to belong there in that mystical hollow. It'd be like stealing from a church. So I take a few pictures and leave them there, with the white half-flowers of the naupaka blooming between Mom's words.

At school we learned a legend of separated lovers, one cursed to stay mauka in the mountains, the other forever doomed to roam makai by the shore. The naupaka flower testifies of their loss and sorrow. There's two different kinds of naupaka plants and both have flowers, but one grows only by the sea, and the other grows only in the mountains. Both bloom with a half-flower, never a whole, because the other half of their heart is trapped far away. When our teacher told us the story, he held the half-flowers together, one from the mountain, the other from the sea, to show how they fit together to make one whole flower.

What better plant to bear a message from my mother who's trapped somewhere far across the sea? Did she pick that plant on purpose? A message inside a message? Or was it a happy accident?

We scramble off the rocks and Malia splashes toward the beach, but I look back up to our secret cave and wish I could find a new message from Mom every time I climbed inside. It's a silly wish, and I know wishes don't make it real, but just in case, I pluck a white half-flower from the bush overhead, cup it in my hands, and whisper, "I love you too. Come back soon."

With my heart's greatest wish carried on its petals, I blow the little flower off my open palm and watch as it tumbles into the sea. If branches and leaves can send me words of love, who's to say my flower of legend can't carry my wish all the way to Mom?

"Alex, you coming?" Malia shakes a piece of seaweed from her rubber slipper. "I got hula lessons in twenty minutes."

"Yeah, yeah. Coming." I splash out of the waves and run past her before she can catch her balance. "Race you to the bikes!"

"Hey! No fair!"

I glance over my shoulder and laugh as Malia sprints after me, but her smile drops as she focuses on something beyond me. She reaches for me with fingers spread wide. "Alex, stop!"

Something huge bellows and *roars!*

I'm so close I can't tell what it is, but deep and loud, the roar fills my ears, and I flinch, my feet skidding in the sand as I wheel back from the sound, my heart racing.

Malia catches me before I fall, and we scramble away as a massive gray seal rears up from its sunning spot on the beach and roars again, its lighter underbelly disappearing beneath its girth.

The four-hundred-pound seal wriggles to face us, flesh rippling against the sand. White whiskers fan out from either side of its muzzle, and pale gray spots dot its back and neck.

Stumbling, almost tripping over our own feet, we retreat toward the rocks of the point, but a lady waves her arms from the tree line. "Get away from there!"

"We're trying!" Malia grabs my hand and we run past trees with dense leaves and cave-like hollows beneath their branches. We don't stop until we're a hundred feet away, the distant seal no more than a gray bump on the beach—at least until it curls up to scratch its head with a flipper.

"What were you doing running at a Hawaiian monk seal like that?" The lady shakes a roll of caution tape at us. "They're endangered and protected. You were way too close—you scared her!"

"We didn't mean to," I gasp, my hands on my knees. Scared *her?* I left my lungs back there on the beach somewhere.

"We didn't know it was there." Malia tugs my arm farther from the shore. "We'd never bother a seal on purpose. I swear."

The protector lady waves at a guy carrying a caution sign and mallet through the trees, the stern lines of her face softening as she considers us again. "I suppose if you really didn't see the seal, you probably had quite the fright as well."

"Oh gosh, yes." I clutch my shirt. "I thought I was gonna die right there of a heart attack."

She chuckles, "I can see that. You're lucky to see a seal like this at all. Most people never get the chance. But next time, use the rule of thumb." She holds her arm out straight in front, her hand in a thumbs-up position, and squints down the length of her arm toward the seal. "See? If I can cover the seal's whole body with my thumb like this, I'm far enough away. Never go closer than that."

"You bet. Next time hopefully I'll see it *before* I hear it." I watch the seal roll to her side and lift her head, maybe watching us.

The lady leans against a tree, her frizzy red hair flying away from her ponytail. "I never get tired of seeing them. This one's probably trying to rest up ahead of the storm coming in tonight. Every time I see one of these seals, it feels like everything's all right in the world again. Like for that one moment, there's still magic." She coughs and shifts the tape from one hand to the other. "I know that seems silly."

"No. Not silly." I clasp Malia's hand and gaze across grass and sand to where the cave hides high in the rock—that special hollow where Mom's words of love came to me as if whispered across the deep. "I think you're right. It does feel like magic here."

CHAPTER SEVENTEEN

A Promise
Is for Keeps

The stupid tin is locked down tighter than an oyster. Unbendable. Immovable. But it's not Mom's fault. There must've been a flaw in the metal when they made it. Now corrosion flows all the way around the rim in a cankering wreath of rust.

Last night, while storm winds and rain beat against the windows, I scrubbed the tin with water and baking soda and left a thick paste of the stuff over the corrosion to sit overnight while I worked on my Mavis Batey report. And still, the rust will not let go.

With today being a teacher's workday even though it's Monday, I've used the morning off from school to try every trick I could imagine to get the box open. When that didn't work, I searched online and followed all sorts of advice that was supposed to work like a charm to clean off rust, but none of it did a thing. I hope Mom didn't put anything breakable inside this one, because my next trick is called . . . *Hit it with a hammer!*

Well, technically, a hammer *and* a screwdriver.

With the tin on its side, I slide the tip of a flat-edge screwdriver against the rim and raise Dad's hammer overhead. "Please don't break, don't break, *don't break!*"

The hammer swings down and, *bam!*

The tin cracks open, each half falling to the table with a *clink!* Inside, a folded gold paper sticks to the sides of the box, a jagged tear down the center.

"Oh, man." With tweezers and Q-tips I tease the damp paper out of the tin and spread it out on the desk.

Dark smudges have ruined most of the message, but a metallic shimmer still glistens across the words: *Chocolate Factory.* And centered over the rip is some kind of symbol with three bumps.

I smack the desk. "Ha! Even with the other words lost to salt and sea, I'm positive there's only one chocolate factory on Oahu that Mom could be talking about: Mānoa Chocolate in Kailua. The three cacao leaves on their logo must be what the three melty bumps used to be before all the water damage. That proves the next clue *must* be inside the chocolate factory in Kailua, doesn't it?

I lick my lips just thinking about the chocolate tasting table. "Thank *you*, Mom!" Maybe her next clue can lead to the macadamia nut farm in Kaneohe—or to a sushi restaurant!

After printing out the bus schedule from Laie to Kailua, I circle bus number 60 at 9:30 a.m., and grab my phone to text Malia and the rest of the crew . . . but I promised Dad I wouldn't run off again. Better ask permission for this one.

Knock, knock! My knuckles rap against Dad's door.

"Just a minute!" Dad opens the door while still buttoning up his favorite Hawaiian shirt patterned after bamboo canes topped with green leaves. Like always, a carved nautilus shell hangs from the leather tie around his neck, his golden ratio always close at heart. Button finished, he twirls a hand over the outfit and quirks an eyebrow. "How do I look?"

I smirk. Before Mom was gone for work all the time, back when there was no schedule on the wall, he used to joke like this with me every day. "You look like my dad."

"Ah, yes. That *is* the look I was going for. The prestige of a handsome, brilliant, amazing father figure. I do give autographs, you know. Need anything signed?" He reaches an imaginary pen toward my forehead. "Right here, maybe? My dad is the best—"

"—nose-picker on the island!" The words rush out louder than I meant, and I giggle. Best sentence ever!

"What! I am not." He ribs me gently and then whispers, "At least, not in public. In private though . . . I make no promises."

As he sorts his things, I bite my lip and gather courage. How hard can it be? I ride the bus to see him at Kahuku High all the time. It can't be *that* much harder to go to Mānoa Chocolate Factory in Kailua, can it? I clear my throat.

"Dad, remember how I said I found a tin in the cave at Clissolds Beach?"

"Mm-hmm. Corroded, wasn't it? You need some help getting it open?"

"No. I got it."

"That's my girl." His words overlap inside my head with Mom's voice, her messages in the cave: *My girl.*

A sharp, sudden ache squeezes my throat, and my breath catches. A few quick steps, and I slip my arms around Dad's waist, my face pressed against his ribs. As his arms settle around me, he wraps me in his strength, and it's enough . . . for now.

"You okay?" The teasing gone from his voice, I know *he* knows what's wrong without ever having to say a word; we share the same wound. It just took me by surprise is all.

I wipe my face with the back of my arm and nod. *I'm fine. I can do this.* "The clue inside the tin leads to Mānoa Chocolate Factory in Kailua. I need to go there."

Dad checks his diver's watch. "The place with chocolate from all over the world, right?"

"Yeah, with all the cacao fruit."

He frowns and checks the schedule on the wall against another one on his phone. "I have work in Kahuku this morning and clients all evening. I can't cancel. It's been set up for months."

"I know you're too busy to come, but *I* have to go or I'll never find the next clue—and you said I was running out of time." *So let me go do it on my own. Problem solved.* But Dad's already rolling down the schedule train, and there's no derailing him.

"Honey, we filled in the schedule together, remember? All my appointments are marked there by date and time. I've got no wiggle room this week. We have some expenses coming up—nothing you need to worry about—but we do need every one of these clients. There's no way I can cancel a dive class for a road trip to Kailua."

"Right. You've got no wiggle room, but *I* do. I could go."

He rubs a thumb across his pendant. "No, it's more than the timing. This doesn't feel right. Are you sure you're reading it correctly? Your mom never mentioned adding the factory to the challenge."

"The clue has the three leaves for Mānoa Chocolates. *And* it says chocolate factory. You know how Mom loves their stuff; we got chocolate nibs and tea in the cupboard right now." I hold up the bus schedule paper. "Look, I already got it figured out. I can ride the bus there and back. Easy. I ride the bus all the time to visit you. It's like our family motto, right? Rise where we stand. I can stand on a bus just fine."

Dad shakes his head. "Kahuku is only the next town up. This schedule says you'd have to change busses in another town, and the trip takes over an hour. No. This is too far, too big for you. You can't go."

"The bus schedule is just another code, Dad. It's easy for me. Like math and spirals for you. You don't have to worry—"

Dad rounds on me and holds both my shoulders. "Promise me, Alexis. Promise you won't make that trip alone. I don't care how grown-up you think you are. It's not safe, and I don't want you getting lost." The hard lines of Dad's mouth soften. "I need you to be safe, hon. Give me that much."

How does he expect me to *rise* to a challenge if I can't even try? "I promise I won't go alone. I'll ask Auntie or Uncle, or somebody . . ." My friends count as "somebody," don't they?

"Good." He lets me go and stuffs a binder into his bag, all business again. "Are you keeping up on your history report? We can't get behind. School's important too."

"Yes, Dad."

"Excellent." He taps today's square on the schedule and checks his watch again. "Time to go."

I barely feel his kiss on the top of my head as he sweeps his case and duffle bag with him out the door.

"See you tonight. Don't forget to text."

"I'll text," I mumble as he disappears out the door.

As soon as the door swings shut, I'm on my phone messaging everybody: Malia, Jack, Ekolu, Naya, Tehani, and Kase.

Who wants to go with me to Mānoa Chocolates? We leave in an hour. My treat! Any chocolate U want

If that doesn't get Jack here in the next five minutes, I don't know what will. He'll be all over that free chocolate for sure!

He answers: *Sorry. Working.*

I scowl at the phone. That's *it*. He's been abducted by aliens or something. I don't know who this kid is, but he's not the Jack I know. Little green men must've sucked out Jack's brain and replaced him with a responsible, hardworking mutant. Not really a way to take over the world, but they gotta start somewhere, right?

Maybe they're all still in bed? I check the time.

Malia texts: *When and where?*

My thumbs tap fast. *Bus stop. By Temple Beach. 9:30. Don't be late.*

K—hope it's as fun as you want.

What! Why say "hope"? Of *course* we'll have fun. The perfect Malia-style response pops into my head and I grin as I type it in: *I find your lack of faith disturbing.*

. . .

Three little dots flicker on the screen and I wait for her snarky response—but she never finishes what she was saying.

The dots disappear. So I wasted a perfectly good line on a no-response? Maybe she's waiting to say it in person. That's okay too, I guess. Because today's gonna be awesome. With Malia, I won't be alone. Promise fulfilled. I stuff the phone in my pocket. "Another couple hours and then Kailua, here we come. Oh yeah!"

The long bus ride means bonus study time for me if I bring my Mavis Batey report. Way efficient, right? I sort my notes, rough draft, bibliography, and notecards into my favorite backpack. A bus ride to town seems like a bowler hat kind of day, so I snatch my black one with the red band off the hook, smooth my hair back, and tug it on to keep leftover storm winds from stealing it away.

Turns out I didn't need to worry because there's hardly any wind outside at all. The storm must've used it all up last night. The buildings seem okay, but palm fronds taller than me litter the sides of the road all the way to the bus stop. I hop from open space to open space like it's the world's biggest game of hopscotch.

Even with all the hopping, I get to the bus stop fifteen minutes early and beat Malia here, but I'm not worried. Her schedule is tight, but she's dependable as the tides.

Last time Mom took us to Mānoa Chocolates, Jack came with us and spent forever tasting the chocolate from cacao trees in different countries. Real chocolate tastes different depending on where it was grown, so it's all packaged separately.

I smile, remembering how hard it was for him to pick just *one* bar. I think Mom ended up getting him three just so we could go home. My favorite is the Tanzania bar 'cause it tastes like raisins, but Mom likes the Waiahole blackberry one.

Dad's fav is a little nutty, which fits him when he's in a teasing mood . . . but I can't remember what country that one's from.

A horn honks and I check the street again. Malia's cutting this one pretty close.

9:20 a.m. I send Malia a text: *At bus stop. Where R U?*

9:25 a.m. *Malia!!! ?? Where are you?*

I watch her street. Is there enough time to run get her? What if her sisters give her a ride in the car and we miss each other? Then *I* would be the late one.

9:28 a.m. *Hey! PLEASE ANSWER!??*

A minute later, bus number 60 pulls up and the double doors swing open right in front of me.

With shoulders wide enough to carry a canoe and intricate black tattoos covering his strong brown arms, the bus driver gives me a warm smile and waves me up. "Howzit! Where you headed?"

"I, um . . ." I scan for Malia again.

Where is she?

"You here for the bus?"

My ears burn. "I am, but—my friend isn't here yet."

"Were you tryin' to catch the 9:30 bus?"

"Yes, this one. For sure. She said she'd be here. Can you wait just one minute? My friend is coming with me to Kailua."

"I see. Your friend's running late, hah?"

"Yeah, but she'll be here. She said so. She's probably coming around that corner right now." We both watch the empty corner for a heartbeat.

No Malia.

He glances at the half-full bus and checks his watch. "I'm

sorry, but I can't make all these nice people late. I only have one more minute before I have to go."

Come on!

I text: *Malia where are you? Bus is HERE!! You leave your house yet?*

Faces watch me through the window. Some curious. Some annoyed by the useless stop for the keiki whining about her friend. My ears burn hotter. If Malia wasn't gonna show, why didn't she say so?

"Maybe you come now and she gets the next one?"

I *could* go without her—except I promised Dad I wouldn't go alone. But the whole reason I'm going is to solve Mom's challenge, so shouldn't I do it as fast as I can? I have school tomorrow, so it's got to be today! "Umm . . ."

"Time's up. You coming?" The bus driver grabs the lever to close off the stairs, and my hand shoots forward to block the door, but it's no good. I pull back and stare at my toes peeking out from my rubber slippers. I guess I didn't need to wear them after all.

"Hey, cuz." The seat and steering wheel seem kid-sized in his strong hands. "No worries. The bus'll be back. Maybe I drive you next time, hah?"

I nod and step away.

One of the ladies in the windows rolls her eyes, but most watch with pity while the door closes and brakes hiss as the bus rolls on.

Gotta admit. I'm not real happy with her. Kinda mad, even. And with Dad too!

Standing in front of all those watching eyes . . . I've never felt so small.

But stupid or not, I did promise. And if I break a promise, it'll make me a liar.

The bus coasts down Kamehameha Highway and disappears around the corner on its way to Kailua—without me.

Part of me wants to check on Malia and see what happened, but she already has my unanswered texts. She can text back when she wants to.

I adjust my backpack and start for home.

Halfway there, my phone rings and Auntie's picture lights up the screen. "Hello?"

"Alex? Can we borrow you?"

I shoot one last glance to where the bus disappeared. I'm not doing anything else. So why not? "Sure. When?"

"Now, please. Do you need a ride?"

"Naw, I'm just down the road. Be there in a few."

I don't bother hopping over any palm fronds on the way back. Instead, I kick a few and mash the others into the ground.

When I near Auntie's gate, I can hear Uncle yelling before I even reach the gate. Sure, he's grumped about this or that plenty of times. Heck, the first time I came over last week, he was ornery as I've ever seen, but it was nothing like this.

I duck through the entrance and hurry around the lanai to where Auntie stands by *Sarge's Barge* with her hands on her hips while Uncle tugs a huge chunk of blue netting out of the sand. Netting is bad news, but that's not even half of it. The storm washed empty plastic water bottles, cups, rubbish, Styrofoam, and all sorts of things up onto Uncle's beach.

"A'ole, we go now. No can . . ." Wind and surf carry most of Auntie's words away as she scolds Uncle. A few leftover plastic bags undulate like jellyfish as waves rush in and slide away again.

"Whoa. There's so much." That storm must've blown right through the floating Pacific rubbish patch and swept all this with it. It's scattered across nearly every square foot of sand! Over by Hukilau Beach, a bunch of tiny figures rush about cleaning, but there's a whole lotta beach between here and there.

Sarge bounds from one pile of rubbish to another and brings Uncle an old shoe, then a bottle. Uncle grabs them and shoves them both into an already bulging rubbish sack.

I'm pretty sure if he could find someone to blame, he'd grab them by the ear and make them pick up every last speck of plastic.

"Careless! No thought for anything. Reckless, dumb fools!" Grumbling through gritted teeth and his face red as lava, Uncle's not just grouchy—he's *mad!*

CHAPTER EIGHTEEN

Waterproof

Sarge's ears perk when he spots me, and he lopes over to give me a good sniff—which mostly means he slimes my leg. I scratch his ears. "That's a *lot* of rubbish."

Uncle stoops to pick up one piece of plastic after another and shoves them into the sack, his face getting redder each time he bends over. The muscles in his jaw clench over and over as he chews on all the words he shouldn't say.

Auntie Kama taps her finger against the hull of *Sarge's Barge*. "Matthew! You must put this anger away. Work careful, not careless. Come, sit down."

Sarge shakes his head in a whirlwind of flapping jowls, ears, and drool, then trots off and snatches another empty water bottle to give to Uncle in their strange new game of fetch.

"How can I sit?" The bag of rubbish shakes violently in his hands as if absorbing all the anger his body cannot hold. "What if they hatch? How can they go through this—" He sweeps an arm at the filth-covered beach. "—on their way? No! I can't allow it. All this must go."

"No, *you* must go. Your doctor appointment is today. We need to go now or you'll miss it," Auntie chides.

My mind catches on Uncle's word *hatch*. Is something out there in the water, waiting to hatch? I'm not sure I like the idea of some creature spawning close to shore. Maybe a kind of fish, or crab—or eel? Chicken skin erupts across my arms, and I shiver at the thought of baby viper moray eels wriggling out of their egg sacks and squirming through the surf. Just one more reason for me to stay *out* of the water.

"So, reschedule then! We must clean this up. It's not right. Not safe . . ." Beads of sweat speckle Uncle's forehead, his shirt and long, thin ponytail damp with sweat. "Not . . ." He staggers.

Auntie rushes close and steadies him by his arm. "See now? You need this appointment. We must go. And look, our Alex will help clean up while you're gone. She can watch over everything and keep them safe."

Breathing heavy, Uncle looks from me to the beach, like he wants to protest. "But . . ."

I cross my heart. "I promise, I'll work really hard the whole time here on the beach. Sarge and me, we'll clean up loads of rubbish."

Uncle holds my gaze, and Auntie whispers in his ear, "What good are you for the ocean or your honu, Saisei, if you are not well yourself? Come."

Waiting for his answer, I can't help but remember how he told Auntie that the day he invited anyone in to cause trouble would be the day pigs fly. Seems to me, he's got plenty of trouble as is and I didn't bring any of it. Flying pigs or no, he doesn't look good.

At last he nods. "Start there, near the bush to the side. Clear a path from there to the water and work across."

"No problem." I grab a pair of gloves from the shed.

Sarge whines as they get in their car and drive away, but follows me when I walk to the shoreline.

Big and small, rubbish lies in all shapes and sizes. The storm took whatever it touched and threw it back on land. All the way down the beach both ways, rubbish of every color mars the pale sand. How can one person make a difference against something like this? It's endless.

Like a tide pulling sand from beneath my feet as it scurries back to sea, the sight steals my courage out from under me. No wonder Uncle was upset. One person can't clean the whole beach; it's impossible without an army to help.

Something cool and wet touches my fingers, and I glance down at the empty bottle Sarge presses to my hand.

No one told Sarge the job is too big for a girl and a dog, so he waits for me to open the sack, and we go to work.

I message friends that Uncle needs help but don't stop to wait for anyone. Piece by piece. Step by step. We clean until a small path of sand stretches from Tanaka's fence line near his bushes to the sea. When we reach the water, we turn toward the bushes again. Makai, mauka. Toward the sea, toward the mountain, back and forth, we fill the bags.

When we clear a four-foot strip from the yard to the water, Sarge's black ears perk and he trots between me and Auntie's house as Tehani skips around the corner, sunlight sparkling off her kitty-ear headband. Kase, Naya, and Ekolu follow behind and throw me a shaka.

"You came!" I take a few steps toward them, but Sarge is

faster and runs to head them off. He leans against Tehani and blocks their way.

"You got choke rubbish, hah?" Ekolu gazes from one side of the beach to the other but stumbles back as Sarge nudges Tehani into him, herding my friends with his big shaggy behind.

"Sarge! Leave them alone." I run up to grab his collar, and he sits down with a *whump*.

"My foot!" Tehani squeaks.

"Oh, come on. We need their help!" We let Sarge smell everyone's hands and I hold his collar and scratch between his ears while everyone slips past us to the beach. He's not fooled, though; his tongue might be out, but his eyes follow their every move. "They're friends, buddy. It's okay."

With all of us working, it goes a lot faster. Naya and Kase handle the ghost nets and heavy stuff while Tehani, Ekolu, and I pick up all the rest. Sarge stays by my side and brings me super helpful stuff like a broken milk crate, a sun-bleached rubber ducky, and a smiley-face emoji disc still attached to some wilted balloons.

I tie off another sack and smile at how the clear patch of sand at the end of the yard is growing. Even better, far down the beach, miniature people with buckets come to the shore by twos and threes, then whole groups as the coconut wireless spreads the word: *You like go save our beach?*

It must've taken a lot of hands to throw all this into the ocean, but today we have even more hands working together to pull it all back out.

"Hey, Tehani! Like one new skirt?" Ekolu sways with a net held in a fist at each hip.

"Naw, it looks good on *you*, brah. But you need a hat." She tosses a broken laundry basket at him and he catches it but holds it out to me.

"Alex is the girl fo' hats. You like try?"

"Naw." I shove a handful of musty plastic bags into the rubbish sack and touch the brim of my bowler hat. "I already got one. That's all yours."

Still grinning at us, Ekolu jogs sideways and shakes his net-skirt on the way to the rubbish bag.

"Watch out!" Faster than I've ever seen the big guy move, Kase lunges to push Ekolu off his path. "Man-o'-war."

Ekolu sprawls on his hands and knees over a weathered milk crate. "Hey! Why fo—?"

A clear, blue bubble the size of a fist with a raised sail shines on the sand, dark blue tentacles sprawled across the path. One more step and Ekolu would have felt the awful stings for hours and probably carried the scars for months.

"Ho, thanks brah." Ekolu scrambles up, and we all check the sand around us for any more blue bubbles hidden amongst the rubbish.

"Never turn your back on the ocean." Tehani murmurs the words we all know by heart, a reminder that the ocean changes from one blink to the next.

As if I could forget.

I shudder as Ekolu and Kase poke the blue bubble with a stick to see how long the tentacles are. Uncle says the ocean makes him feel safe, but that makes no sense when creatures like this can wash up on the shore. Seems more like a sly trap to me.

When we find no more of them on the beach, we scan the water for clear tiny sails bobbing on the surface with their terrible tentacles trailing below, but none seem to be around.

Naya grabs a shovel from the shed, scoops the man-o'-war up, and carefully slides the mess into Kase's rubbish bag.

The danger gone, my friends relax and we laugh, and I keep expecting Malia and Jack to walk in, but they don't. Kase says he saw Jack hauling palm fronds out of someone's yard, but he didn't have time to talk, and nobody's seen Malia. That makes at least two days of hard work for Jack. *And* he turned down chocolate besides. What's up with that?

By the time the boys leave, everything by Tanakas' yard is bagged and in the rubbish bins by the front gate. All that's left is a streak of micro-plastics speckled in a wavy line across the sand.

With kitty-litter scoops, Tehani, Naya, and I shovel bright patches of scattered plastic and shake it so clean sand falls through while bits of plastic stay caught. Sort of like panning for gold, except the prize is a bucket of junk and a clean beach.

Naya might be extra big and strong, but after lifting and dragging all the heavy stuff with Kase, she starts to slow down. So I run into the house and grab some cheese sticks and sweet bread out of the kitchen to refuel. Snacks make everything better, and we talk while Naya and Tehani pull the cheese apart. I sit and nom on the sweet bread, but stuff the cheese stick in my pocket for later.

We fill half a bucket with the tiny colored bits and bottle caps before Tehani and Naya have to go work on their reports, which is probably what I should do since I can't go to Kailua anyway.

There's still lots to do up and down the beach, but I think Uncle will be happy with what we did when he gets back from the doctor. Good thing he went, too. I've seen him grumpy gobs of times, but never with his face all red and his hands shaking so hard like that. He sure didn't look good. Maybe he needed more of that noni tea?

With a last look around, I dump the bucket into the bin, the pieces rattling all the way down inside to the bottom. That done, I jog to the sitting logs and reach for my backpack. "Bye, Sarge. Uncle will be back soon." *I hope.*

But when I try to swing my backpack onto my shoulder, Sarge is faster. He catches the strap in his teeth, stealing it right out of my hand!

"Hey, bring that back!" I grab for it but miss.

Tail wagging, Sarge prances backwards, my bag dangling from his jaws.

I wrinkle my nose as a line of dog drool drips down the strap and across the bag.

Good thing it's waterproof, but still.

"Drop it." I point at the ground. When I packed my stuff this morning, I was imagining a dry bus ride, not a slobbery game of keep-away. "My whole report's in there. I'm not playing."

But Sarge thinks we are, so every time I lunge for the bag, he leaps out of my reach and wags his giant tail like crazy, flinging sand and water drops all over. He's so goofy, it's hard to be mad when he only wants me to stay and play.

"Give it." I sprint to the side, but he whirls and dashes toward the beach. "Hey, wait!"

My half-smile crumbles as Sarge bounds right over the waterline and into the ocean.

Splashing gleefully, he shakes my bag, tossing it like a cat playing with a mouse. He looks toward Hukilau then back at me, his feet dancing with excitement at our new game.

"Don't you dare!" I shake a finger at him, and he shoots off through the shallows, streaking up the beach. My bag flaps up and down with every bound as water streams behind him.

Great. "Stop! Not funny!"

I try to watch for blue bubbles as I jump over nets and dodge empty jugs. For once, I'm glad I got my slippers. A few houses away, he waits for me belly-deep in the water. Waves lap at my bag and he gives it another playful shake. Sure, it's supposed to be waterproof, but I've only ever tested it against *rain*.

"Sarge, stay." I try to sound like Auntie. "Big lug! You give it back, eh?" Hand outstretched, I ease closer while he watches me with a doggy grin. No blue bubbles on the water, and no shadows under the waves, but the ocean has fooled me before.

One step into the water, then two. My heart skips along, beating faster than Sarge's tail.

"Got it!" My fingers graze the bag, but he jerks it with him and plunges along the shore into deeper water. His white and black coat spreads out, floating around him as he paddles away, my bag bobbing in the water beside him.

"No!" I grab the rim of my hat and pull it down hard, thinking fast. "No, no, no! My backpack—my report! Sarge, please!"

I pat my pockets frantically, pull the cheese stick out, and hold it up. "Look Sarge, cheese! Want cheese?"

Please come back, please, please!

Out in the surf, Sarge turns and swims parallel to the beach, his eye on me as I unwrap the cheese and waggle it high for him to see.

"Yummy cheese. Bring it back and I'll trade you!" I try not to think of what might happen if there's a hole in the bag.

My notes could be soaked already. "Come here, Sarge. See the *cheese?*"

Paddling faster, Sarge turns toward shore, but in his hurry, he lets my backpack go.

"No!" I run till water splashes halfway up my calves and point behind him. "My bag! Come on, boy. Go get it!"

Ignoring my pleas, he torpedoes right for me, jowls billowing with every leap in the waves. His feet touch down and he shakes, a hurricane of water drops flying from nose to tail.

I cringe, closing my eyes for a split second—but it's too late, his tongue slurps the cheese from my grasp in one quick gulp. Thick slobber drips from my hand.

My poor backpack bobs on the waves more than thirty feet away, but with every wave that dashes over top, it sits lower in the water. Waterproof or not, it's going down. One more piece of rubbish lost to the sea.

I clench my fist and scan the water. Clear waves in front and whitecaps off to my right should mean I'm close enough to Hukilau to miss the reef, but still, I can't be sure. Was that flash a blue bubble? No, just sunlight reflecting on the water. But what if I'm wrong? What if there are eels and tentacles and things waiting just out of sight?

The bag sinks lower, and I bite my lip. All my notes. All my work—can I let it go? If I lose it now, I'll never have time to do it all again, and Lowen will win the award for sure.

No report means no grand prize. No photo to go on the wall beside Mom's award pictures—and I *need* to be in that picture. People say, 'like mother, like daughter,' but it takes a *lot* to be like Mom. She's extraordinary, but I'm just me, ordinary Alex. Winning is the only way I can be sure I'm good enough. Without that report, any hope for the grand prize sinks right here with my backpack.

I try to pretend it's no big deal, that it doesn't matter to me—except it does.

"Go get it," I order, more to myself than Sarge. This should be easy. It's so close, I can swim it in less than a minute. Maybe even walk out and grab it without swimming at all! I can see the bottom below it—nothing but sand. Am I really going to let my report go because I won't walk across sand with a little water on top? "You can do this."

A couple rollers rush across the surface and dunk my bag.

Once,

twice,

three times.

My bag flips under the water.

Lower and lower.

What does the bag mean to me? The question jumbles in my head and changes into, "What does Mom mean to me?"

Everything.

Sarge hops beside me as I retreat above the waterline and set my slippers on the sand with my hat, phone, and glasses carefully tucked in the middle. If I lose this pair, all I've got left is swim goggles.

Keeping an eye on the shrinking brown blur that is my backpack, I slosh into the water.

It's not so bad—not by the reef. Just a little farther, I chant inside my head. *Like a swimming pool. Not by the reef. No place for things to hide and jump out at me.* Every time I start to freeze up, the blurry, sinking backpack spurs me forward again. *It's not that far. Just a little ways. Not in the reef. Nowhere near the reef.*

Still ten feet away from the bag, waves steal my breath as the ground drops away and water swells up to my armpits. A wave breaks against my face, and then there's nothing beneath my pointed toes.

Another wave hits me and I strike out swimming. Images of eels and urchins and hidden things fill my head, but the backpack is so close. Just in and out. Not far. I imagine clear sand beneath me and cling to that picture as I close the last few feet.

My backpack sinks all the way under, and I reach with my next stroke to grab it, then spin around and kick for shore. Is that a shadow below me? Something big and dark crosses between me and the sand. Maybe I'm imagining it, or maybe not. I kick harder until my fingers curl against the sandy bottom and I rise from the waves and scramble to my feet.

Dripping wet, I stalk to my pile of things on the sand and scowl at Sarge, who trots alongside me with happy splashes like that was the most fun ever.

The backpack zipper sticks the first time I tug, and I hold my breath until it releases, revealing a mostly dry bag. A tiny dribble of water pools in the bottom corner, and I tip the bag to pour it out.

A tight knot in my gut lets go all at once and I sigh. *It's okay. I'm okay. I made it.*

"*Huff, huff!*" Sarge barks as he prances around me splashing and wagging his tail.

"You stink," I growl, but he nudges my hand with his nose until I scratch his ears. "I *don't* forgive you," I tell him, and his tongue rolls out in a delighted doggy smile. As we walk back to the yard, he stays by my side, nudging my hand for more pets.

How can I stay mad at that?

My phone buzzes with a text from Malia: *So sorry! I fell asleep. U need me at Uncle's?*

With my bag secure on my back, I stare at the words. If she had been there for me, I wouldn't have missed the bus. I could have the clue figured out by now . . . except then I wouldn't have been able to help Uncle. I thumb a reply: *No. Thnx. Already done. U okay?*

The three bubbles appear and disappear a few times as she types a response, but when it comes, it only says: *I will be.*

Tomorrow I'll corner her at school and see what that means, but for now, it's enough to just put one foot in front of the other. By the time I make it back to Uncle's beach, my legs wobble and all my energy leaks away—lost somewhere between here and the shallow waves filled with imagined shadows.

I focus on one foot in front of the other, my hand fisted in Sarge's thick fur as he pulls me home. At the edge of Uncle's yard, where the beach creeps into the grass beside the bushes, I slump onto the warm sand and tuck my backpack under my head for a pillow.

Dad always said a few minutes in the sun could recharge his batteries, maybe that's all I need too. A little recharge, only a minute and I'll be fine. I won't even close my eyes.

I yawn, and Sarge lies down between me and the people cleaning farther down the beach.

I never meant to fall asleep, but with my bowler hat shading the side of my face like a tiny dark cave, I drift off. When I open my eyes again, I'm not alone.

Saisei the turtle basks on the sand beside me.

CHAPTER NINETEEN

Face to Face

Saisei raises her head, her pale yellow throat puffing in and out as her mouth moves as though she's chewing on something. But instead of a smooth curve to the hard, flat shell like other green sea turtles have, a dent creases Saisei's back in the middle, forming a slight double bump instead of one continuous line. The old scar circles her middle like a shark tried to bite her in half but spit her back out.

A few golden plovers sweep down from the trees overhead and land on the shoreline somewhere behind Saisei. Their mellow *qui-lee-lee* songs sprinkle bursts of melody over the sound of waves, but Saisei doesn't seem to mind.

She rests on her hard belly and elbows with fins pulled back near her shell as she tilts her head up to soak in the sun. With thick scales covering her whole body, she is regal and ancient, as if my imagination pulled her straight from a Triassic world where dinosaurs ruled before birds ever took to the sky.

In the depths of her half-lidded eyes, a silver-gray ring shines through the dark and focuses on me as we lie together on the sand.

She bends her neck and uses her elbow to wipe sand from her scaly face, but I stay still, hardly daring to blink. Part because I don't want to scare her, and part because she scares me—not terrified like with the eel, but more like a shiver prickling along my skin. At four feet long and maybe three hundred pounds, she's so big—it shakes me a little that something this huge could crawl out of the ocean to sit next to me. And if something this big can come *out* of the sea to find me, what else can live in the deep where no one can see?

The eel found me. The turtle found me. The blue bubble hid right on the shore. What else might come looking?

I wait, tense, ready to bolt for the lanai should she get tired of chewing on air and decide to munch on me instead . . . but she doesn't.

We stay that way for a while, Sarge snoring at my back, Saisei lounging a half-dozen feet in front of me. Under her watchful eye, I'm rooted, caught in this place and time as if captured by a ghost net.

Minutes slip by and my ears fill with the sound of surf, birds, and rustling leaves. But Saisei doesn't move any closer. Bit by bit, my muscles relax until I'm limp again.

Maybe she's not coming closer because she thinks I'm a lumpy pile of rubbish or a weird piece of driftwood.

Maybe, but I don't think so. I'm sure she sees me.

More than that, it feels as though she sees right through me. As if she already knows everything that I could tell her.

Fascination fills the space where fear used to be, and I know I could watch her forever.

Sharing the beach with her like this, if someone told me that Saisei knew all the secrets of the universe, I would believe them. I can't help but wonder, what secrets would she share if she could speak?

"Have you crossed the ocean?" I whisper. "Gone to the bottom of the sea?"

She blinks, her throat still puffing in a quick, steady rhythm.

"Did you ever travel as far away as my mom? Have you seen a typhoon?"

Her chin touches the sand, though she doesn't look away. Uncle says she's shy, but she doesn't seem to mind my words, softer than the plover's tones. Maybe she thinks my voice is only a murmur of surf and sea. Or maybe Saisei saw me cleaning and decided I wasn't so bad.

"When you saw the typhoon—were you scared? Or did your shell protect you?" Did Mom feel protected in the belly of the submarine with its shell of metal instead of bone?

Sarge groans as he stands and walks away while the plovers fly off in a flutter of gray wings, but with the turtle so close, I don't turn my head. With my legs tucked against my belly and my spine curved, I pretend we're the same—even if Saisei probably outweighs me by two hundred pounds.

"Did your mom leave clues so you'd know what to do?" I imagine a little bitty turtle searching the whole ocean for her mom with no video chats or phone calls—just tiny flippers alone in the middle of one enormous ocean. In that moment, I feel like she knows me, and I know her. An old soul and a girl. Both of us alone, but surrounded by life.

Saisei closes her eyes and the connection fades, but even as it drifts away, I reach for one more moment, clinging to the magic between us long enough to murmur a final question. "Were you ever scared you'd never find your way home again?"

Sarge huffs, his collar tags tinkling against each other as he dances near.

"Saisei's found her way home over and over, even when I tried my best to send her away." Uncle's voice is calm, but I still sit up and scoot away from the turtle. What had the protector lady said the rule was? Be far enough away to cover the seal with your thumb? If it's the same rule for turtles, I'm way too close. Normally, I'd *never* get this close to a turtle. But *she* came to *me*. And I was asleep besides. But still, I cringe. I know better.

I glance up at Uncle, but instead of being angry, he seems at peace, with none of the rage and pain from before. He watches Saisei scratch her nose with her elbow again. "She's like family to me now. Some are born to all the family they need, others hānai the family of their heart. Saisei and me, I think we adopted each other."

"Is that what you and Auntie did with Mom?" I ask.

"'Ae, foolish of me to forget how much power a little girl can wield." At first I think he means power as in "powerful cleanup," like what we did for the beach, but in his quiet mood, I'm not sure. Prickly words are easy to use with barbs that sting and jab. It's harder to scoot the spines aside and leave the soft heart unprotected—but I think he's trying.

He takes a few halting breaths like he wants to say more but doesn't know how. Probably he needs more practice.

"Are you okay?" I glance from Uncle to Saisei and back, half-expecting our turtle friend to hurry away when I talk loud, but she raises her head to peer up at Uncle instead. You'd think a turtle's beak would make it hard for them to smile, but I swear she does, and he beams down at her as if she were a beloved child instead of a turtle.

"I'm well enough." He takes a long sip of noni tea. "So you and Saisei, good friends now, hah?"

"Maybe—but I'm not sure. When she moves her throat like that, does it mean she's tired?"

"Oh, no. Her ribs are part of the shell, so her lungs can't expand to breathe unless she moves some part of her body outside the shell. It could be a flipper, but she likes to use her neck for that."

I try to imagine living with my ribs all cemented together in place, but my lungs hate the idea so much I take a big breath just because I can. "I thought maybe she was showing off— like swelling up to seem bigger like a puffer fish." Not that *she* needs to look bigger. She's already huge.

"No. One time, I met a turtle who moved his *tail* to breathe."

"Like a dog?" I glance at Sarge with his tail whipping back and forth and try to imagine Saisei wagging her tail like that. So weird.

"No, it was more regular, with a constant steady beat. He wagged out and in so his hindquarters around the base of his tail could expand out and make room inside his shell. It was just his way of breathing."

Turtles breathing with their butts. Who knew? For the first time in forever, I *want* to know about a creature of the sea. Not knowing the difference between breathing and acting tough or being tired is a rookie mistake. It's like Uncle said, knowing about sea creatures is kind of like knowing a secret code, and the more I know, the less I'm afraid. My knowing stuff won't let Saisei actually talk to me like a person can, but if I understood her special codes, maybe she could talk back in different ways. I clear my throat. "What else can you tell me?"

"About green sea turtles?"

"Yeah, like why do we call them green? They're brown. There's nothing green on them at all. Yellow maybe, and kinda white in parts, but the rest is brown and black."

He sniffs and takes a drink. "The green is there, but you can't see it. There's a green layer of fat under the shell between the bones and the organs."

"Eew, that's gross. What else don't I know?"

"Plenty," he chuckles. "They have favorite colors—red, orange, and yellow, I believe. And their hearing isn't very good unless it's low frequencies that humans can't really hear. But their sense of smell is keen. They use it to find food, mates, and predators."

"Is that how they know where to go? Can they smell their way home?" Fat lot of good that would do Mom. She can count a whole load of things faster than Sarge can swish his tail once, but she's not gonna sniff her way home.

"We don't think smell has anything to do with how they navigate the ocean. They use it to avoid danger and find food for short-term detours, but that's all."

"So, how do they find their way back home then?" Maybe whatever it is could help Mom find her way home too.

Uncle sweeps a cupped hand around an imaginary circle. "They follow magnetic signatures from the earth. So, no matter how far they roam, the earth guides them home. Sort of like a compass they can't lose, but it tells them more than just which way's north."

My lips twist. Pretty sure none of that turtle stuff can help Mom. She's smarter than almost anybody, but she'd still need a compass and a good boat or sub to get home.

Auntie steps up beside Uncle, reaches for my hand, and pulls me up. "Cheehoo, such good job, Alex. Pau cleaning already? You're this big—" She snaps her fingers. "How did you do so much?"

I brush sand from my side and pick up my bowler hat. "My friends helped, and so did Sarge . . . kind of."

"Ah, yes. Always helpful, that one." Uncle nods gravely, but Auntie laughs.

"Helpful as a wool blanket in summer, and just as in the way."

Uncle walks over and peers under the bushes as if looking for any rubbish we might have left. "You did well. No digging here?"

"No, why?" The micro-plastics didn't reach up that far. We scooped farther down, midway between water and grass.

"What, you want all my secret treasures at once? Saisei's not enough for one day?"

The twinkle in his eye says he's kidding, but I answer anyway. "Saisei is awesome."

"She is a treasure—and some treasures are best protected and left alone."

Before I can ask what he means, laughter from a cleanup crew echoes down the beach, and Saisei turns to push herself toward the water with halting flops. Her flippers leave straight, paired marks in the sand as she drags her shell along, push by push, her tail carving a last line behind her.

"What happened to her shell?" I'm not sure if the scar is exactly in the middle or not, even though I stared at her for long enough. Were there more scales on one side than the other? I should know—Mom would know, but I never thought to count.

Should I have counted?

"Twenty-seven years ago, I saw a flipper waving out there like this"—Uncle wiggles two fingers in a quick up-down wave—"from a floating pile of wood and netting. I paddled out and found her all tangled up with net around her neck and fins. I thought I'd cut her loose and let her go like usual, but when I pulled her up onto my kayak, she had this plastic ring cemented into her shell all the way around."

"A diving ring?" I've played with them in pools before, but never in the ocean.

"No, it was a Frisbee ring, the kind people throw for dogs to catch. She must've swam through it and got stuck. By the time I found her, she'd carried it for so long, her shell had started growing around it."

Uncle watches Saisei as if seeing her as she was back then: small, caught, and helpless, but still struggling to live. "A turtle's shell isn't like stone. It's alive and grows with them with blood flow and nerves from the bones of a turtle's ribs and spine, which fuse to make up their shells. I'm sure she felt pain when it dug in, but she survived—at least until she got tangled in the net."

Auntie slides her arm around Uncle's waist and leans her head on his shoulder. "It was all he could talk about. The turtle this, turtle that—we named her Saisei because she's reborn."

"What color was it?" I ask.

He glances at Auntie. "I think the net was green."

"No, I mean the Frisbee ring."

"Ah, it was sun-bleached, but it used to be red—remember I said they like red? We had to surgically remove the embedded plastic and treat a stubborn infection where the Frisbee cut deep. Healing was a slow process, but eventually we released her right here."

"And here she's stayed." Auntie smiles softly. "She has good taste."

Waves wash over Saisei's misshapen shell as she pushes forward and slips into the sea, her awkward, dragging gait giving way to grace as the ocean welcomes her home and gives her wings. A regular turtle living a regular life. If it weren't for the scars, you'd never know anything was ever wrong.

Uncle drains the last of his cup and sighs, "She's lucky to be alive. I've seen studies of a few others who've survived more shell damage than her, but haven't seen them in person. There's a red-eared slider who was stuck in a six-pack wrapper that shaped her shell like a peanut—so that's what they named her. And I believe there's a snapping turtle they called Mae West because she crawled through a tiny milk jug ring when she was a baby and got stuck halfway through. Think of how small that is—a ring of a milk jug. Cinched tight around her waist, it gave her an extreme hourglass figure as she grew everywhere except in that one spot still bound by that little ring. It's a miracle it didn't sever her spine."

I push my cat-eye glasses up and squint at the water, trying to catch one last glimpse of Saisei, but she's already gone to wherever turtles go under the waves.

Uncle gives Auntie's shoulders a squeeze and steps away from the shore. "You want to stay for dinner? When does your dad get home?"

"Um . . ." Did Dad have time for dinner on the schedule? I can't remember. "I don't know."

"Ask him when's the best time, and let us know." Uncle nods and walks toward the house. "It's been too long since we've had company."

I blink and watch him go. "Did Uncle just invite us for dinner?

Auntie pats my back and murmurs, "Fo' real, seems pigs *can* fly."

CHAPTER TWENTY

No Mistake

Dad doesn't answer his phone, so Auntie takes me to pick up grindz at Laie Chop Suey before bringing me home. She's putting on a strong face, but after spending all day at the doctor's with Uncle, I think she's even more tired than I am. I don't want to pry, but she says something about Uncle's tremors messing with his blood pressure, and when he didn't take his medicine and got all upset, it made everything worse.

"Ask your dad about dinner, yeah?" Auntie echoes Uncle's words as I step out of the car.

"Okay!" I kick off my slippers at the screen door, set the Chop Suey bags on the table, and check the wall calendar.

Dad's schedule has him on a dive today, tomorrow, the next day . . .

I scowl and run a finger along the week. Every single day? Even if Uncle invites us again, it'll have to be only me, because Dad's too busy to do anything at all. And what's with the extra red lines under my parts of the schedule? The report is under-lined twice, and Mom's challenge is underlined three times. A few stars even sprinkle the lines on the weekend—whatever that means. He colored it without me. Not cool.

I shouldn't feel disappointed. I mean, I know he's worried about money and Mom. That's why he added lots of jobs this week. He's doing his best, but it'd be nice to go do something together because we want to, not because he scheduled it ahead of time.

The pot stickers cool off long before Dad gets home, but he swirls a pot sticker in shoyu sauce with chopsticks and pops it into his mouth anyway. "Aren't you glad you were there to help and not off in Kailua on a goose chase?"

Goose chase? I set my chopsticks across my plate and fold my arms. *He's* the one who keeps underlining my schedule like I'm running out of time. How am I supposed to solve anything if I don't go find the next clue?

"I'm glad I could help Uncle and everything, but if I'd gone to Kailua, I coulda been back already with the new clue. I woulda gone if Malia hadn't missed the bus. I wanted to go—almost went anyway, but I promised not to go alone, so I didn't. And now I don't have the next clue." I don't say the *it's-your-fault* part of why I don't have the clue, but the way he raises his eyebrows as he chews, I'm pretty sure he gets it any-way. I nod to myself. *See, Dad? Look at me being trustworthy all over the place.*

He swallows and clears his throat. "Malia missed the bus? I thought the plan was for Auntie, Uncle, or someone to take you."

"Malia is someone." Okay, maybe it only counts as *mostly*

trustworthy. I feel him watching me, trying to decide if he's gonna be mad or disappointed or not. I carefully study my chopsticks as the silence drags on.

Finally, he exhales. "Why'd you want to go to Mānoa Chocolate Factory in the first place? I'm sure Mom wouldn't send you out of town without telling me first. What's the clue you're looking for?"

My head jerks up. "Wait, you talked to Mom? When? Why didn't you tell me?"

"No. No word yet, but it's only been a few days. I'm sure she'll call as soon as she can."

If Mom hasn't called, how would Dad know if she wanted to send me anywhere? I shut my mouth as a tide of angry words surges through my head and breaks against my closed lips.

He *should* know where Mom is. In fact, he should call her right now and sort this out—ask *her* if I should go to Kailua. It's her challenge and not his.

I glare at my plate while my insides swirl from one current to the next. Waves of irritation, fury, logic, and fear crash and roll till I don't know how I'm supposed to feel.

"You know I'd tell you, right? I wouldn't keep that secret." Dad's words are an anchor as I fight the tides inside.

I shrug like it's no big deal, but that's not how I feel. I *know* it's not his fault that Mom hasn't called. Logically, I do. But I'm mad anyway. Mad at him, or Mom, or me. I try to scrape the anger off, but it clings like barnacles, fouling me and weighing me down.

"What made you think you needed to go there? Show me the clue."

When I pass the golden ticket to Dad, he turns it over and holds it up to the light. His thumb slides across the smudge. "This is why you want to go to Kailua? Because of this ticket?"

"Yeah, it says chocolate factory. You know how Mom loves that place with the good cacao fruit and stuff." Easiest clue yet—except for the whole seal-giving-me-a-heart-attack part.

"I think this ticket go to a different sort of factory." He traces the triple bump line with his finger. "One with snozberries and rainbow drops."

"It says chocolate factory right there. And there's no such thing as snot berries." Real chocolate is made from cacao fruit. Doesn't he remember the tour at all?

"There is, but it's snozberries, not snot berries. And part of the writing is smeared away, so this is trickier than it was meant to be." He walks to the bookcase and runs a finger along the line of books by Mom's old textbooks before sliding a worn paperback from the shelf and handing it to me. "Here's your factory."

A kid smiles on the cover, a golden ticket in his hands: *Charlie and the Chocolate Factory.*

The book can't be that old—I mean, there's a pretty good picture on the front, but it's in really bad shape. Our librarian would have a fit if she saw this book; the dog-eared pages, stains on the cover, corners worn round instead of square from being carried around in a bag so much. "What happened to it?" Maybe it fell out of a car, or got thrown in with the laundry?

"The book?" He checks the cover. "Oh, nothing's wrong. This was your Mom's favorite book when she was little. A kid's favorite book is kind of like a velveteen rabbit. They make friends with the characters and carry the book everywhere. The more tangible the tale, the more tattered the pages." He passes it back to me. "No, nothing's wrong. Except maybe she loved the story until it became real."

Real or ragged? Maybe it means the same thing for Mom's story. I turn the pages. On the inside cover, a long list of moves lines the page. I read down the list, but they seem like commands from an old Battleship game: A3 to J6, B9 to H8 . . .

I flip through the pages in order, but the broken spine flops open to a fat white envelope jutting out of the middle.

Mom's handwriting scrawls in neat, clear lettering across the top. "*Almost there.*"

My mouth forms an O, and I feel Dad hovering over my shoulder as I pluck the card from its hiding spot. I *was* wrong. And *Dad* was right. Mom didn't send me to Kailua.

She sent me home.

If Malia had gone on the bus with me, how long would we have crawled around the Mānoa Chocolate Factory looking for clues that weren't there? Probably till they kicked me out for acting all weird. Maybe I owe Malia a thank you for missing the bus—even if it was an accident.

In the middle of the envelope, something bulky pushes against the sides with raised lines and ridges—probably another one of Mom's paper creations. They used to fold them just for each other, but after I was born, most of the new ones ended up hanging from my ceiling because I like them too.

But when I open the flap and pull the folded paper from inside, it's not some intricate dragon or bird—it's a simple paper airplane. It's not even as detailed as the origami jet plane hanging with my flock of origami over my bed. A simple paper airplane. "Um, am I supposed to throw it—fly it somewhere?"

Dad's trying his hardest not to smile, but his dimples give him away.

"You know what this means, don't you?" I accuse. "You know the answer to this whole thing."

He checks the calendar. "It's too early for me to say. If you haven't figured it out by the end of the week, I'll tell you what I know."

Dad basically figured out the last clue for me, so no way am I gonna let him do this one too. "I can do it."

"I never doubted that you could," Dad calls as I carry the envelope, airplane, and paperback to my room.

With my notes all taped up on the walls to dry, my desk sits bare except for my computer, which is pushed to the side—it's easier to pretend it's not there right now. A few pages of notes curl at the corners from water damage, but most made it through Sarge's swim with only a few drops. That's pure luck, though. If I'd been another minute or two later, the small leak would have filled the whole backpack and ruined everything in it. I sit in my roll chair, swivel my knees under the desk, and lay out each new item.

Other than Mom's note saying "*Almost done,*" the envelope seems pretty normal. But with a sneaky brain like hers, anything could be part of the puzzle. I set it aside in case it hides another invisible message made of lemon juice or something.

The airplane holds more promise, with parts of numbers and lines poking out from seams like cockroach antennae got caught in the creases and smashed inside when Mom made the plane. Slowly, I peel the layers apart and lay it flat.

Spread across the paper, a bunch of numbers line the edges of a circle that sprawls across the page. A ring of numbers? No, not just a ring—it's a clock. Where the numbers of every hour should be to mark the time, three small groups of numbers cluster around each mark. I try substituting them for letters, or dashes or dots, and all sorts of things, but none of it works, and the clock seems to laugh at me.

After another hour, it's pushing bedtime, and I'm starting to really hate that clock. I give up on the time thing, turn the book over, and scowl at the smiling kid on the cover. I've already searched the pages for any notes or codes written in the seams anywhere, but even though the outside is worn enough to be used for a teddy bear, the inside seems pretty clean except for the inside cover.

I bend the book a little and run my thumb across the edge of the pages, letting them slip by in a blur in case some sneaky stop-motion animation pops out at me. Backwards and forwards, I watch the page numbers race past, growing bigger and smaller, but there's nothing else there. No missing pages. No highlighted words . . . Maybe I'm supposed to actually play a Battleship game so the boats or misses can make a pattern?

"Ugh," I grumble in a voice that would do Uncle proud. "What's the point of hiding this in a book if it doesn't make any—*oh!*" The page numbers sync with the clock inside my head. I must still be tired or I'd have seen it right away. It's not a code, it's a cipher. The numbers have to mean page numbers, how many lines to count down, and how many words to go across—like a map to find the word Mom wanted me to find inside the book. Using the first group of numbers I flip to the page number, count down, and slide over till my finger rests on a word: *Pony.*

I circle it with a pencil, and write the word down on scrap paper.

Hmm. One by one, I count off page numbers, lines, and words then circle whatever I find. I add squirrel, together, family, goose, parent, child, sheep, father, and mother, to the list.

A family of animals? Other than Sarge and the geckos, my family doesn't have pets. My grandparents on the mainland have cows and stuff on their farm, but not sheep. It's got to be something else.

After a while, Dad peeks in. "You ready for bed?"

"Almost." I brush my teeth and flop onto the mattress. Why have the animals on a clock instead of a line? What kind of sense is that to have a clock with no hands? Everyone knows they move clockwise, so maybe the hands aren't important? I yawn. "But still, why no hands to go round the clock?"

An echo stirs in my head. "Which way does the clock go round?"

I sit up and stare at my notes on the walls. Mavis Batey's boss said something about looking at things from a different point of view, 'cause a clock goes clockwise for everyone *except* the clock. A view from behind the hands would make them move backwards. Counterclockwise.

I fall asleep still puzzling it out and dream of animals trotting around a clock with little battleships shouting, "*A3 to J6!*" But it's not till morning sunlight hits my origami flock that any of it makes sense.

Every string that holds an origami creation is hanging perfectly spaced from every other—all of them together forming a square grid. And at the corners, moving counterclockwise, are a pony, a squirrel, a goose, and a sheep.

My flock must represent the grid for the numbers from the inside cover of Mom's book—like how a chessboard marks all the squares with both a letter and a number. I read the clue again. A3 to J6. A dragon hovers in the A3 square, but I can't move her to the J6 spot because that's where the origami bat hangs.

I flop onto the bedcover again. What I really need is a blank grid I can move all the origami figures to. A flat surface with empty squares. A regular chessboard would be way too small, because my paper flock can't fit onto such a tight space. I need something bigger with huge squares, like . . . my eyes fall on the chessboard marked on my wall.

"Sneaky Mom." A slow grin creeps across my face as I count the squares of the chessboard painted on my wall. How did I never notice there were too many squares? "No time to finish, she says, *hah?* We'll finish it later, together, *yeah?*" Hiding in plain sight, Mom's unfinished wall chessboard is a perfect place to transfer them. Seems it was no accident that she "ran out" of time.

I pull the dragon down and tape its string to the middle of the square, but it feels incomplete. Maybe there's clues on the inside? I unfold it.

There's no new message, but the colorful paper that used to be my best dragon is the exact same size as Mom's chess square. Like *exact* size. No way was it an accident. I tape it to the wall in the J6 spot on the grid.

Each instruction calls for me to pull another origami down from my flock, and every one of those unfolds into a pale water-colored square. None of them make a picture on their own, and none have words or anything, but as I tape them in their assigned squares on the wall, an image takes shape. I rotate a few that seem wrong until their lines and colors match the ones beside them like a giant puzzle with all square pieces.

Finally, I step back just to say, *wow!* Mom's chessboard is transformed into a humongous watercolor painting that takes up most of my wall. The colors and blurs form a picture of a V-shaped waterfall spilling over a rocky cliff into a round pool filled with deep blue water and rainbows.

"A waterfall?" I tilt my head, trying to match it to any of the waterfalls I know. I've been up the trail to Laie Falls loads of times with Castle Crew, but it's not as big as this. Waimea Falls, maybe? That's not right either.

I glance at the clock. If I don't leave in five minutes, I'll be late for school—*ho*, the coconut wireless would be all over that. Probably Dad would know I was playing hooky the minute I stepped out the door. But still, how can I leave now with a paper miracle unfolding right in front of me?

My origami flock has been on my ceiling since I was little, and they're the same origami creatures . . . aren't they? They must've been swapped, but it still feels like magic.

For the millionth time this week, I wish I could ask Mom how she did it, or talk to her, or *anything*. I pause. More than asking how she's done all this, I want to ask her if she's okay. Dad said they'd call as soon as anyone had news. That subs can "go dark" for a long time since they have everything they need to hide and cruise underwater.

Her envelope said, "Almost there." And that was *before* I found the waterfall painting, so I've got to be really, really close.

But which waterfall is it? Koloa, or Wailele Falls maybe? Last time, I jumped at the wrong answer for the chocolate factory and was totally wrong. I have to be sure this time.

The rainbow draws my eye again and again. I'm sure I've seen it before, but I can't— My eyes widen. *The sappy picture!*

My feet slap against the tile as I run to the framed pictures by the kitchen.

Behind my smooching newlywed parents, a rainbow arcs across the splash pool at the base of Rainbow Falls. It even has that V shape. It's got to be the one!

I pull the picture off the wall and check the back, but there's nothing written or stuffed in the frame. Just to be sure, I pull the picture all the way out of the frame and check between the picture and the backing, but there's nothing there either. It's the only picture we have of Rainbow Falls, and there are no clues on it anywhere.

What am I supposed to do? Swim there to look for clues? Rainbow Falls isn't even on Oahu. It's on the Big Island in Hilo—that's like two hundred miles away. Dad didn't even like the idea of my almost-Kailua trip. And no way would Dad let us sail there in his boat. First, I don't think he's ever taken his boat out that far, and second, I'd rather get run over by wild pigs than sail through that much water. No way.

My phone chirps and I groan. I'm officially late.

But when I tell myself it's time to go out the door, I end up back in my room in front of the Rainbow Falls watercolor.

I'm sure I have the right falls. It's just like the picture on the wall—except without the mushy stuff. To look there for clues, I'd need to take a plane—something way sturdier than Mom's paper plane from the envelope. That's for sure.

Well . . . I don't know. And I'm out of time. Better late than never to school, I guess.

I walk under what's left of my origami flock to get my backpack by the desk. My ceiling seems so odd without them all hanging up. Folded creations still dangle from the edges, but the rest are mostly gone, leaving an empty star-shaped hole in my ceiling. Except, the middle isn't empty.

My steps slow as I eye the last origami left inside the star shape: a jet hanging in the exact center of the flock.

I pull the string down—but the jet feels heavier than it should.

Layer by layer, I unfold the paper, until it lays open on my desk—with an airplane ticket to Hilo in the middle.

It *is* Rainbow Falls, and I've got an airplane ticket with my name on it to prove it!

Dad laughs when I call him all breathless on the phone. "I have a ticket! Mom's clues lead to Rainbow Falls, in Hilo!"

"I knew you could do it."

"I can't believe Mom hid the next clue on the Big Island! How'd she do it? Did she stop there before she left?"

"No, hon. There are no more clues. You solved the challenge, and a trip to the Big Island is the prize. That's why I've been working extra these last few weeks. I thought it would be fun if Auntie and Uncle came with us."

"I solved it?"

"Yep."

I yell into the phone. "Are you serious? I solved Mom's challenge?"

"That's right. You did. Better pack your bags; we leave in three days."

CHAPTER TWENTY-ONE

Never Turn Your Back on the Ocean

The Castle Crew freaks out when I tell them we solved the challenge. Even Malia's excited—after I shake her awake at her desk. "Finished? That's awesome." She stretches and winks. "Done well, you have."

Kase makes a big deal out of putting his shades on. "And thus, the spymaster apprentice becomes a master. Oh yeah!"

"We knew you could do it." Jack taps his pen against his math book.

"What say we go Sam's store for grindz?" Ekolu ribs Jack with his elbow. "Celebrate!"

"No can; gotta work—and missing assignments to make up."

I'm not sure what to think of this new Jack who suddenly cares about his homework, won't go to Sam's store, and doesn't have snacks in his pockets. I figure, either he's trying to be healthy all at once, or there's trouble he's not telling us. Either way, if Castle Crew can help me figure out a challenge as hard as Mom's, we should be able to figure out what's up with Jack no problem.

The next three days fly by as I pack and dive into my history report so hard, it's mostly done by Friday. With all my notes about Mavis Batey and Bletchley Park, I'm sure to be one of the best—except I want to be *the* best.

If one example of coded messages in action is cool, three examples should knock those judges right off their boards.

I already have a cardboard replica of the top of an Enigma machine. No way can I make all the inside gears, but the top part looks awesome. I painted it and everything.

My second display was gonna be a cryptex, which is a tube thing that destroys the message inside if the user doesn't open it with the right code. But it turns out, they don't exist in history! Super rude. I thought Da Vinci invented them ages ago, but nope; an author made them up.

So instead, I made a Caesar cipher with two cardboard circles stacked on top of each other like a little sand dollar sitting on top of a big one, both with the alphabet written all the way around the outside. Rotate one and the letters all shift to change the code. Probably I'll make up a few messages so they can try to figure them out.

I'm still deciding on the third one, but other than that, my report is basically done—except I have to copy it off my papers and type it up. And that will have to wait till I get back from the Big Island, since Dad says the schedule is too full to work on it there. Either way, when I'm finished with the displays, it's gonna be epic!

Take that, Lowen!

Dad calls Mom's work every day for news, but he doesn't have Mom's clearance or connections, so when he calls, the answer is always the same. "The sub has gone silent. We have no further information at this time. We will contact you as soon as we have anything to tell you."

He says she's safe though, because the news would have said something if a sub had sunk, and there's been no rumors like that at all, so we just need to wait, and I shouldn't worry.

Now if only I could make myself *believe* that. I do trust Dad, and if he says things will be okay, I'll do my best to believe him. But after the super typhoon and all the footage that night, I don't think I'll really believe she's safe until I see her with my own eyes and hug her for all I'm worth. So that's where I'm at: I *mostly* believe Mom will be home soon-ish.

Uncle and Auntie will fly out of Honolulu tomorrow to meet us in Hilo, but Dad has me out the door way early—which is right on time, according to him. On the way to our gate, Dad leads me through the cultural gardens in the middle of the airport before our flight. He put it on the agenda because Mom loves the living island garden there, and she was supposed to be with us. My favorite part is the koi ponds, but Dad gets fidgety if I linger too long in one spot. I'm not sure if that's because I'm taking too long or because Mom's missing one of her favorite spots.

My stomach makes a dash for the ground when we take off, and Dad lets me hold his hand till the bumps and drops are over. The best part is when white haze covers the cabin windows all at once and rushes past in misty threads as we rise above the clouds and break into the sun. From so far up, it's like I can see the whole ocean—or at least I could, if I had a telescope. Long before an hour is up, the tilt of the plane changes and my ears pop as our pilot eases us in for touchdown in Hilo.

When Dad pulls the rental car into our Airbnb in Hawaiian Paradise Park, Song of India trees line the driveway, with thin yellow and green leaves clustered like fireworks over our heads. Deep blue, purple, and pink orchids hover between the boughs as if leaning out to say hello from their hidden balconies.

"Wow." They must've had a real tall ladder to tie the orchid roots to the branches so high up.

Dad pops open the trunk. "What say you explore the yard and report back?"

"Okay."

Spiky shrubs, each with a baby pineapple growing in the center, dot the yard and lead the way around back. In the nearest corner, I spy a golf ball–sized snail creeping over the grass beneath a grove of guava trees.

Near the other side of the yard, I peek under the cover of the catchment, which looks sort of like a round aluminum kiddy pool, but is really for collecting rainwater. And behind that, an isle of coconut trees stands tall, surrounded by thick foliage with wide, glossy leaves. But I'm pretty sure Dad's favorite plant will be the banana tree with its long, dark purple stem that drips like a strange elephant trunk tipped with a violet flower.

Someone worked really hard to make the yard beautiful with fruits and flowers all over, but my favorite plant is a weed. Sure, sleepy grass has thorny seedpods and stems that are murder on bare feet, but when I blow on their thin branches, the leaves fold up super quick, like a hundred tiny doors slamming shut to hide from giant-sized me. Probably I shouldn't play with it, but it's just so cool.

I help Dad put the rest of our stuff away while telling him about the backyard—and I'm right about the banana tree. He loves it.

Once groceries are put away, Dad pulls a poster-sized photocopy of a new, more detailed schedule from his bag and spreads it over the table. "Okay, we've got a lot to see in a few days."

"Wait. You brought the schedule?" My lip curls almost as much as Elvis's, and I wipe my mouth to hide the grimace.

"There's so many places your mom likes to visit here, and I'm not sure which ones she wanted you to see, so we're going to hit as many of them as we can and hope we got it right. You're gonna love it." Dad pats my shoulder. "Tomorrow we'll hit the Hilo Farmer's Market early, pick the Tanakas up from the airport, and head to Rainbow Falls."

Dad lists destination after destination, but there's so many, they feel more like assignments to check off than adventures.

". . . Picnic lunch at Laupahoehoe park, and a quick trip over to 'Akaka Falls before we head back down to the Rainforest Zoo. The next day we'll. . . ."

"*Co-qui!*" I turn my face to the window screen as the first coqui frog begins his song. "*Co-qui! Co-qui!*"

"But you'll have to wait and see where the last destination is. I'm positive Mom would want us to save it for last just in case she can make the grand finale for your special trip."

My head snaps up. "Wait, Mom's meeting us there?"

Dad leans back in his chair, lifts both hands, and lets them fall in his lap. "That was the plan. She was supposed to meet us here when we first arrived, or at least before the last stop of the trip, but I still haven't had any word that she's off the sub."

So weird, having "Mom's special trip" without Mom here at all. I sit up, "Are you sure they'd tell us?"

"Tell us what?"

My fingers tap thumb to finger in sequence as I try to sort the words inside my head. "So, hypothetically, let's say a submarine was destroyed or captured—would they really tell us?"

He pulls me in for a squeeze. "No one is conspiring to keep her away. I already told you she'll come home to us safe and sound. All you need to worry about right now is enjoying the adventure she set up for you. She loves you. Never doubt it."

"I know."

"So, what do you think of the schedule?"

"Sounds . . . busy."

"It's a matter of priorities. It's like my dad always said, the early bird catches the worm—used to drive me nuts."

I wrinkle my nose. "But wouldn't you rather have bacon?"

"We—what?"

"Eggs would be good too, or toast, or strawberry pancakes—really, *anything's* better than worms."

"Haha, funny girl." His voice is flat, which only tickles me more. "Now get some sleep. We have a big day tomorrow."

"Okay." I kiss his cheek and run get ready for bed, but when I turn the lights out, I leave the window wide open and let the song of the coquis spill into the room.

I try to hear the deep, hollow pulse of the Hawaiian tree cricket, or the higher, tinny chirp of the Uhini iki cricket that should be there, but the night is filled with frogs. "*Co-qui!*

Co-qui!" Unrelenting, their high-pitched call eclipses all other night sounds until the forest rings with their singular plea. An orchestra overwhelmed and silenced by one piercing instrument. So small, and yet such a powerful voice. Demanding, pleading, calling, needing.

As the nightly rain patters on the catchment cover, I drift off wondering who they're looking for, and whether they'll finally be satisfied when they've found them.

In my dreams, I search the shore for something I need, but I can't remember what it is, so I pick up everything I find. Rocks, shells, driftwood, and plastic fill my pockets and pile on my back like a hermit crab. Each precious new find presses my steps deeper into the sand as I stagger under the weight of my treasure. But it's never enough. So I try harder, search longer, as my shell grows big enough to blot out the sky.

When Dad shakes me awake and chases my dreams away, they flee to the edges of memory and hover in that shadowy space between reality and imagination.

Only a thread of the idea remains, enough to remember desperately searching for something, but not enough to remember why.

It haunts me a little as Dad and I walk between booths of every kind at the farmer's market, like I should pay extra good attention in case I run across . . . something. Under the wide market tents, booths overflow with fruits, baked goods, colors, and creations of all sorts. At one end, I spot Mom's favorite local artist with his images of reef and waves painted with light, and beside him, strong guys chop coconuts open with machetes. Dad lets me pick out sweet apple bananas, rambutan (*yum!*), local papaya, mochi, lumpia, buns, lilikoi jam, and a few small gifts besides. We carry our bags of treasures to the car.

When we pick Auntie and Uncle up at the airport, I bounce right up to give them the treasures I picked for them at market: a turtle necklace for Uncle and a flower hair clip for Auntie.

"It's beautiful." Auntie hugs me and climbs in the back seat beside Uncle, who gently turns the turtle over in his hands and puts it on. "Thank you."

"You're welcome." I pretend it's no big deal, but inside, I'm super glad they like what I found. Maybe I needed to prove to myself that I *could* find things if I wanted to.

"How goes the cleanup?" Dad signals and pulls onto the road.

"They finished yesterday." Uncle leans forward in his seat. "One group said their goal was to reach the clean swath by my beach, so they kept going."

"That's my girl." Dad pats my knee. "Hear that?"

"I didn't do it alone; my friends probably did more than me." I shrug, but a pesky smile catches my lips anyway.

My phone lights up with a text from Malia:

Jack's dad lost his job.

What! When?

Couple weeks. Kase says rent is overdue. Might have 2 move.

Castle Crew without Jack? I chew on that thought, but it's sour. He belongs with us. Well—us and Sam's store. We can share.

You sure? What did Jack say?

Nothing. Didn't want us to know.

We text a few more times, but Jack should know better than to keep secrets from us. We're stronger together. And as soon as I get back, I'll tell him so.

A few tour busses already dot the Rainbow Falls parking lot when Dad pulls in, but we still find a good spot beside the stone wall to watch the falls. Even though the falls are more root-beer color than blue today, a wide rainbow glows so bright in the mist it seems almost solid.

"Do you know why Mom used this waterfall for the painting? What makes this one special?" I ask.

Dad looks to Auntie, then Uncle. "Correct me if I'm wrong, but wasn't this one of the first places you traveled after you took Elizabeth in?"

"She was still new to us then, but she was ours just the same," Auntie says. "Elizabeth is our hānai child—the child of our heart if not from our blood."

Uncle slides an arm around Auntie. "She was young, so I don't know what she remembers of here, but yes, we brought her here for the first of many family trips."

"You should have seen her," Auntie laughs. "Small kine thing with frizzy hair, all knees and elbows. Skinny as a lost kitten, but so inquisitive. Always wanted to know everything. She stole our hearts—how could we not open our home?"

Dad crooks a thumb at the falls. "She said it was her rainbow after the storm."

"So . . ." I peer over the stone wall to the colors sparkling in the mist. "This is where you became a family."

"We were already ohana. Maybe this is where she knew it was real," Uncle says.

"It's a place of legend and rainbows," Auntie agrees. "Maybe that's how she remembers it."

"Actually—" Dad clears his throat, his eyes bright as he slides into teacher mode, "the best way to see a vibrant rainbow is to come in the morning when the sun is still low in the sky behind you."

"Mom told me she saw a rainbow from her airplane once, but it was shaped like a giant full circle below the plane."

"That's true," Dad says. "You'd have to be really high to see the full ring a rainbow makes around you, but you're always in the center of it. Down here, the earth gets in the way, so we usually only see a part of the curve."

"I thought you were a math teacher." Uncle folds his arms, but we all know he's only pretending to be grumpy. He's got that twinkle.

"Elizabeth loves rainbows, and I love her. So, I learned how to get her the best I could. A little planning makes a big difference."

They keep talking, but an old man totters by with a basket full of luahala leaves and settles onto the grass. Within minutes, his calloused fingers twist and weave the first handful into a bird, and he sets it on the ground beside him. He makes a turtle next, then a dish, and then a hat.

"Alex, time's up." Dad nudges my elbow. "Ready to go?"

"Okay," I say, but I keep watching as the man crafts an angelfish. "He's so good."

"Hey, we'll take that one, hah?" Uncle buys one and passes it to me. "An angelfish for our angel of the beach."

"Thanks." I turn it over in my hands.

Our day goes on like that, from place to place with barely

enough time to walk in and see what Mom liked about the area, then out and gone to the next. In and out with no time to linger.

We wind down and down and down the steep, narrow road past tsunami warning signs to the sheltered oasis of green below: Laupahoehoe Point, where slow, unbroken swirls of pahoehoe lava once flowed into the sea.

At the shore, waves smash against concrete formations and rocket into the air with sprays that would do Laie Point proud. Uncle says the Army Corps of Engineers made the cement as a special breakwater to stop the ocean from eroding the land.

Dad says we've got twenty-five minutes, so I climb up the hill on a staircase of roots and try to guess which waves will make the biggest splash.

Uncle walks the other way to a little hill, where Auntie stands in front of a white stone marker.

I hop back down the tree stairway and catch up to Uncle as he curls Auntie's hand in his.

"What is it?" My steps slow at the many leis of shells, leaves, and flowers carefully arranged at the base of the stone, which reads:

IN MEMORY OF
THOSE WHO LOST THEIR LIVES IN THE TIDAL WAVE
APRIL 1, 1946

Two columns of names with ages fill the rest of the stone—most of them kids.

"There was a school here before the tsunami." Auntie takes a string of tiny brown seeds and spreads it beside the others. "Your mom was always quiet here. Peaceful and still, without the usual restless energy to trouble her. No counting. No finger tapping. And she always left a lei to honor them."

I don't have a lei to give, but I do have something that might work. I run to the car and hurry back with my new angelfish made of lauhala leaves and place it beside Auntie's lei as a splash of green beside nut-brown beads and pale yellow shells.

When we load into the car, the quiet fills all of us until we pass the tsunami signs and turn onto the road again. We stop to eat the buns with sweet pork from the market, but I barely have time to swallow my food before Dad bundles us back in the car for a short hike by ʻAkaka Falls.

Dad charges up the path. "This way!"

But I keep pace by Uncle, who practices new grumbling techniques all the way up the steep incline. "*Hmph*, since when did this trail go straight up?"

"Looks like same path to me." Auntie touches a flower beside the path. "Same trees, same mountain, same waterfall . . ."

"Yeah, yeah. Same birds, leaves. Rocks," he mumbles. "Always with the hiking."

"I think Dad is going for adventure." I jog backwards up the path. "Exploring the wild blue yonder and stuff."

"No wild blue up here." Uncle nods toward the ocean. "Out there is the blue. You want exploring? Give me a kayak at sea and we'll get somewhere."

"I think maybe you're right," Auntie says.

"Of course I am," Uncle nods. "Wait—right about what?"

"One change from before." Auntie's voice is solemn. "I see it now. Big one."

Uncle glances ahead and back. "Yeah? What kine?"

"More complaining!" Auntie laughs, and I giggle, but Uncle scowls.

"Bah, the both of you."

I keep wondering what Mom would say or show me if she was here. Would she be happy we came without her? Sad she missed it? Everywhere I look, she's there at the front of my mind, like my glasses have Mom's picture stamped on the lens.

We sail through the sights with Dad at the helm, his will pulling us like kite-surfers bound to the wind. It's exhilarating, and wonderful, and lonely, and sad. But I play along because I've never seen him try so hard. He needs me to pretend everything's fine, so I do.

At last, we drive to the Rainforest Zoo, but the farther we go, the slower Auntie walks, Uncle at her side, hand in hand. Though when we stop at the white tiger habitat, it's Uncle—not Auntie—who leans against the rail with his face all red.

Dad watches Auntie wrap her arms around Uncle, and suddenly wherever else we were supposed to go after the zoo magically disappears from the schedule.

That night, as Uncle sips his tea, we play Uno and Hearts. Turns out, Auntie is wicked good at both, but Uncle is the one to watch out for.

"Again?" Auntie waves her cards at Uncle. "What! All the time, waiting fo' the last minute to steal my victory? One minute almost asleep with your tea, the next you take it all."

Uncle shuffles his cards with a straight face, but he's laughing on the inside. I can tell.

"He's like the sea," I tell Auntie. "One minute he's calm and gentle, and next thing you know, he whooshes in with a rogue wave and sweeps everything away."

"Exactly." Auntie leans across the table and fake whispers to Dad, "This one's smart, hah? He can't fool her."

Uncle chuckles. "Well, it's like they say, never turn your back on the ocean."

🐢 🐚 🦀 🐟🐠🐟 ⭐ 🐚🐙🐚🐙🐚🐢.

CHAPTER TWENTY-TWO

Family Crest

Spam and Hawaiian fried rice make for a super yummy alarm clock. First the crackling of Spam and eggs sizzling on the griddle with the rice. Then the smell! It's a sneak attack of savory deliciousness that fills the whole house. I breathe it in and wake with the taste on my lips.

I eat so much for breakfast I almost have to roll myself into the car for our drive.

First stop on our schedule is Hawai'i Volcanoes National Park. Dad says the museum that was always Mom's favorite was perched right on the edge of the cauldron with a lookout down into the crater, but after the 2018 eruption, more than a thousand earthquakes shook everything all up inside. All the shaking made the museum too unstable to ever open again. Now it's pau, finished. Closed forever.

Instead, we go to the Kīlauea Visitors' Center. It's still near the crater, but far back from the ledge. All my life, I've heard stories of Madam Pele, Goddess of Volcanoes and Fire. How could I not? They say hers is the power to create or destroy. And when Kīlauea erupts with smoke and fire . . . she is creating still.

"Such teamwork, yeah? Six volcanoes working together to make our island: Mahukona, Kohala, Mauna Kea, Hualalai, Mauna Loa, and Kīlauea." Uncle passes his hand over the diagram, pausing at each peak. "You'll see a lot more of what Kīlauea can do before we're done today. Kīlauea isn't like cartoon volcanoes that poke straight up in a tall cone and erupt out the top. She's full of lava tubes and caverns that spread out from the center and carry magma sideways into vents and fissures all over the place. On Oahu, we see where the volcano has been. But here, she lives and breathes beneath our feet."

"Want to know my favorite volcano?" Auntie sidles up beside us. "The one building Lō'ihi, the brand-new Hawaiian island growing under the sea."

"Maybe in a hundred years you'll get to see it," Dad says. "But today, it's time to go. We still have a lot of ground to cover."

We drive all the way down to Punalu'u Bake Shop to taste Mom's favorite malasadas and get sweet bread for later, but Uncle's way more excited to backtrack to Black Sands Beach, where green sea turtles *and* Hawaiian hawksbill sea turtles sun on the shore. People come from all over the world to snorkel and watch turtles munch on limu, swimming with seaweed. There's plenty of turtles to see without ever going in the water, but when Dad starts dropping hints that we could plan another trip someday to come back and snorkel here, I say no thanks.

I hate disappointing him, and it puts me on edge sharp as lava rock 'cause I know he's hoping I'll change my mind if he keeps asking. When Dad says it's time to go, I get all wobbly with relief, but Uncle begs for five more minutes.

I can't help but tease him a little. "If you keep looking at all these other turtles out here, you're gonna make Saisei jealous!"

He presses a finger to his lips. "Shh. I won't tell her if you won't."

It takes a while to get to our next stop because we have to drive the mauka roads all the way back around before we can wind down to Kalapana-Kapoho road. Travel on the Big Island can be kind of tricky when lava keeps eating up all the roads.

We drive over new lava fields where the molten flow sliced across grasses and trees and left barren, black rock. Surviving islands of green stand scorched around the edges, surrounded by rivers of stone. Instead of flowers, yellow painted lines add splashes of color to new sections of road paved over desolate black.

I try to imagine what it must have been like when the land was burning, but it's so immense and powerful, it's like someone trying to imagine a tsunami when all they've ever seen is a bathtub. "It's so weird how there's trees, then nothing, then trees again. Is it because the ground is tall underneath? Did it used to be a hill?"

"Sometimes, but I've seen places where lava took a whole neighborhood and left a single house right in the middle," says Dad. "I'm sure there's an explanation somewhere, maybe a slope or ridge in the landscape, but it seems like lava goes wherever it wants."

"It's incredibly hard to predict where lava will flow." Uncle leans forward from the back seat. "Especially with a shield volcano like this that created so many fissures for lava to slip through—twenty-four this time. Teams of scientists at the college study it. When lava's hottest, it can move really fast, and it slows when it cools. It also changes depending on viscosity—thin and runny or thick and chunky."

Chunky peanut butter sounds great. Chunky 'a'a lava? Not so much.

Then jungle surrounds us again—some places so dense, the canopy arches over the whole road, a living tunnel of vines and branches.

A big truck comes from the other way and we pull to the side to let it pass on the narrow road. Beside my window, a tidy line of rocks borders a break in the undergrowth where someone cleared the brush away and planted grass. On one side, yellow and white flowers peek from between mangrove tree roots. Behind those, more coconut trees stand beside a banana tree heavy with young fruit.

It always seems weird to me that bananas grow upside down with the pale green fruit curved up toward the sky. At home, we hang banana bunches from their stems so the ends of the fingers point down, but on a live tree, the stems of bananas are on the bottom of the hands, and the bunches grow up from there.

"There's your mom's favorite. See it?" Auntie taps my arm, and I pull my gaze away from the purple flower trailing below the banana cluster to follow her lead.

"Where?"

"See the blue on the trunk to the side? They have a rainbow tree in their yard."

Turning almost backwards, I spy a flash of blue and red streaking up a trunk to the far right. "What is it?"

"That's a rainbow eucalyptus. Not so many around here, but there's a grove of them on Kona side," Auntie says. "Remember how it looks, because you'll never see the same one twice. They're always changing."

I peer at the trunk that is brown *and* green *and* blue *and* red *and* orange—a real rainbow of colors *all* worn by the very same tree! Like drips from melted crayons, bright streaks speckle the length of it all the way up. It's easy to see why it's Mom's favorite. If it weren't for Castle Tree, I'd pick it for my favorite too. "How do they do that?"

The truck rumbles past and Dad speeds us back onto the road.

"The rainbows?" Uncle sways as the car rounds a bend. "It's all about layers. As the trees grow, their thin bark curls and flakes away from dark green bark underneath. The longer it's exposed, the more the color changes. The older the tree, the more colors they wear."

"So, it's like natural tree-bling that never fades, yeah?" Greens and browns blur past my window as I watch for more.

"I have a picture from last time we went to Kona." Auntie scrolls through her phone to a picture of Uncle standing beside a tree draped in neon blue streaks as bright as glow-in-the-dark play dough. That *can't* be real. It looks like taffy from the chocolate factory in Mom's book. "How do you know it's real—not painted or anything? Can we go back and see?"

Uncle chuckles. "They're real."

"Ah, the schedule's pretty full." Dad checks his watch. "Maybe you can have your phone ready on the way back and take a picture out the window. We still have Pohoiki Park and Uncle Robert's to get to before our last stop."

I bite my lip as another tree zips by too fast to get a good look. The forest could be full of rainbow trees for all I know, but we're going too fast to see more than a glimpse of anything. What's the point of "seeing" all this stuff if I never get to actually *look* at it? Can't we have one day without a schedule?

At home, it's easier to ignore because it's part of my regular routine . . .

But here?

The schedule should be bolted to the wall in our house. Not copied and carried with us. We're always tied to it, and I'm sick of it. Sick and tired of being ruled by a stupid piece of paper that's more important than seeing Mom's tree.

"So . . ." I lick my lips. Do I really dare say it?

Another tree flashes by.

Yep. I dare. "How about we *don't* go to the other places?"

"What?" Dad glances from the road to me and back again.

"You know, like we could *stop* and go back, and see the rainbow tree—and when we get to the next stop, we could stay there and look around, like *without* a time limit. We could walk around." If Mom were here, she'd have held my hand and walked all over the trails by the volcano center, and especially around the Black Sands Beach with the turtles. That's what we do. We walk. We look. We notice. And we take our time!

"Sorry hon, sunset's at 5:50 p.m., and we can't stay another day."

It's so unfair. *I* finished Mom's challenge that she made for *me*. So why can't I have a choice in what we do? A familiar heat swirls inside, but this time, I don't want to push it back down. Why do I have to pretend it's fine when it's not? That stupid schedule is ruining everything! "But I didn't get to look at the tree at all. Maybe Mom wanted me to see it. How do you know? What's the point of all this if we miss the thing she wanted me to see?"

"Alex, we've got a schedule to keep—"

"Can't *I* be more important than the calendar for once? "We might be racing all over for nothing."

"It's not for nothing!"

I flinch at Dad's sharp tone as his hands open and close on the steering wheel like he wants to bend it. He takes a deep breath and tries again.

"True, I don't know exactly what your mom wanted you to see. It was never the plan to do this without her. But when the unexpected happens, we do the best we can. That's why I'm trying to cover all the bases. I know her end goal—our final stop. And we're almost there, but we don't have much time." His voice cracks, and I glimpse how tight he's holding on to control.

My heart cracks a little to match. He told me once that having a schedule anchors him when he's tossed in a sea of chaos and uncertainty. If he's holding on this tight, he must feel the same tempest inside as I do.

Auntie pats my shoulder. "What? Don't want see the whole island in one day? Don't worry. Your dad knows what he's doing. Patience."

After that, Dad and I drive in silence, both of us trying to get salt out of our wounds, while Auntie and Uncle tease and murmur in the back seat. I'm not mad at him, not really. But we dance around this fissure where Mom ought to be—but isn't—and sometimes it fills up with all the things we don't say until it swells into a boil and spills over, venting our hurt and frustration.

He needs me to pretend, I know. But it's hard to stuff all the feels back where they go when this hollow ache keeps spitting them back out. Auntie pats me on the shoulder and hums a tune, and I remember she and Uncle are trying hard too. They came all this way to be with me and Dad. For Auntie, I'll try one more time to be strong.

When we pull into Pohoiki Park, Dad sweeps around to my side of the car and opens my door with an extra twirl of his hand. "Welcome to the newest black sands beach in Hawaii. You can walk around and look all you want . . . as long as you're back in the car in twenty minutes."

I look from his tired eyes to his offered hand, then reach out and take it. I can be strong for him too. "*Gee*, thanks, Dad. Twenty whole minutes?"

"For you? Twenty and a half." Dad lifts my hand to his lips and makes kissy-noises as if I were a princess, and I laugh, dart out of reach, and wipe it off on my shirt.

Even though we both know he's totally putting on a show, I smile with him, and hold on to Auntie's advice that it will turn out okay.

We walk onto a side road and I follow the yellow lines down the center, hopping from one to the next until the last one disappears under lava rock where a thirty-foot wall of lava marched right over the pavement and swallowed whatever came next.

I squint up at the top, but I already know what it looks

like up there—same as all the lava fields we already drove over. "Where did this road used to go?"

"This road led to many good places." Auntie gazes at the rock as if she had X-ray vision to see right through. "Ahalanui Warm Springs Park, Kapoho tide pools, homes, orchid farms—some of the best flowers in all of Hawaii."

Dad's phone rings and he glances at the screen, twice. "Uh, I need to get this. Matthew? Can you tell Alex about the park?"

"Sure." We walk to a shady area beside the road where lava gobbled up trees and grass and ate half a picnic table—but left the other half stuck part in, part out of a solid wall of rock.

"Whoa." I duck to look underneath, but the table isn't hardly scorched at all. How'd that—

"What do you mean, oversight?" Dad paces far down the road. "How long ago?"

Uncle's gentle hand turns me from Dad as we walk through the park and out to the boat dock. He points toward the lagoon at the base of a ramp. "One of the last people to escape got out right over there."

"I thought everyone was evacuated?"

"Everyone else was, but it's hard to leave a life's work behind. So, with the roads closed by lava, a boat came in right here and they made a dash for safety just in time. Right after, the flow pushed through to the ocean over there, and when fire met water, rock *shattered*, forming this black sand beach almost overnight."

Below us, the boat ramp slants down into a small lagoon completely cut off from the ocean by a solid wall of black sand. What a race it must have been with the lava eating up everything all the way to the sea.

I glance at Dad as we walk out onto the new black sand, but he's still talking and pacing.

Auntie takes Uncle's hand, and I follow them across the beach. When we pass a stack of lava rocks, Auntie tsks, and we stop to spread the rocks back out to a natural state, 'cause stacking rocks is not pono—and rock stacks are contagious. First one tourist does it, another copies, then another, and they keep making more, never stopping to think whether or not they should.

Too soon, Dad waves and shouts from the car, "Hey! Time's up!" and we hurry back.

After he pulls the car back onto Red Road, I ask, "What was your phone call?"

"Don't worry about it. Everything will be—*is* fine." Dad flashes a fake smile and pats my knee. "So, what do you think of the new black sands beach?"

By the time I answer all his questions, we're already part of a line of cars headed to the next stop on his agenda: Uncle Robert's.

Lava rock surrounds the parking lot and most of the buildings, but it's older than the flow by Pohoiki. We pull into the sandy parking lot, and Dad waves me out of the car and swipes at his phone. "I'll be right there."

I scowl as he takes forever to finish whatever he's doing. What about Dad's precious schedule? Weren't we in a hurry? I bite my lip. The call must've been something bad for him to be careless with time. I turn toward the music playing under a pavilion below us where people crowd around market booths and dance to a live band.

"We go." Uncle leads the way, but instead of heading down

to the pavilion, he crosses to a sandy path through a wide lava field. Swirls of slow pahoehoe lava curl underfoot in beautiful lines; jagged 'a'a lava pokes up here and there where the flow must've moved or cooled too fast.

When we reach a high spot, Uncle nods toward the vast lava field beside us. "That was Kalapana Village."

"Under the lava?" I scan past young palm trees for any sight of a building or town beyond, but there's nothing but lava.

Auntie says, "Not much left, but Uncle Robert's was spared."

"So, Uncle Robert's is the name of the marketplace down there?" I ask.

"Yes, but Uncle Robert is a real person—a revered kupuna and Hawaiian sovereignty activist." Auntie watches the people way down below. "Though when we say 'Uncle Robert's' now, we usually mean his place with the farmer's market and music. When the eruption happened and so much was taken back by the volcano, lava came right up close to his house, but didn't take it. After that, his family helped make it a gathering place like it is now, and they made this path across the new lava flow to the ocean."

"So, when the eruptions happen, can't they . . . I don't know, make it go around the towns? Maybe build a trench or something?"

"Oh, they have," Uncle says. "They've dug trenches and built up walls. In Hilo they even bombed the lava tubes once to try and cool the lava before it could reach its end."

"Bombed?" I look to Auntie, who nods.

"With bomber planes. But none of it works for long. Lava flows where she wishes. Only the volcano can stop the flow."

"Sorry about that." Dad jogs up the path and takes my hand before checking his watch. "Okay, ah . . . I wanted to show you the market inside Uncle Robert's there, but we'll have to skip it."

He clears his throat, stands up straight, and puts a hand on his chest. "My lady Alexis, you've reached the end of your quest. Allow me to escort you to Kaimū Beach."

"*Cheehoo!*" Auntie teases as she and Uncle follow us. "Lead on, noble knight."

Dad's hand is clammy around mine as we walk over sand and lava on the worn path to the ocean. Whatever the call was, it shook him.

Plants of all kinds sprout from the rock beside the path— even dragon fruit with its flat, segmented vines. The closer we get to the ocean, the more palm trees dot the lava, some tall as a house, but most less.

With the sun dipping toward the horizon, streaks of orange, yellow, and red fill the sky over my right shoulder as we reach the end of the path. In front of us, waves rush up a narrow black sand beach and beat against the rock ledge that stretches out to either side as far as I can see.

"Did you find it?" Dad asks.

"Find what?" I glance at him, but he's looking at his phone again with his lips mashed into a tight line.

"Dad? What's wrong? Is it Mom?"

"It's nothing, hon. Nothing to worry about. Your mom left something here you need to see." He pats my back like all is well, but the pinched wrinkles around his eyes say different.

"It's here, sis." Auntie pats the trunk of a tall coconut tree and waves us closer. "This is your mom's tree."

"What? Here?"

"Our Elizabeth went crazy for these young trees putting down roots," she says. "That next day, we brought a coconut for her, and she left it here on the rock."

Uncle taps lava at the base of the tree. "No dirt. No care. Nothing to make a good home—only one good seed with the will to grow."

"Next time we come, we found her tree with roots reaching down into the crack here." Auntie points where the crack extends beyond the reach of the roots. "Every time we come after that, we check her tree. Watched it rise. And it grew up strong. Strong like your mother."

"Strong like the sea," Uncle agrees.

Dad steps beside Auntie. "Do you see it now? Imagine a coconut sitting there at the foot of the trunk. Does it remind you of anything?"

I tilt my head. The circle of a coconut with a tree growing—not just growing, *rising*. "Is it the tree on our tapestry?"

"Now you know where your family crest came from, and why your mom wanted to share this place with you," says Dad.

I always thought the circle was supposed to be like the world or maybe the ocean, but it's a coconut. Looking up at Mom's tree, I can almost hear her voice whispering to me, *Rise where you stand.*

"She felt a kinship with these trees," Dad says. "Your mom didn't have an easy start either, but once she put down roots . . . "

"It's a choice." Uncle waves for me to join him, Dad, and

Auntie by the tree as he talks story. "Sometimes, life is hard. Unfair. A mean one. Maybe seems like you're alone. Maybe seems like no one cares. Maybe hard things make you want to hide inside your shell. But—believe in yourself always, and when you get the chance—"

"Rise." I touch the trunk of Mom's tree and smile.

CHAPTER TWENTY-THREE

The Cure

When Dad gently shakes me awake, a few coquis still call to each other in the dark of early morning.

I rub my eyes and yawn. "Is it time to go already? It's still dark."

"Almost. But first, I made something for you." He uncurls my fingers and sets a delicate paper coconut tree in the palm of my hand.

"*Oh!*" I blink at the intricate creation. More sculpture than origami, the little tree stands with flowers at its base, precisely cut fronds at the top, and little coconuts hanging underneath. It must've taken him hours. "When did you make this?"

"Last night. I couldn't sleep." He turns his face to the window, where black outlines of real trees stand tall against the lightening sky. "We need to talk. Maybe I should have told you yesterday, but I didn't want to ruin the day for you—not when it meant so much to your mom."

Despite my warm blanket, a chill settles inside my chest so fast I feel frost creeping inside my skin. I set Dad's tree on the nightstand. "Talk about what? I knew something was wrong. Where's Mom? What happened?"

"She's okay—or rather, she's going to be." He gathers my hand in his and explains how during the typhoon, Mom's submarine went deep below the storm, and Mom got very sick. She thought it was just seasickness, but when the storm passed, she didn't get better. By the time they figured out what was wrong, her appendix had already burst, and she was delirious with fever and pain. Dad smooths the cover on my bed. "Someone was supposed to call us, but something went wrong, and I didn't hear anything until the phone call last night. They said she's being moved to a new hospital, and she'll call us this afternoon after we fly back to Oahu."

"So, she's okay now?" My voice cracks as all the walls I've built inside to stay strong come crashing down. Mom was sick and hurting, and we didn't even know it. I felt it though, didn't I? When I ran to Castle Tree, was she crying or counting the same time as me? My chin trembles.

"She will be. Hey, *shh*. It's okay." Dad pulls my head against his shoulder. "I'm sorry. I probably should have said something last night, but it hurt to know she'd gone through all that alone, and I struggled with that. I was afraid I'd fail her again if last night didn't go as planned. It had to be right." He kisses the top of my head. "I didn't know what else to do."

I pull away and shake my head as I wipe my cheek. "Some things don't fit on a schedule."

"I know." He gives a watery laugh. "You're right."

"You sure she's okay? Was she there when they called?" I still can't believe it's true.

"I'm sure, and no, she wasn't. But they said she's recovering well and in good spirits. The worst is over, and we'll have her home soon."

"When? How soon is *soon?*" I kick the covers off, shove my glasses on, and grab my hat, ready to run to the airport this very second. "Will we be home in time to meet her?"

Dad chuckles and squeezes my hand. "You bet. Maybe a few days. As soon as she feels well enough and the doctors give her the okay, she'll fly home."

Mom's coming home! I want to scream those words out to the world, but instead I hug Dad's arm as tight as I can—so hard my eyes mash shut, and a shuddering hiccup squeaks out my throat. "I can't wait to see her!"

"Neither can I." He bows his head to mine and murmurs, "What a story she must have to share."

I nod and gaze at Dad's little tree on the nightstand. We both do. I've followed Mom's clues every step of the way from Laie to Hilo, and now *finally* we're both headed home—except there's one more story I'd like to tell. "Dad? How much time do we have before we have to go?"

"About three hours, why?"

"There's one last stop I want to make before we go home." I lift up Dad's tree and smile. "One that's *not* on the schedule."

When the first fiery slice of sun peeks over the ocean horizon, we pull up to the crossroads where Highway 132 used to lead to Kapoho, the tide pools, and Vacationland before lava from fissure eight took it all back in one night.

I climb up the embankment of 'a'a lava, where wisps of steam still vent from deep inside the cracks. Uncle says that the Goddess Madam Pele added over eight hundred acres of new land to the shoreline—about two square miles—but the field of broken lava is so vast between us and the sea, it's hard to imagine the size of it all.

All around me, coconuts rest where loving hands wedged them into cracks and furrows in the lava, and at the top of each, a tender young tree grows from a split in the shell.

At the crest of a mound, I duck to peer into a wide fissure where red-tinted roots dangle from a coconut shell across open air until they reach lava rock and cling tight, a solid anchor for a new tree.

Uncle, Auntie, and Dad wait near the car while I clamber up one little hill of 'a'a lava and down another—careful to avoid the steaming places—until I find the perfect spot and wave to them. "This is it."

Dad climbs across, passes me a coconut, and waits while I tuck it into a groove in the rock.

I brush my hands on my shorts and snap a couple pictures of my new almost-tree from different angles. Maybe it will grow, maybe not. But I like to think it will rise just like Mom's did.

"You ready to go home?" Dad asks.

I scan the barren new land one more time, trying to fix this spot in my mind for when I see it again someday—*with* Mom. "Yeah, I'm ready."

Well, I'm happy to report that Uncle rules at Scrabble, Auntie's the queen of charades, and Dad . . . well, let's just say he's really bad at Pictionary. Like, really, *really* bad. (Auntie thought Dad's clown fish was a reindeer.)

Dad invited the Tanakas to wait with us for Mom's call because it's all any of us could think of the whole trip home anyway, so we might as well distract each other. I thought maybe I was the only one with my guts all twisted up like I ate a pile of sea slugs, but when the phone finally rings, Dad pounces on it so fast, he knocks the mahjong board right off the table.

Mom's voice is quiet, tired, but *hers*. And that makes everything else okay. I start to tell her all about the Big Island, but Dad writes "She's tired" next to his clownfish-reindeer and I shorten it down to "I miss you."

"Miss you too. I can't wait to see you and hear all about your adventures, reports, and anything else I've missed."

We take turns asking questions, and Mom says she's getting stronger every day—but she still sounds pretty weak to me. If I close my eyes, I can imagine her like she is when she first wakes up. Curly brown hair in a messy tumble down her shoulders, a soft robe wrapped around her waist, her tablet tucked under one arm, but not turned on yet.

"The doctors say I'm doing better and will be home soon." She sighs. "Or I would be if I could just get this blood pressure under control. I waited too long to get help and got really sick, so it went low at first—and they fixed me. I'm sore, and most of the infection is gone now, but they think I might be reacting to something or have an underlying condition because now it keeps spiking up."

Too soon, her nurses come to help her walk some more to get her digestive system working right again, and Mom promises to call again soon.

When the line disconnects, the grown-ups talk while I stare at the phone. Mom said they'd let her go home sooner if her blood pressure got under control. Fix that, and she can come home, right?

I interrupt. "Uncle? Didn't you say your tea helps with your blood pressure?"

"Maybe. I think so."

All these weeks, I've been trying to solve Mom's clues and work out her challenge because that was all I had to feel close to her. But what if I could make something to help her? "If I gather enough fruit, can you show me how to make it? Maybe it could help Mom too."

"She's already under doctor's care—" Dad begins.

"But there's still a chance it might help her. And the faster she feels better, the faster she comes home, right?" My voice grows stronger with every word. "If our island helped her grow and put down roots, it only makes sense that it can help her get better, too. Will you help me?"

Uncle glances at Dad and Auntie, then nods. "I'll teach you."

~~~~~🌊~~~~~

It's tricky to have basements on a volcanic island where the ground is mostly solid rock, and digging down is really hard—especially with seawater sneaking in through old lava tubes and sandy soil. With Uncle's house on the makai side of Kamehameha Highway and the ocean in his backyard, he can't have a basement like my mainland grandparents do. But I'm learning that Uncle doesn't let a little ol' thing like solid rock get in the way of what he wants.

No basement? No problem; he built the next best thing.

There's a crevasse in the lava beside his house where 'a'a lava pushed up in a chunky wall and smooth pahoehoe lava swirled down low beside it. So Uncle built some walls around it and mounded earth for a windowless shed.

This is where Uncle lets stinky cheese fruit sit in special small tanks forever until it's ready to harvest the bitter golden liquid that's left at the end.

"Wait, it takes how long?" I blink, waiting for my eyes to adjust to the dark of his step-down shed—more above-ground hobbit hole than a basement.

He taps a bottle. "Two months to make this. But longer to make it a dark brown color. It goes darker when it ages."

"But we can't wait months."

Sarge barks, and we peek out of the shed in time to see Sarge lay across both of Malia's feet.

"Oof!" Her arms whirl to keep her balance, but her eyes are bright and clear. "Hey Uncle Tanaka, next time you need a smaller dog. Like a bear, maybe."

"Or a moose," I agree.

"Bah, he's perfect size. Not his fault the rest of the world is too small. Sarge!" At Uncle's call, Sarge heaves himself to his feet and ambles to Uncle's side, Malia following after.

"I thought you'd be busy." I give her a hug and she rubs Sarge's head as he wedges himself sideways between us.

"While you were on the Big Island, I talked with my mom about feeling burnt out, and we went over all the stuff I've been doing. We found a pretty good compromise, I think. I'm still doing a lot of things, but not *everything* all the time anymore. So you know what that means . . ." She wiggles her eyebrows.

"You get to . . ." I try to think of what else she'd want to add to her schedule, but I can't.

"I get to sleep in," she fake whispers. "It's this thing people do sometimes. It's glorious."

A message from Jack pops up on my phone. *Howzit - Why Malia say you wan pick stinky cheese fruit?*

To help my mom.

But. The SMELL.

Yeah, yeah. You gonna help us?

But but but THE SMELL!

I roll my eyes and tuck the phone back into my pocket. "Jack might come later to help, maybe. Uncle, tell us what to do."

Sure, noni plants are all over the place, but the one in Uncle's yard only has two fruit pale and soft enough to be ripe. The rest are all way too hard and green. I worry we won't find enough, but once the coconut wireless gets wind of what we're doing, my phone starts chiming all over the place for places we can go pick ripe fruit.

A couple hours later, Malia and I trudge back into the yard with two whole sacks full of the stuff, which seems pretty good until we see five overflowing bags at Jack's feet as his dad visits with Auntie, who must've just got home from work at PCC because she's all dressed up in her pretty skirt, flowers clipped up in her hair again. Uncle chats too, except he's bent over holding onto Sarge's collar to keep him out of trouble.

Spying us entering the yard, Sarge swings his behind around so he's between Uncle and these newcomers. With his precious human protected, he lets his tongue loll out and wags his tail.

"Holy cow." I thought we got a lot of fruit, but they must've used super-speed. "What'd you do? Steal all the noni in the whole town?"

"Naw, naw, Dad and me been going door to door, trimming trees and cleaning up palm fronds for people for a while. We asked them if we can take noni for you, and they said yes." Jack cups his hand beside his mouth. "Did I mention they stink?"

"Hey! Be respectful." Jack's dad ruffles his son's hair, pulls him back against his chest, and winks at me. "So sorry. What can I say? I teach him manners, but look what happens?" He lets Jack go, and they grin at each other.

"If my manners are bad, it's 'cause I copy you." Jack smooths his hair, but it's still sticking up all over the place.

Malia and I snicker, but Jack catches another whiff of cheese fruit and turns a little green.

The Tanakas show us how to wash and prepare the fruit so some goes into day jars, some in the hobbit hole tanks, and some we slice up to dry on racks. With Malia, Jack, his dad, and me all working, we fill every jar and drying rack Auntie and Uncle own—which is a lot.

By the time Malia's mom comes to pick her up, we've got everything as prepped as possible. Jack and his dad leave with the half-full bag of leftover noni, but I'm pretty sure we heard Jack complaining about carrying the smelly bag all the way across Kamehameha and past Laie Elementary.

Auntie goes inside to cook dinner, but I keep looking from the sliced fruit drying in the sun, to the big clear jars, to the dark tanks. I like how it feels to see it all done, like unlocking a bonus level on one of Mom's challenges.

"You work hard today." Uncle sits on a chair under the lanai and wipes sweat from his forehead with a trembling hand. "Real hard."

"It was fun. And who knows? Maybe it can help."

"Perhaps. You have enough ready for a year, yeah?"

"Yeah."

He pulls a small, dark vial from his pocket. "Until your noni is ready, you can take this one with you. It's finished and aged. Maybe it's right for your mom. Maybe not. Remember, could be her doctor says she can't take any. You respect what your parents say, even if you don't like it, okay?"

"I will. Thank you." I hold the vial as if it's more precious than gold—because to me, it is. Gold can't make my mom get better, but maybe this little glass bottle could help. I carefully tuck it into my pocket.

"Good. There's something I want to show you." He scoots forward and takes my hand when I reach to help him up. Our long day of work must've been harder on him than I thought. When he tucks my hand into the crook of his arm and leads me around to the beach, he shuffles more than he steps, and I feel the trembling all the way through his elbow.

I open my mouth to ask him what it means for him to have Parkinson's, but I don't know how to say the words, and worse, I'm scared he'll clam up again like he used to. No, not clam up. That's not right either. More like a squid that squirts black ink all over to blind and confuse threats before shooting away to hide. The squid is here and gone before anyone even knows they're scared. But Uncle can't hide from me anymore; I know him too well.

When we reach the sand, I think I spy Saisei playing on

the waves, but she's pretty far out so I can't be sure. We stop beside the corner bush, and Uncle pats my hand. "Would you like to know a secret?"

I hesitate and he clarifies, "Not a secret from your parents, no. Nothing like that. But a secret from the rest of the world."

Sarge sniffs at the base of the bush and wags his tail.

"Sure."

Uncle smiles. "I have buried treasure on this beach."

I narrow my eyes, but play along with Uncle's joke. "Treasure, huh?"

He points with his chin to the waves. "You heard of green sea turtles nesting down Bellows Beach?"

"Yeah, they had to close the beach to protect them, right?"

"They did." He nods. "But my Saisei does what she wants. I tell her to go with the others but she only listens sometimes—or maybe she did and came anyway. It's possible for a female turtle to lay on more than one beach."

"Lay?" I blink. "Wait, are you serious?"

"Saisei's eggs are here."

I drop to my knees and peer under the overhang of the bush. "How many?"

"Most nests hold around a hundred and ten eggs. But we'll know in about a week when the sixty-day incubation is over. You can count them when they climb out of the nest on their way to the sea."

"A hundred babies! We get to watch?" Not that I'm admitting to squealing or anything—but I totally did.

"Some of my colleagues will be here to record and observe the hatching. Late in the season like this, and in the shade . . . mostly male offspring, we think."

"That's so cool. I can't wait to see them."

Uncle's next answer comes slowly. "I knew you would like that. But I been thinking—do you really only want to see half of it?"

"Half of what?"

"They call the young years of a turtle's life 'the lost years,' because they are so small we can't track them, but if you wanted to follow them a ways, you could see if they go into the reef, or over it, or where they go."

"You think *I* can find out where baby turtles go?"

Uncle chuckles. "No, no. Only to see them off on their journey from a distance. One more look before they disappear."

"I bet they're gonna be so cute." Images of baby sea turtles flapping those adorable flippers fill my head . . . until my brain catches up about how "following them" means that I would have to be in the ocean too. I purse my lips. "Is this a trick to get me back in the water?"

"No trick. Only opportunity. You are too strong to let this fear have power over you all your life."

"But you're scared too." I heard him say so himself.

"True, but when I get the chance to see something on the mainland—something far from the sea where I feel safe—I go anyway. You're stronger than me. Stronger than you think you are."

"I'll think about it." For now, that's enough.

"Good," he grunts. "But one more thing. When you went with me in the kayak, you were afraid of tipping, yeah?"

"Yeah." Sweat pricks the back of my neck just thinking about that day.

"I found something to help you with that too." He folds his arms all proud of himself, but I can only shake my head.

"I don't want to go in—"

"How is this report you used to talk about all the time? With the Bletchley Park codebreaker?"

"Mavis Batey? Uh, good, I think. I typed it up and made models and stuff for the codebreaker machines. I really want to win." That would make an awesome welcome home for Mom. *Hi, Mom! Here's my trophy, same as the one you got.*

"If you want me to look at it, I might be able to help. I taught your mom everything I know about secrets and codes, and look where she ended up."

"In the hospital?"

Uncle's mouth opens and closes and I can't help giggling.

"See? You need supervision. Young people these days. No respect. Where's your family anyway, hah? Who taught you to be so obnoxious?" The grouch in his words never touches the laughter in his eyes.

"My family?" I point to him. "One of them is right here. But I wouldn't ask him if I was you. I hear he's grumpy."

"Bah!"

CHAPTER TWENTY-FOUR

A Report and a Test

The school librarian loves my history project! Once she saw the Enigma machine model, she tried to get me to leave it at school like Lowen left his, all covered, but at school and ready to go—except I've heard how Lowen keeps snooping around other people's projects and I don't want to give him the chance to ogle at mine. He's got his tied up so well, there's no way to peek without him knowing. I already caught him prowling by my backpack twice today, but he never figured out what's in it 'cause I've got it safely packed inside the biggest cardboard shoebox I could fit inside my waterproof backpack. I'm not letting it out of my sight. When I set it up this Friday, Lowen won't know what hit him. *Boom!* Best report evah! *Oh yeah.*

My report will be a surprise-sneak attack. Sort of like when Mavis Batey deciphered an Italian message in 1941 that said, "Day X minus 3," and figured out that enemies were going to attack British ships in three days. But the British were sneaky and pretended they didn't know about the attack. The admiral of the British fleet even pretended to go golfing on the big day—with golf clubs and everything—but he snuck out and led the British fleet in a preemptive strike! Not only did Mavis's info save the British fleet, but it wrecked the enemy's navy for the whole rest of the war. How amazing is that? Her code-breaking skills defeated a whole navy.

Not that I actually want to hurt Lowen or anything; the only battle I want to win is the one for the trophy. I just don't want him to see my report coming. Because *that* would be cheating, or at least spying, or sleuthing, or espionage? *Whatever.*

Surprise report attack for the win!

I gather my things and stuff my feet into slippers for the walk down the covered walkways to the giant gecko garden by the front office.

Even though it's awesome that the librarian loves my report, there's one person who loves it even more: Uncle.

It makes me grin just to think about it. When I set my report up at Uncle's house to show him, he got real close, looking at every detail of my machine. Then he called Auntie in to show her. I hardly had to say a word to tell Auntie about Mavis Batey, because Uncle remembered all the things I told him and was so excited, *he* pretty much gave Auntie my report all by himself.

All day, I've been trying to puzzle out what Uncle might have done to the kayak to help me not be so scared of it, but unless the kayak suddenly grew wings, I've got no idea what that would be. Maybe make a big bubble all the way around it? We could climb inside and bob around on the waves inside a clear bubble so we could see everything under the surface—except we couldn't steer or paddle or breathe—yeah, no idea. Hopefully I'll figure it out when I check on Saisei's nest with Uncle today.

When I make it to Tanakas' gate, Sarge's deep huff echoes across the fence line. Silly dog, he's barking like crazy, and when I grab the gate handle, he hits the door so hard it rattles. Great, did he forget me since yesterday? Or maybe he's mad I brought Jack and his dad over.

I cup a hand to my mouth. "Uncle, call Sarge! I'm coming in!"

Probably he's already kneeling by the turtle nest, watching for any signs of movement and writing down observations.

"Okay, Sarge, don't squish me, okay? No Alex-squishing allowed." I ease the door open a little, ready to pull my feet out from under his fluffy buffalo-sized behind, but Sarge backs up with a whine.

"Uncle?" I step to the side to peek around the lanai, but as far as I can tell, Uncle's not by the nesting bush. Adjusting the strap of my backpack, I step under the lanai and head for the screen door, but Sarge blocks my path—worse, he barks at me. Not the *huff, huff* I'm used to, but a deep "*Roash! Roash!*" He's so big and loud, I'd probably be scared of him if I didn't already know he's a gentle giant.

"Seriously? You're guarding the whole house from me now? I'm ohana, remember? Come on, Sarge."

A dangling string of drool flips up over his nose and smacks him right between the eyes, and I laugh. "Eww, gross. Keep that to yourself."

The wide car gate swings open and Auntie pulls in. While

the gate closes, Sarge dashes to Auntie's side, then back to me, his foot knocking the empty food bowl into a noisy wobble.

"I think he's hungry."

"He ate this morning. If he tells you different, he's lying." Auntie pulls a grocery bag from the back seat, but Sarge darts in and snags a loaf of bread.

"Hey! īlio pupule, that's our dinner." Auntie holds the rest of the groceries high overhead as she nudges Sarge aside and makes a swipe—and miss—for the bread. "Big gourd!"

I hold the door open for Auntie and call inside. "Uncle! Your dog is lolo."

"You here for Matthew?" Auntie bustles past. "You wan check on the noni already? It's too soon. Try wait till tomorrow at least."

"Naw, Uncle said he had a surprise for me for when we check the nest today." I slip one shoulder out of the strap and lift my bag for Auntie to see. "Oh! And I tweaked a couple things on my project."

"Even betta, hah? That's our smart girl."

A yank on my arm jerks me so hard I spin around and nearly fall. "*Eep!*"

Sarge stands a few feet away from me, his paws prancing, with my backpack hanging from his jowls.

My entire report—the cardboard Enigma machine replica, my paper models, my diagrams—all of it hangs beside strings of drool. My stomach twists like I just drank a whole bucket of rotten noni. "No! Not funny. Not playing. You drop it right now!"

He shakes his head fast, once, twice. Long canines tear the

waterproof covering as he shakes a third time. I swear I can hear things ripping inside, crushing under the force of his jaws.

I lunge for him. "Stop it!"

Mistake.

As soon as I move, Sarge races off around the house toward the beach.

"Oh, no. Sarge, no, no, Auntie! Make him stop!" My throat burns, and tears prick my eyes as he sprints for the water. I'd keep calling, but my throat's so tight I can't talk.

He splashes into the surf, his white underbelly soaked with waves as he pushes deeper into the ocean.

Not fair! Weeks of work destroyed by one stupid dog. He stands chest-deep in the waves, which splash over the holes in my used-to-be waterproof bag. I feel sick.

"Give it!" I kick off my slippers and toss my phone high on the sand, out of the water's reach. With the beach deserted except for tiny figures way down the shore, I don't have to worry about anyone taking it anyway. We're pretty much alone—on land and at sea—and thank goodness for that, because I don't need any witnesses while I tackle this overgrown fuzz-bucket.

I grab for him, but he leaps forward, drops my bag, and stands on his hind legs to keep his muzzle clear of the waves.

"My bag!"

A raw string of barking like I've never heard pours from his throat. Whining, barking, crying, howling, snarling.

"Geez, Sarge. What's your problem?"

A wave slaps my bag, and I spring to the side to catch it before another wave pushes it under. *Got it!* With a heave, I haul it high out of the water. A little wet might have squeaked inside, but probably not enough to saturate the shoebox yet. If the models are safe, all I've got to do is reprint my report. *My project is saved!*

Relief ripples through me as cleansing as the waves splashing over my jeans. If I get it inside and spread it out fast, I might even be able to save the diagrams before—

I turn for the shore, but Sarge cuts me off, splashing a line between me and the shore, then standing on his hind legs again, he wails, "*Yipe, yipe, yipe!*" Rapid and high, the pain in his voice rises almost like a human cry.

"My gosh, what? What is it?" I sling my bag over one shoulder and try to see his feet under the waves. Did he step on a blue bubble man-o'-war, or maybe a spiny urchin?

"Sarge, look at me. I'm right here. What's the matter, boy?"

But he won't look at me. His stare is fixed out on the waves as he opens his jaws, pants, and cries.

I follow his gaze and squint out at the bay. No surfers, or boarders, nothing at all—except for a lone kayak rocking violently in the waves far out over the reef. The tide must've swept Uncle's kayak out this morning, or maybe—

The kayak is not empty.

Chicken skin erupts in icy pinpricks up my scalp as my heart skips in fear—already knowing what my brain refuses to believe.

It's him.

Slumped forward in his seat, Uncle leans to one side, his arm dangling limp in the water.

"Uncle!" The scream rips from my throat. "Uncle! Wake up!"

Sarge *howls*.

I look over my shoulder as Auntie runs from the lanai, her face paling at my scream. "Uncle's in trouble! Call for help!"

She starts forward as if to go after him herself, but with her fancy skirts dragging her down, she'll never make it in time.

She can't help him—but *I* can.

I wave my arms fast across my body and shake my head. "I'll get him. I'll bring him back. You get help!"

I don't wait to see if she listens.

The backpack with my models and pages falls forgotten into the tide as water splashes up to my chest.

I bolt for the ocean. How far is the reef? Fifty feet? Closer? A wave breaks over my face and I swim with long strokes, my feet kicking hard. A shadow passes below and the water temperature changes, a swirl of cold and warm at once. The current shifts too, the waves wrong—same as last time I fell into the eel hole.

Arms churning, I cross over the wide circle of sand below, my breath coming in gasps, but I don't stop. It's wider than I thought before. More than three swimming pools at least. Loads of space for something big to come find me.

I force my body to keep swimming as panic crawls up my throat and reaches with thick, clawed fingers to cage my heart. With every stroke, the wide black reef on the far side looms closer, the sharp coral waiting like a bear trap for me to step inside. And it is a trap, isn't it? Why else would Ocean mock me with Uncle as bait?

With my heart beating a frantic stutter against the tight bands around it, I slow and bob in the waves, looking for Uncle. What if I went the wrong way? What if I only thought I saw him?

Something inside me screams that if I cross that black line, I'll never make it to shore again. I'll die! Something dark and frightening hides in the reef, a vengeful power in league with the ocean. It waits to destroy me like it tried to do before—and I've jumped right in! What was I thinking?

I can't do this, I can't!

"Auntie! Uncle!" Waves rush into my mouth and I choke. Impossible to call for help. I spit saltwater and gasp for air, but wave after wave engulfs my face and presses against my lips. It won't let me breathe!

A swell catches me, lifting me high enough to see another flash of Uncle's kayak before shoving me down into the trough as a second wave rolls me backwards into the eel hole. Bubbles swoosh around my face, but not enough to block the shadow of the thing moving through the water.

Big and dark, a dragon from a cave, it separates itself from the murky black of the reef and closes the distance. A shadow of memory from my nightmares, sweeping right toward me.

CHAPTER TWENTY-FIVE

Rise

The eel. The viper moray, coming for me again. I must be, I must . . .

I open my mouth to scream and water floods in. I kick against the horrid current of the eel hole and reach for shore, but the dark shape turns with me, gliding around me once before breaking the surface.

In my blind panic, a glimpse is all I get, a circle of gray set in a dark eye, a flipper, a tail, scales . . . and the double bump of Saisei's shell.

My relief is so sudden I go limp and start to sink, then scramble to tread water again.

Saisei, Uncle's friend, his companion—maybe his guide. Of all the creatures of the sea, this honu, this green sea turtle who owes her life to Uncle, has my absolute trust.

She rolls to the side and dives, swimming beneath me with elegant flaps as if to show there's nothing to fear. She swims as if flying, free and fearless here in the sea. What harm could the reef do? She's survived so much worse already, and none of it was from the ocean.

Gathering courage from my shelled friend, I search for Uncle's kayak. What had my panic attack cost him? A minute? Two? Anger and shame burn the last of my fear away. If he dies because I was busy thrashing in fright—

No! He's not dead. He can't be.

I grit my teeth and scan the waves again.

Don't fall out, Uncle. Please, please, don't let him drown!

There! A flash of color far ahead between the waves and then gone again, but it's enough. I strike for that spot of hope and swim harder than ever before.

The top of my foot cracks against something sharp, and I flatten out my swim to the surface, the reef only a few feet below me. What if I accidentally touch a wana perched on the reef here, one wrong move and venomous sea urchin spines could pierce my skin.

What if, what if . . .

I shake my head and think of Saisei's steady gaze, that thin ring of gray in her eyes forming a light against the dark.

Some bigger waves roll in, three and four feet tall, but there's less than four feet between me and the reef. The crest rushes closer, rising, rolling—and I duck dive right before it touches me, the peak passing over my back. Three more and I dive under them all, but a fifth streaks from a different angle and I don't time it right. My arm crunches against the reef, but seaweed takes most of the blow so I'm only bruised, not sliced this time.

The kayak nears and I get a clear look at Uncle, *still* slumped in the kayak.

Thank you, thank you!

Waves break over the hull and splash my face, and I close the last few feet. Why hadn't it tipped? He's leaning so far, what miracle kept him upright?

But something is different about the kayak—didn't he say he had a surprise for me? Something to make me less afraid? True to his word, he's changed his kayak for me.

He gave it *wings*.

Attached with metal rods out to each side, long floats bob in the waves, changing his ocean kayak into an outrigger with floats on either side.

Careful not to let my feet drop within reach of the reef, I clasp the side of the kayak, hook my toes on the float, and time the next wave. As it washes over us, I push off the float and sprawl onto the center of the kayak.

I climb into my seat and reach for Uncle, scared to touch him, but even more scared that I won't know how to help him.

A wave lifts us, tipping right then left, and I squeeze Uncle's ankle, tugging and shaking soft at first, then harder. His skin is clammy and chilled. "Uncle, wake up. Please, come on!"

Patting his cold leg with wet little slaps, I watch his face— *is he even breathing?*—and scream, "*Uncle!*"

He draws in a shuddering breath, pulls his hand out of the water, and tucks it beside him.

He's alive! I squeeze hard, and tug again. "Uncle? Are you okay? What happened?"

A moan bursts from his lips, and he murmurs something,

271

but I can't understand. He's trembling, the shakes wracking his whole body instead of just his hands. Beads of sweat glisten on his forehead, and he groans softly.

Seeing him like this, my own hands quiver. For years, I avoided him. His harsh glare, his snapping words full of stings. I couldn't see the man my mother loved, because he was camouflaged better than any cuttlefish. He hid his heart from me, from all of us, but I've seen through his disguise. Where I expected sharp teeth, I found gentle hands. Where I feared spite, I found love.

Seeing him crumpled like this, I'm frightened more by his frailty than I ever feared the creatures of tide, reef, or sea. But instead of leaving me helpless, this new fear ignites a greater fire inside me—one strengthened by love. He is my ohana, and I *will* save him.

Uncle's oar is lost to the waves, but mine is still tied in its place on the side. I pull it off and paddle toward shore. After the first couple strokes, I find my rhythm and pull the blade toward me and behind. Uncle's kayak coasts over the top of the waves, and we drop, rising and falling. We cut across each white cap, my teeth gritted against the jolts. As we cruise closer to shore, my arms strain at the new motion, but I keep reaching with the paddle, dipping down to pull again and again.

Auntie stands waiting in the water, her beautiful skirts sodden and swirling about her knees.

I don't slow, but ride the last of the waves right up onto the sand. Auntie grabs the bowline and hauls us the rest of the way onto the shore like a fisherman pulling her net from the deep.

Restless, Sarge prances back and forth, sniffs Uncle's face, and licks his cheek.

"Matthew? Matthew! You hear me?" Auntie pushes Sarge aside, lifts Uncle from his forward slouch, and leans him back before slapping his cheeks with quick, soft smacks. "Matthew Tanaka, where's your medicine? You *will* live. Hear me? You're not done yet. You gonna let Alex grow up with no one fo' talk story with? Don't you leave. I forbid you to go!"

Sarge knocks me over, trying to wiggle close to his master, his whines mixed with yips of joy. He pushes between Uncle and Auntie, who snaps her fingers to keep him back. "Alex, tie him. Over there by the fence. The ambulance is coming."

"Got it." Sarge would get in the way, and the wire leash ending in a clip isn't far away, but dragging an excited Sarge where I want him with arms more seaweed than bone is like telling a hurricane to mind. After a few failed attempts where Sarge dragged us both back to Uncle, Auntie rolls from her knees to her feet and grabs his collar. "You come now!"

With Auntie here to take charge, the pillars of stone that held me upright crumble, and I sag against the kayak.

Sarge barks toward the front of the house, and Auntie disappears around the corner to let the paramedics into the yard.

I lace my fingers through Uncle's chilled hand and lean close to kiss his forehead, but something jabs my hip. Sliding my hand into my pocket, I pull out the precious vial of aged noni medicine. None of the other medicine is ready yet. If Mom flies to the island today and I don't have this, she might never be strong enough to come home.

What should I do?

What would Mom want me to do?

Uncle's eyes flutter, and he moans again. His dark eyes

open, but not seeing. Not really. He whispers through cracked lips, "Elizabeth?"

Sometimes I forget, he loves my mom too.

And then the decision is made. He is rooted in my heart as strong as any tree. He's mine to protect, so I must trust Mom to be strong on her own for a little bit more.

Across the lawn, people in medical jackets with stretchers and boxes come running, though they're blurry because my glasses went in the water with me, but didn't make it out. It doesn't matter though; I don't need perfect eyes to see the path for my next step.

Gently, I open Uncle's hand and press the glass to his palm, the dark liquid inside sloshing from one end to the other. I curl his fingers around the vial and tuck his fist against his chest. "You have the noni juice, Uncle." I tap his hand that holds a bottle filled with hope as much as medicine. "Your noni, Uncle. Your medicine is here."

His eyes clear for a moment, and he nods, his fist drawing close to his heart.

Bright jackets rush between us, and I'm moved out of the way as they go to work.

Only then do I remember my backpack with the report. I look to the shore, but it's not washed up anywhere that I can see.

It's gone.

Fact is, I don't even remember putting it down. I wait for the dismay to hit over the loss, but it slides past without touching me. Of the two treasures lost at sea today, I saved the one that mattered.

Auntie's arm cradles me against her side, her wizened heart

bending low with the storm. I buoy her up, standing tall as I can, a young tree clinging to the rock with all my might. Each of us lending strength to the other.

And when they lift Uncle to carry him away from the sandy beach he loves, we rise together and follow.

CHAPTER TWENTY-SIX

Into the Sea

Weightless.

I drift at the edge of the reef, where fine white lines creep up dark purple coral. Beyond that, baby pink and purple coral lean away from yellow brain coral—all of them, bright spots between the brown.

Here a reef trigger fish, there a wrasse with brilliant blue and a red bands around its middle.

How had I ever thought the reef was all dark?

Facedown in the water, I float over an entire world, and air fills my lungs as if I have gills—but really it's a snorkel. My prescription goggles bring each tiny fish into focus, but best of all . . . *there are turtles!*

Saisei was not alone out here. Turtles soar through the eel hole, over the reef, and on to Hukilau and beyond. Sometimes we swim together for a while, but never too close.

She has her family with her, and so do I. *All of them.*

My face breaks the surface and I scan the shore until I spot the one I'm looking for: *Mom.*

With my widest sun hat on her head and a lavalava draped over her legs, she waves from her chair on the beach, and I wave back. If I were a dolphin, I'd do flips to show her how much I love seeing her there, waving at me. She laughs at something Dad says, and I dive, carrying her smile with me into the sea.

With open-heel fins, I kick along the edge of the reef while butterfly fish and convict tangs swoop out of my path to hide in the coral.

I've kept an extra close watch for shadowy holes in the reef, but I haven't seen a single viper moray eel. *Not one!* Baby eels no bigger than licorice whips wiggle through the open spaces in their dash for the other side, but comparing those babies to a viper moray is like comparing earth worms to anacondas.

The hidden life below the surface is amazing, but the real magic runs deeper than that: I haven't had a panic attack since the day I pulled Uncle to shore.

The ocean is wild, fierce, and dangerous—same as always—but it's also exciting, beautiful, and wondrous. A reckless sort of majesty.

Where I used to see shadows lying in wait, now I see a world waiting to be explored. If I ever do see a viper moray eel again, I'll just be patient and let it swim on by. And should a riptide take me, I know to swim parallel to the shore as long as it takes until it lets me go. It's not near as scary now that Uncle and Dad taught me how to read the codes that make up life in the ocean.

An odd bump on the sand catches my eye and I swim closer to check it out, but before I can reach it, it moves. A fist-sized octopus scurries into the rock and changes from gray to brown, hiding from the scary monster floating overhead.

It still stings a little that my history report prize went to Lowen, even if the librarian did give me an honorable mention from the preview she saw before my whole project sank into the sea. The written report was good and all when I printed it off again, but my display was what made it really stand out, and after Uncle and Mom came home, it sort of fell through the cracks.

Something wriggles in an anemone perched on the reef, and I watch as a clown fish sneaks out, then darts back into the safety of those swaying tentacles.

I think, if I had to make a trade—an award for all of this—I'd let Lowen keep the award. I'd rather stay here with my ohana by the ocean.

A boogie board bumps into me, and I surface, nose to nose with Malia. "It's getting close, you better come."

"Oh, yeah!" I kick toward shore, but Malia calls after me.

"What's the deal? You trying to make up for years of staying out of the water all at once?"

Make up for my lost time? No. Even though things were hard, I wouldn't change how it all turned out. Sometimes storms bring hardship and pain, and sometimes they cleanse away the old grime and let people start over.

As I step out of the waves, Auntie helps Uncle walk to a chair. Sarge, of course, watches Uncle's every step. Now that he finally got Uncle back, Sarge refuses to leave his side. Not that he's mean or anything, but it's amazingly hard to move a hundred-and-fifty-pound slug. Besides, Sarge wouldn't hurt a fly . . . unless that fly got too close to Uncle, then Sarge might sit on it and crush it to bits with that enormous, furry behind.

The doctors say Uncle's new medicine should even things out for him so Auntie can stop watching him like a sea lion protecting her cub.

"I'm fine!" Uncle grumbles. "I don't need a chair. Leave me alone."

"Of course you don't need a chair. Why would I think that? But ho, here's one sitting here on the sand for no reason. Shame to waste it," Auntie says as she eases him into the chair and pats his cheek.

"Bah!"

Across the narrow, bowl-shaped path that leads from the nest to the ocean, Dad stands with his hand steady on Mom's shoulder. He said having her home again was like surfacing for the first time after a deep dive into darkness. Lucky for Mom, Dad doesn't follow her around refusing to leave her side like a lost puppy—not at all. Dad prefers to gather Mom in his arms and carry her *with* him wherever they go. Much more efficient that way.

"Don't forget your sweet noni juice." Dad passes Mom the cup, but she turns her face away.

"There is absolutely nothing sweet about that drink. I tell you, the name is a lie. They should call it 'fractionally less bitter' instead of sweet." Mom grimaces.

"You'll get used to it," Uncle says.

"Maybe next time Alex can make me mango juice instead. I could drink mango all day long, but cheese fruit?" She downs the glass and shudders.

"Next time, we'll add bananas and coconut milk to mask the flavor for you," Dad promises.

Mom opens her mouth to tease Dad some more but then

sees me coming and reaches for my hand instead—something she's been doing a lot lately. "You ready?"

"Yeah. Have you seen anything move yet?"

"Not yet. Can't rush these things," Uncle murmurs.

I glance at Dad. What if it takes too long and we have to go? Better to know now than be surprised by it later. "So, Dad. What else is on the schedule? How long can we stay?"

"As long as you want." Dad rubs Mom's shoulders. "Today we are here, and that's enough. We'll worry about the rest later."

"Hear that?" Malia bumps me with her elbow. "You get to stay!"

I throw her a shaka and she returns it with a wicked smile. *"Cheehoo!"*

The rest of Castle Crew waits down the sides of the furrow, all of them scared to leave and miss the big moment.

Jack's dad would be here too, except the coconut wireless told someone who told *someone* who told the hiring manager at the Polynesian Cultural Center about this hardworking man that Auntie saw harvest enough noni to feed an army in a fraction of the time. He'll come see Jack when he gets off at five. And in the meantime, Jack's got his phone ready to record it all for his dad.

It's happening!

A hush settles over the crowd as the sand covering the nest rises and falls, soft as breathing.

A crack,

a rustle,

a surge,

a *collapse!*

Then a new hollow chamber boils with tiny flippers, shells, and bodies as they clamber over each other, climbing, falling, tumbling, then pushing, fighting, and swimming through siblings and sand, relentless in their drive to reach the sea.

Oh my gosh!

They're so cute!

Look at that one!

He's stuck! Oh, there he goes.

How many are there?

There's so, so many . . . and still so few.

When the last one presses his way up onto the damp sand and flaps toward the sea with all his might, we follow him, cheering him on for his great journey.

You can do it!

Be brave.

Come back again someday!

His head sinks under the water and his clumsy fins become wings to speed him on his way. Uncle said I could swim after him—follow as he slips into the reef—but I've already explored out there today, and the view from right here is better.

I gaze at my ohana: Uncle, beaming like a proud grandpa with Auntie, content at his side, Mom and Dad, with nowhere to rush off to, and me, grateful for every second with all of us together.

I search the waves for a fleeting glimpse of Saisei's last baby, and I see him! Or maybe one of his brothers, but still, I whisper, "Be safe, and grow strong, little one." A wave sweeps over and he dives beneath the spray, each small but fierce stroke building speed as he soars beyond my sight and begins his secret journey. I wave and wish him well. "Grow strong like my family—strong like the sea."

Author's Note

I fell in love with Laie, Hawaii, in kindergarten, when my big sister—AKA the coolest person in my five-year-old universe—moved there to go to school. Her letters home were filled with posters, li hing mui candies, leis, pictures of geckos and giant bugs *in her room* (so cool), and a multitude of adventures. Her Polynesian dormmates taught her how to make their favorite foods like pani popo, kalbi ribs, bulgogi, lumpia, and many more dishes that quickly became family favorites for us.

As I grew, so did my appreciation and respect for Hawaii and her people as I've visited Oahu, stayed with my sister on the Big Island (she's still the coolest), and made friends on both islands. If readers would like to learn more about any local words or foods I've included in my story, I suggest visiting local Hawaiian websites and resources. I've especially come to love sites where native speakers share what these words, foods, and concepts mean to them personally. With that in mind, I asked my local friends to share what *they* love about living in Hawaii in their own words:

DARREN TANAKA, OAHU

There is much to love about living on the island. I love the food here. With all the different ethnicities, potlucks are always spectacular. Imagine a feast with three kinds of furikake rice, Auntie's special pasta salad, kimchee, a sushi plater, pancit, kalua pork, spaghetti and garlic bread, chicken katsu, hot dogs, chili, butter mochi, Liliha Bakery coco-puffs, homemade brownies, short ribs, steak, and three kinds of ahi poke. With such abundant variety, there's always plenty to share, and the friendship is as rich as the food.

I love the fact that you can go hiking in the mountain trails and look out over the island from a summit, then hike down and swim in the ocean, both in the same day.

I love the smell of the air after the morning rain in Kaneohe. Light and fresh. It lets the quiet peace of the island seep through. It makes me feel that there's hope and good things to come.

S. MAILELAULI'I NAKI, OAHU

My favorite thing about Hawai'i is that our islands have a deep history that has been passed down from generation to generation through our oli (chant), mele (song) and mo'olelo (story). Our 'ōlelo Hawai'i (Hawaiian language) flourishes as our 'ike (ancestral knowledge) from our kūpuna (elders) is passed from generation to generation.

From our Kumulipo (Creation Chant), we learn how the islands were formed and how we are descendants of our 'āina (land) to the travels of Hōkūleʻa that proves our ancestors could circumnavigate the world. It is this ʻike that brings pride to our people, our ʻōiwi. It is this deep history that resonates in all that is Hawaiʻi.

KAMAKEʻE LINDSEY, OAHU

I love and am grateful for ohana. Family is everything. We love on and share our love with many keiki in our ohana. Biological "gifts" are great, but names are given with love as gifts. That care and energy imbibe the names with power and hopefully protections and connections to ohana members past, present, and future.

K. DUDOIT, OAHU

What I love about my hometown of Laie is the small-town feel. Many families have been here for generations, and it shows around town. Everyone goes to the same high school, and sports events are so much fun with the entire community there to support their children.

The feeling of family permeates all aspects of public life in my hometown with how everyone constantly looks out for each other, and the saying "It takes a village to raise a child" really applies. Coconut wireless is a part of it, but a bigger part is how the older community members are hands-on mentors for the youth.

CRYSTAL GANCINIA,
BIG ISLAND OF HAWAII

I love the Aloha spirit that is here on the islands. Aloha has a lot of meaning. It can mean "hello" or "goodbye," but it's also the way people carry themselves here. You can see it in the way people treat one another.

The Aloha spirit is also seen in how we treat our kupuna—which is the Hawaiian word for respected elderly. We respect and listen to them. We hug and kiss each other on the cheek when we say hi. We always take off our shoes and slippahs when we go into someone's house.

When we go to someone's house we don't just sit down and let that auntie or grandma do all the work. We ask auntie if she needs any help to clean or cook or do stuff. There is a local song that says something like:

> We go grandma's house
> on the weekend clean yard,
> If we no go
> Grandma gotta work hard

When you have that Aloha spirit, it's infectious and contagious. You make friends easier, and everyone knows who you are. You are quick to say hi to people, to befriend people, you naturally meet more people that way.

When we moved to the Big Island, Hilo side, new town with a baby, we knew no one. So we would have a BBQ and invite neighbors and new families to come for dinner. We'd share a meal, get to know them, and become new friends.

I grew up eating poi my whole life. Poi is traditional food made from taro roots. I grow my own taro and have a bunch growing in the backyard. We can use the leaves for different things like laulau and squid luau. When I was growing up, my dad would mix the poi, but as I got older the responsibility shifted over to me. I learned the difference between one-, two-, and three-finger poi—which is how to tell the thickness. I was taught that the poi should be smooth, not lumpy, and to keep the sides of the bowl clean.

Another cultural tradition I enjoyed growing up was dance. I grew up dancing hula and Tahitian. My parents met dancing at PCC, the Polynesian Cultural Center, and that's where I later danced while attending college nearby. I just love that you can tell a story through dance. It is a beautiful expression, like in local weddings, the bride will do a hula. I've seen hula done at a funeral. If you look at the history of the hula, it is really important because there was a time where Hawaiians could not speak Hawaiian or dance the hula, because it was forbidden.

I love the pidgin slang. I love the way we talk, I love the beaches, I love the way we treat each other, the way we were raised to treat kupuna, and treat people as family. I love how people come together for a cause, like to clean the beach if rubbish washes up, we band together and look out for one another.

It's a beautiful place to live, but it's more than that—it's the people. It's the way we show love, compassion, affection, and kindness to one another.

E aloha kekahi i kekahi.

"Love one another."

SUDEVIKA KEALANI OKEAHI, BIG ISLAND OF HAWAII

I love the mood of Aloha the most and the warm loving energy of the islands.

I find it's the same on all the islands—just a little different mood to each island, Hawai'i being the most laid back. The Big Island has this energy that is very calm and laid back yet a hidden deep fire with expanding energy. The island is always changing, transforming, and growing, and when people come here, they transform and grow too.

Maui has a more rich business vibe, very windy and a little more fast-paced and passionate.

Oahu has all the beauty of the other islands but feels like New York City too, you could find things from everywhere in the world there.

Also, Hawaiian geckos are usually good houseguests. They eat bugs and don't make a mess on windowsills. Good luck, too. They make a cool sound when you say something true.

TRIESTE MAMO PA'A'AINA, OAHU

The Hawaiian language is full of beautiful words and meanings. I teach my daughters these things so they will not forget their Hawaiian heritage. One of the words that I love in Hawaiian is my maiden name, Pa'a'aina—it means holder of the land. I always thought it sounded like it held a very important sense of responsibility. I have four girls, and each have two middle names, one being Pa'a'aina to connect them to their Hawaiian ancestry. The second word I love is ohana, which means family. Ohana is not limited to family by blood. I have a lot of friends that I consider my family.

REBECCA, DANIEL, AND EIAN CARLSON, OAHU

One thing I love about Laie, and Hawaii in general, is that everyone takes time to stop and talk story. You'll see cars parked in the middle of the street with windows rolled down and drivers chatting away. I love to sit on my front porch in the evenings and visit with both friends and strangers who pass by. Another thing I love is the fact that I can walk from my own front door to a jungle hike in the mountains or an afternoon of snorkeling on the reef.

Maybe the most amazing and important thing is the way others watch out for you. If word gets around that someone needs help, you'll have an instant small army coming to the rescue. It makes me feel like this community could work any miracle it set its mind to.

I asked my sons what they loved best, about Hawaii:

Daniel: "I love the community here because everybody is friends and everybody is family here."

Eian: "I love the people because it's nice to have a supportive neighborhood, and there's always great people to meet."

Eian is high-functioning autistic, and I get teary-eyed every time I think about how much the other kids at school take care of him and watch out for him. They know him and know his needs and are constantly making sure he can participate with everyone else. The KIDS do this all on their own, no prompting from adults. There's a mindset that everyone here is family, even the ones who are different.

ANNE AND LINCOLN WORKMAN, OAHU

The fact that Mother Nature is so dominant here—letting you know she's in charge through sun, salt air, rust, and tides—keeps people humble and focused on their people and experiences, rather than on things. When I have lived away from here and look back on photos from Hawaii, I'm always struck by how much color there is in every photo—even photos of everyday moments. Life here is vibrant and colorful, warm and rooted. And it is, every day, breathtakingly beautiful.

My son, Lincoln, says, "Living in Laie makes you feel you rule the world as a kid. Walking around barefoot, surrounded by friends, the whole town seems your own. Sunny days, sparkling water, green trees blowing in the breeze, you can appreciate every detail."

Acknowledgments

This story was a labor of love and a huge community effort. I would not have been able to finish without every one of the following outstanding people.

First, I must thank my family and parents for understanding and supporting me in my writing adventure as I disappeared to write through dinners, family events, and even farming.

To my agent, Stacey Glick, thank you for believing in me and my writing.

The awesome folks at Shadow Mountain who helped guide and encourage me in this writing journey. Specifically, my wonderful editors, Tracy Keck and Lisa Mangum, as well as Chris Schoebinger, Heidi Taylor Gordon, Richard Erickson, Emily Remington, and Breanna Anderl. I am so grateful to you all.

I would especially like to offer my deepest gratitude to my

Oahu and Big Island of Hawaii friends who did their best to help me understand life on the islands. Thank you for answering my countless weird and random questions about island life, for reading and offering invaluable feedback on how to improve my story, and most of all, thank you for your friendship.

To Darren Tanaka, the coolest rock-star librarian I've ever met, I've treasured our conversations about all things Hawaiian in the wee hours of the morning, and to his students at Kailua Elementary who helped brainstorm both challenges and prizes for Alex and her friends, thank you! To Kamake'e Lindsey, who showed me how to scoop plastic from the sand with kitty litter scoops at Hukilau Beach, and shared her love of ohana with me at the cemetery and through numerous messages over the last year; mahalo, my friend.

To Rebecca, Daniel, and Eian Carlson, who snorkeled the eel hole, kayaked around Hukilau and Temple Beach, and hiked all over Laie, often filming on location so I could *see* and experience the answers to my questions in their real life, I hope to return and snorkel with you IRL. To Anne and Lincoln Workman, who gave me the best "kid tour" of Laie ever—over rocks, under bridges, inside Castle Tree, and all over; thank you for showing me your world from a barefoot kid's point of view.

To Joe Plicka, who showed me around the university and allowed me to visit with his excellent students. To S. Mailelauli'i Naki for teaching me, and sharing your love of both the Pidgin and Hawaiian language with me. To K. Dudoit, the best elementary tour guide ever. To Allison and Michelle Buchanan, who shared videos and photos of their many Hawaiian ocean dives and fielded my many diving-related questions.

Huge thanks to my other Hawaiian readers who gave excellent feedback: Tetoa Tofa, Crystal Gancinia, Sudevika Kealani Okeahi, Trieste Mamo Pa'a'aina, Naine Marie Tai Hook, and Teradee Thornton. And also beta readers Nicky Stanton, Cammie Jensen, Tami Waldrup, and Krista Isaacson. Heartfelt thanks to Marcy and Corey Curr, who fed me grapes, jerky, and caffeine, and to Deanna Ketring, who helped me turn my drawings into Alexis's secret code message for readers—you guys rule.

Sincere gratitude to Bryony Norburn for answering my queries and pointing me toward Mavis Batey and the other amazing women from WWII, and also for sharing details from her research and interviews with the late Mavis Batey.

To Debbie Frampton, Angela Busselberg, Don Carey, Jolene Perry, my writing group, and everyone else who encouraged, taught, corrected, and helped guide this story. I will always be grateful for your help.

With humble thanks,
Wendy

Code Key

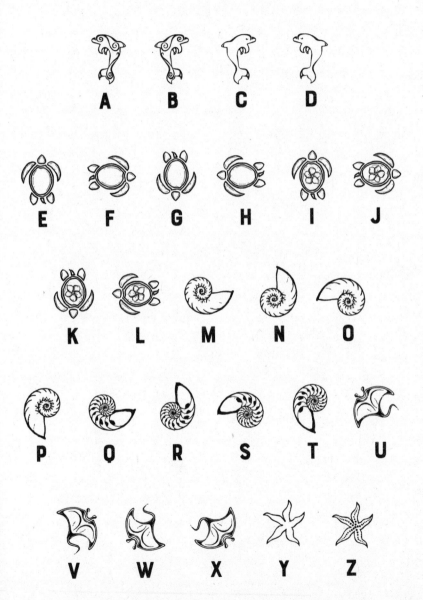